SUMMER OF THE EAGLE

SUMMER OF
THE EAGLE

Julian Jay Savarin

This first world edition published in Great Britain 2005 by
SEVERN HOUSE PUBLISHERS LTD of
9–15 High Street, Sutton, Surrey SM1 1DF.
This first world edition published in the USA 2005 by
SEVERN HOUSE PUBLISHERS INC of
595 Madison Avenue, New York, N.Y. 10022.

British Library Cataloguing in Publication Data

Savarin, Julian Jay
    Summer of the Eagle
    1.   Muller, Hauptkommissar (Fictitious character) - Fiction
    2.   Police - Germany - Berlin - Fiction
    3.   Suspense fiction
    I.   Title
    823.9'14 [F]

    ISBN 0-7278-6208-1

Typeset by Palimpsest Book Production Ltd.,
Polmont, Stirlingshire, Scotland.
Printed and bound in Great Britain by
MPG Books Ltd., Bodmin, Cornwall.

This is for the Clan of S

One

Pappenheim eased his bulk out of the passenger seat of the gleaming seal-grey Porsche Turbo, and waited for Müller to get out.

He looked up at the bright-blue sky of the August day, and stared at the peculiar shape of a single wisp of cloud, high up, that marred the otherwise unspoiled emptiness above him.

'Summer eagle,' he remarked softly.

'What?' Müller said, looking at Pappenheim as he squeezed the remote to lock the car.

'When I was a kid, my father told me this kind of cloud was a summer eagle.' Pappenheim had been born on a farm. 'He used to say this eagle was riding on a high wind that predicted stormy weather to come, even though the bad weather was itself nowhere to be seen. The eagle could ride it, where others could not. Scientific it wasn't; but he was always right – about the bad weather, I mean. I'd take his word over those TV doxies with their charts any day of the week, month, or year.'

Müller looked at him tolerantly. 'Are you quite finished?'

Pappenheim fished out a packet of Gauloises Blondes, slipped out a cigarette, returned the pack to its hiding place somewhere on his person, lit up, and took a long satisfying drag, after his abstinence in the smokeless zone that was Müller's car.

'Yep.' Pappenheim allowed his eyes to rake over the huge mansion before them, then glanced at the thin cotton gloves Müller was wearing. 'Perhaps you're the eagle, about to bring the storm. You should feel at home here,' he went on, 'rich man like you, *Graf* von Röhnen, *Polizeihauptkommissar.*'

'Are you ever going to stop saying that?'

1

Pappenheim stretched his lips across his teeth, between which the cigarette was firmly gripped. 'Nope.'

'Just wondering.' Müller looked at the building. 'I don't think what we'll find in there will be anything I would want in my own home. At least, not the people.'

Pappenheim gave the building his own critical scrutiny. 'So this is where Reimer had his sexuality challenged by the homicidal Mary-Anne, last July . . . sitting astride him, while she put his own gun into his mouth.'

'And was saved by a belle named Berger.'

Pappenheim chuckled. 'She never lets him forget it.'

Müller gave a fleeting smile as he glanced over to his left, where, a little distance away, six big saloons were parked in line-abreast formation. All were black. All had drivers sitting in them.

One of the drivers was so engrossed in his picture-book newspaper, he did not see the Porsche arrive.

Following the look, Pappenheim commented after another drag on his cigarette, 'I see Barsch is improving his mind again. He will be surprised to see us . . . if he can tear himself away from the doxy in the bikini.'

'Let's not disturb him. Besides, we've got company. Ready?'

'Oh yes.'

The company turned out to be a tall man who had appeared at the high, arched door of the building. He was dressed all in black: black polo neck, black jacket, black trousers, black shoes. His close-cut hair gleamed a bright blond. He came purposefully towards them, face still, grey eyes unwelcoming. He carried a two-way radio in one hand, pointing downwards, like a weapon that could be brought up for instant use.

He stopped before them, but gave himself distance. His eyes raked the Porsche, then back to Müller and Pappenheim.

'Not a bad car,' he began as an opening gambit.

'It struggles along,' Müller remarked with a straight face.

The man did not smile. 'Do you have an appointment? The general is busy.'

Müller glanced at the black saloons. 'I'm sure he is. I'm also certain he'll see me.'

The man pointed the radio as if about to shoot them. 'Not

2

today.' He jerked the arm down, as if about to snap to attention.

'Ah,' Müller told him mildly. 'Our first disagreement. And we've only just met.'

The man remained totally impassive. 'I'm assuming this passes for humour. The general . . . is *busy*.'

Müller again glanced at the cars. 'See that one over there? The one with the driver who can't take his eyes off the girlie paper. His passenger is my boss, *Polizeidirektor* – probationary – Kaltendorf. We call him the Great White Shark.'

'Not to his face, you understand,' Pappenheim joined in.

The grey eyes flicked in the direction of the still-engrossed driver. 'And who might you be?'

He stared with deliberation at Müller's single earring, pony-tailed dark hair, gloves, and lightweight Armani suit, before giving Pappenheim's crumpled appearance the same treatment. All without the slightest break in the severity of his expression.

Müller was getting tired of the stand-off. He glanced at Pappenheim. 'Who might I be?'

'Well,' Pappenheim said, fixing the man with deceptively innocent, baby-blue eyes. He blew a stream of smoke at the general's seemingly immovable underling. 'To the lower orders like yourself, he is the *Graf* von Röhnen. To his friends, he is Jens. To the normal citizen, he is Müller, *Polizeihauptkommissar*. And he hates officious functionaries. And I'm Pappenheim. *Oberkommissar*.' Pappenheim blew another stream of smoke. 'I hate them even more. Does that cover it?' he added to Müller.

'It does.'

Both of them stared at the man, who blinked.

'I'll inform . . .'

'No one,' Müller interrupted, and began moving past him. 'We'll see ourselves in.'

Pappenheim followed.

'You can't . . .' the man began, then hurriedly spoke into his radio.

'Calling the cavalry,' Pappenheim said as they moved on without pause.

'That won't help.'

3

'Oh we are in a foul mood.'

'Not yet.' Müller paused. 'Not yet. That is still to come.'

'I can hardly wait.'

Müller glanced at the cigarette. 'Going in with that?'

'Would I deprive myself now, after courageously abstaining in your car?'

'Don't deprive yourself.'

They went up the short flight of steps to the arched doorway, urgently followed by the black-clad man, who was still speaking into his radio in sharp, barking tones.

'He is excited,' Pappenheim said.

'He'll be a lot more excited soon enough.'

Pappenheim smiled beatifically, and took another long drag as they reached the door.

The blond man hurried to bar their way. '*No* smoking!' he snarled.

For reply, Pappenheim blew a steady stream at the man, who blinked, and coughed.

'You need more exercise,' Pappenheim advised unfeelingly. 'You also need some manners. You can let us through, or we'll go in through you. Your choice.'

The man stared at them, radio again held like a weapon. 'The general is *busy!*'

'You do like repeating yourself,' Pappenheim told him with a dangerous calm. 'I'm fed up with you, and the *Hauptkommissar*, despite his silence, is seriously fed up with you. Out of the way!'

Pappenheim was about to give the man a stiff-armed shove, when a voice called from within. 'The general says to let them in.'

Müller looked at the blond functionary with cold eyes. 'Now that is more civilized.'

The man reluctantly moved to one side, allowing them to enter.

Pappenheim glanced about the wide hall, which owed its genesis to a few centuries. 'Very baronial,' he remarked, before looking at the tall slim man who stood there waiting.

Immaculately dressed in a well-cut business suit, he introduced himself. 'Helmut Reindorf,' he said. He did not snap

4

to attention, but looked as if he would at the drop of a hat. 'The general's advisor. How may I help?'

'According to you, the general said to let us in,' Müller told him, eyes nailing Reindorf. 'So . . . would you please take us to him?'

'I'm afraid . . .'

'I hate it when people begin sentences like that,' Pappenheim said, blowing a smoke ring towards the ceiling.

'And the general does not allow smoking in the house!' Reindorf said with sharp disapproval, glaring at Pappenheim.

'Doesn't he? Good thing I'm not his employee.'

'It would be manners, *Herr Oberkommissar*, to respect the house owner's wishes.'

Pappenheim smiled at him. 'Would you believe I just told the window dummy he needed some manners?'

The window dummy was hovering by the door, slate-like eyes watchful. They twitched at Pappenheim's description.

'You do realize,' Müller began to Reindorf, as if having a pleasant conversation, 'we'll remain here all day, if necessary. And I would hate that. I am very busy, and the *Oberkommissar* is also very busy. I am certain the general is very busy as well. It is therefore most definitely in the general's interests to see us immediately. I am trying very hard not to shout at you, Herr Reindorf. If you do force me to shout, things will go very rapidly downhill from then on.'

'He's speaking very quietly,' Pappenheim said. 'Always a bad sign.'

Reindorf stared at them in turn. 'What is this? A double act?'

'Not one you would enjoy,' Pappenheim told him.

'You are mere policemen,' Reindorf said sniffily. 'Don't overstep your boundaries.'

'Spoken like a man used to the joys of command.' Pappenheim gave Reindorf one of his most innocent smiles. 'I don't think I'll jump to attention. Not today. Tomorrow . . . who knows? You could get lucky.' He smiled again, and blew more smoke at Reindorf. 'What were you? A colonel? Certainly not a general.'

'The general, please, Herr Reindorf,' Müller said with quiet patience.

Reindorf continued to glare at them, reserving the most poisonous for Pappenheim. 'You have no idea what, or whom, you're dealing with.'

'And that,' Pappenheim said to Müller, 'is another kind of remark I hate.'

'Tell you what, Reindorf,' Müller said, deliberately dropping the polite address. 'We'll bang on each door we can find, until we find the general and his pals. You can follow if you wish. Coming, Pappi?'

'Right behind you.'

They strode off to the first door, a wide, baroque creation of solid wood. Pappenheim raised a massive fist, ready to pound.

A scandalized Reindorf hurried to stop him. 'If you two will insist on destroying your careers, who am I to stop you? Follow me!' he snapped, and marched off, not bothering to check if they were following.

Behind them, the window dummy stared malevolently, and spoke into his radio.

Reindorf led them through several vast rooms, each guarded by the ubiquitous, solid baroque door. Expensive carpets adorned highly polished floors.

'Did I see a Ming vase?' Pappenheim muttered to Müller.

'You saw more than one.'

'I knew that. So he's actually richer than you?' Then Pappenheim answered his own question. 'Nah. Don't think so. These things are all fake.' He looked about the room they were walking through. 'Wonder how he made his money. Not his salary, even as a general, That's for sure.'

Up ahead, Reindorf paused and turned briefly to stare at Pappenheim. 'If you must continue smoking, *Oberkommissar*, watch where your ash falls. One of these carpets is worth more than your pension.'

'That puts me in my place,' Pappenheim murmured. He flicked some ash on to a carpet as Reindorf turned to continue walking.

Müller glanced at where the ash had fallen, but said nothing.

It took a good few minutes to reach the inner sanctum where the general was holding court. They paused before a door that seemed even more solid than all the others they had seen on their maze-like journey.

'Will we be able to find our way out again, Herr Reindorf?' Pappenheim asked as Reindorf prepared to knock. He was again looking about him. The arched corridor was festooned with ancient coats of arms, swords and shields. 'This part looks almost like a crusader castle. Are we back in the middle ages?'

He finally took the virtually dead cigarette from his mouth, pinched out the dying ember, and put the stub into a jacket pocket.

'Have your fun if you must, *Oberkommissar*,' Reindorf said, looking on with disgust. 'And that's a filthy habit.'

'My smoking? Or pinching out the cigarette and putting it into my pocket?'

'Both!'

Pappenheim smirked.

Giving him a last cold stare, Reindorf knocked with discreet respectfulness on the huge door.

It seemed to boom, discreetly. Its handle looked as if it had once been part of a battleaxe.

Reindorf turned the handle to the left. It moved with a silence that was somehow ominous. He pushed the door gently open, its soundless movement matching the handle's.

Low voices were suddenly heard as if a volume knob had been turned up, and, just as suddenly, they fell silent in anticipation.

With Reindorf leading the way, Müller and Pappenheim entered a gentleman's study that seemed as big as an entire apartment.

The vast room was bright, but not through natural lighting. Though there were many large windows, rich heavy curtains were fully drawn across them, ensuring that no one could look out but, perhaps more importantly, no one could look in, even clandestinely, from a distance.

Despite the promised warmth of the day, the room was at an evenly balanced temperature. A barely perceptible hum betrayed a sophisticated climate control system at work.

Pappenheim stared at the walls and ceiling. If anything, the arched corridor outside the room paled into insignificance.

'My . . . God!' he exclaimed softly as his eyes took in the pristine examples of medieval armoury of all kinds that decorated the place. 'Now this *is* a crusader's castle.' The room was littered with priceless artefacts.

Müller said nothing. His attention was focused on the six people seated at a solid, baronial table. There were only two faces which were not familiar.

The general looked back at him with the air of a predator watching prey it believed was itself predatory. A man in bishop's mufti studied him with uncertainty. Another in a business suit appeared to be seeing him for the first time. Both Müller and the man in question knew this was not so. Neither gave the slightest indication of this. The fourth familiar face was Kaltendorf, who was looking constipated. The two unknowns looked on blankly.

It was the general who broke the silence.

He got to his feet slowly, approached, and stopped a short distance from them. 'The famous Müller and Pappenheim. Or should that be . . . infamous?' He did not smile. 'To what do I owe this unexpected pleasure?' Unlike his companions, the general was in shirtsleeves.

Müller's cold eyes looked upon dark, reptilian orbs that brimmed with a feral menace in a chiseled, pitiless visage.

'I do not think you would find a visit from us pleasurable, Herr General,' Müller replied. 'Not today. Not at any time.'

The general gave a brief, thin smile, and nodded slowly to himself. 'To the point. I like that in a man. So like your father.'

Müller's face was still. 'My father. Yes. My father.' He paused. 'I hold you, General, and others, responsible for the murders of my mother and my father, among numerous other things. I will ensure that you pay for them.'

The general stared at him. 'Most definitely to the point.' The thin smile came again, then disappeared as if a switch within had been turned off. *'You come into my house uninvited, and accuse me of murder?'* he roared. *'How dare you!'*

Müller was unmoved. 'You have no idea how daring I can be.'

'Now *look* . . .'

Müller took a sudden step forwards, causing the general to

unwittingly take a corresponding step backwards. It was, inescapably, a subtle shifting of power.

'*No!*' Müller interrupted, raising his own voice with a suddenness that took even Pappenheim by surprise. '*You* look! I came here to give you a warning. I will see you either dead, or behind bars. And your friends with you. That is not a threat. It is a promise.'

Standing with his back against a wall and watchfully surveying the unfolding battle of wills, Pappenheim noticed out of the corner of his eye that Reindorf was sneaking out. He waited until the door had quietly shut behind the general's 'advisor', before changing station to position himself at a strategic point near it. He was certain that Reindorf had gone for reinforcements.

By now the general's face was beginning to look as if he had spent too much time on the sunbed, and was turning an apoplectic hue of darkest red. The reptilian eyes had also grown darker. But astonishingly, the general uttered not a single word for several seconds. Then the darkness of face vanished so quickly it might never have been; but the feral shadow within the eyes remained.

The general actually smiled. When he spoke, it was not to Müller.

'Heinz,' he began softly to Kaltendorf, eyes remaining fixed upon Müller. 'What are we to do about your underling?'

Kaltendorf looked as if he wished the general had not spoken to him. He took long seconds before replying, and as if emulating the general, he did not speak to his questioner, but to Müller.

'You should leave, *Hauptkommissar*,' Kaltendorf said, 'before you dig yourself deeper. Correction. I am giving you an order. You *will* leave. *Now!* I will discuss with you later your behaviour in this house, and your immediate future, in my office. Now *go!*'

Pappenheim's eyes lit up with renewed interest at this development, as he waited to see how Müller would react. With the information they both had on Kaltendorf, the *Polizeidirektor* was on very shaky ground, and in no real position to order Müller to do anything.

Müller did not budge.

'He's not listening, Heinz,' the general said, eyes still fixed upon Müller. 'He is not listening at all. Who is the *Polizeidirektor* in this room? You seem to have got a pit bull on your hands. Unstable creatures, I've been told. Frequently have to be put down.'

Pappenheim, ready for anything, prepared himself to ensure he could draw his automatic quickly, if need be. He kept a tracking eye on the door, on the general, and on the men at the table; the bishop included.

What Müller did next surprised everyone. He walked past the general, and went to the chair the general had recently left; but he did not sit down. He moved the chair back, then stood at the head of the table, in the general's place.

The general was forced to turn round to look.

'Be careful when you vacate a position, General,' Müller said conversationally. 'You never know who might take your place.'

Pappenheim smiled to himself, but did not relax.

The general was outraged. He opened his mouth to say something, but Müller beat him to it.

'I see none of you are wearing your rings,' he went on. 'Did you slip them off your fingers when you heard we were coming?' Müller began to slowly remove the cotton gloves. 'I've got mine,' he said, removing the gloves completely.

He placed both hands upon the table in display, supporting himself on them, and looked at each man in turn. The lone signet ring on each little finger sent a ripple of shock through them. The general was no exception.

'I carry both rings of the Semper,' Müller continued. 'By the rules of the order, you are duty bound to show hospitality, respect, and to give aid whenever it is demanded of you. The rings I am wearing also demand *total* respect for the rank they convey upon me . . . from each of you.' He looked at the general. 'You too, General.'

It took the general a good thirty seconds to find his voice.

'*This is a travesty!*' he shouted. 'You are *not* a true member . . .'

'So you admit that the Semper exists?' Müller asked with deceptive calm.

The general clamped his mouth shut.

Müller smiled. There was a chill in that smile that even Pappenheim studied warily.

'No matter, General,' Müller said. 'The rules of the order also state, quite unequivocally, that a member of such rank can bequeath it to his first-born heir. In this case, you're looking at him. These are my father's rings, which he bequeathed to me.'

The general could not help himself. 'Your father was a traitor!'

'*Is that why you had him, and my mother, killed?*' Müller snarled with a savagery Pappenheim had never heard before.

Again, the general, fearing he would trap himself, cut off whatever response he had intended to make.

'No matter,' Müller repeated, reverting to his normal calm. 'I'm hunting you all. You six are merely the tip of the iceberg. Perhaps not even that.' He looked at Kaltendorf. 'I will continue digging, but not the way you think . . . sir. I would like to believe . . . sir, that you are a fool who has got in deeper than he expected. If so, I will do all I can to help. If not . . . I will take you down with the others.' He looked back at the general. 'Don't run away, will you? So time-consuming, chasing people; but for you, General, I *will* make an exception. Clock's ticking. Are we finished here, Pappi?'

'Not quite,' Pappenheim replied. 'I think we might have more companions of the order paying us a rushed visit. Reindorf sneaked out.'

He had barely finished speaking when the heavy door swung open with some force and the window dummy, darkly gleaming sub-machine gun in hand, charged in.

But Pappenheim was ready. A powerful arm went around the man's neck with a speed that anyone first seeing Pappenheim and fatally misjudging, because of his size, would never have expected.

The window dummy had made that mistake. Pappenheim's large Beretta automatic was against his temple, hammer back.

'Don't . . . even . . . tremble,' Pappenheim told him with a cold gentleness. 'The hammer is a nervous type.' He glanced at the man's gun. 'Skorpion vz 61. Nice weapon. Put it down.

11

Make sure the safety's back on. You've been so busy with that radio of yours, if any of your friends are outside, you won't survive their entrance.'

'*Stay where you are!*' the man shouted.

'Much, much nicer,' Pappenheim told him soothingly. 'Now then. Safety on. Gun down.'

The man complied with alacrity.

Pappenheim kept the grip on his neck.

'Are you quite finished?' Müller asked.

'I think he's cooperative.'

Müller turned back to the general. 'It would seem we have a situation here, General, as the Amis would say. Two of the nation's policemen, under threat by armed thugs belonging to an illegal organization inimical to the state. It is quite likely that if we are forced to defend ourselves from these people, all six of you might not survive the encounter. So many bullets flying around. What's the fashionable term these days? Ah, yes. Collateral damage. Am I making myself clear?'

'You would *murder* us?'

The chill returned to Müller's eyes. 'If that were not sick coming from *you*, of all people, I would laugh. There are quite a few murders that lead to your door, General, apart from those of my parents. Last July, more were added, including two of our own colleagues, and that of the wife of an American colonel.'

'You are floundering!' the general barked. 'You have no evidence   '

'Quite amazing how disgusting people like you, who would subvert a democratic state, have no problem abusing it's democracy to save your rotten necks. You want "evidence"? Don't worry, General. When I haul you in, you'll be drowning in evidence. And do not forget Pappi, here. He's nursing a grudge for that attempt on his life last May. It is all adding up, General. I am getting very close. But be careful about trying to stop me. I carry the Semper rings. There are rules of the order to obey. So . . . for now, I would advise you to call off your hounds. I am not yet in the mood to shoot your thugs. I have more important work to do. But don't tempt me.'

'Willi!' the general reluctantly snapped at the window dummy, hard eyes on Müller. 'Call them off!'

Willi tried to speak.

'Give him some air, Puppi,' Müller suggested.

'Oh!' Pappenheim exclaimed with almost believable innocence to Willi. 'Sorry. Throat hurting? Get out that radio you love so much. Pass on the general's orders.' He gave Willi just about enough room to manoeuvre. 'No funny business, Willi. The hammer is still nervous.'

Willi cleared his throat, coughed a bit, then spoke into the radio.

'They are standing down, General,' Willi reported when he had finished.

'Oh good,' Müller said, cutting in ahead of the general. 'I think we should take him with us, don't you, Pappi?'

'Definitely,' Pappenheim agreed.

'And I –' Müller heaved himself off the table and with a speed that surprised the general, moved to place his own gun at the ex-officer's temple – 'will bring the general.'

Kaltendorf tried. '*Müller!* You can't—'

'Sir, please shut up. I can, and I will. After you, General. Your cohorts might not be strict observers of the rules; so if you have planned a surprise for us, you won't live to see it. Alright, Pappi.'

'Come on, Willi,' Pappenheim soothed. 'Not long now, and your throat will be fine again. Go out first, shall I?' he added to Müller.

'Be my guest.' Müller glanced back at the table. 'Nice meeting you, gentlemen.' The chill in his eyes raked at the bishop. 'To think that, as a boy, I once had respect for you, bishop. I would suggest you stay exactly where you are,' he went on to them all. 'I am certain you would not want to risk the general's life.' He gave the general a none-too-gentle shove. 'Our turn, General.'

It was just as well that they had taken the precaution. The corridor was full of armed men, led by an unarmed Reindorf.

'Well, well, well,' Pappenheim said. 'Stood down, have they, Willi?' His armlock tightened about Willi's neck. 'If you can't breathe . . . I'm so sorry.'

13

Willi sounded as if the life were being choked out of him.

'Gentlemen,' Müller said to the glowering, black-clad minions of the general, 'threatening police officers with weapons, no matter how much you may not love us, is a serious offence. We will defend ourselves . . . violently. Many of you will die, including the general and smiling Willi here. So . . . do we do this the pleasant way? Or the unpleasant way? And you, Herr Reindorf, please lead the way out . . . with your men. We'll follow.'

There was a long moment when it appeared that the men would call what they clearly thought was a bluff.

'*Down with your weapons!*' the general barked. 'That is an order! He cannot be harmed in this house.'

'The general wants to live,' Pappenheim said to the men, watching them closely for the slightest hint of a wrong movement.

Reindorf's eyes gazed flatly at Müller, then after a few more seconds of pointed stalling, he turned and nodded at the men, who, all with sullen reluctance, put their weapons down.

'Now lead them outside,' Müller ordered. 'For your sake, and the general's, I hope you have left no ambushes along the way. If you have, you know what to do.'

After a few more seconds, Reindorf took out a radio, and spoke into it.

'What a surprise,' Pappenheim commented.

'Is that the last of it?' Müller demanded of Reindorf.

'Yes!' It was a tight-lipped snap.

'Any snipers we should know about?'

'One. He has been stood down.'

'Snipers . . .' Pappenheim murmured. 'We are running a small army.'

'Alright, Reindorf,' Müller said. 'Lead the way.'

They made it outside and to the car without incident. Müller ordered that the men and Reindorf remain in a group close by, where they could be easily covered.

He glanced at the parked limousines. 'Any of those drivers armed, General?'

'They all are. It is a precaution. Kaltendorf's driver is armed,' the general added smugly, as if in justification.

'He's a policeman on duty. There is a difference.' Müller unlocked the Porsche with the remote. 'Into the back, General.'

'*What? Are you insane?*'

'A precaution. You're a fit man. Get into the car!'

'There is no room!'

'Find room! I've had two people sat in there before, and they were not children. *Get in!*'

'You will regret this, Müller!'

'General, I am regretting the day you were born. *In!* Or get shoved in!'

While the general tried to squeeze himself into the back of the Porsche, Müller and Pappenheim noted that the drivers of the limos had all got out of their vehicles to look on – even Barsch, who had forsaken his pictorial newspaper – clearly wondering what was going on. But they all remained where they were.

'Reindorf must have warned them to stay put,' Pappenheim suggested.

'Showing some sense,' Müller said. He peered into the car. 'Settled in, General?'

The general had managed to position himself sideways; upper body behind Pappenheim's seat, legs behind Müller's. He glared back at Müller.

'Alright, Pappi, let Willi go before he becomes attached to you. Take his radio.'

Pappenheim released Willi suddenly, gave him a rough shove and snatched the radio in seemingly one movement.

'Done.'

Willi stumbled, tried to massage his freed neck, and fell in an untidy heap. From the ground, he turned a malevolent look upon Pappenheim. 'There will be a next time,' he promised.

'And I'll be waiting,' Pappenheim retorted. 'Count on it.'

'Better get in, Pappi,' Müller said. 'Not sure how long these wolves will remain at bay. Some idiot might take it into his head to start shooting. Might hit the car.'

'You're worried about your *car*? What about me?'

'You can take care of yourself.'

'Such nice things the man says,' Pappenheim commented

as he got in. 'Anyway, I need a cigarette. Sooner we're away from here, the better.'

Müller waited until Pappenheim had shut the door, then spoke to the gathered men who were looking back at him, a naked lust for violence in their eyes. Only Reindorf's gaze remained flatly neutral.

'In case any of you takes it into his head to shoot at us,' he began, 'remember you will also kill your boss.'

Still watching them, and with his own Berctta 92 still threatening, he got in behind the wheel. Only then did he put the weapon away.

Pappenheim was still training his gun through the lowered window, on Reindorf and the men. He kept it trained as Müller shut the driver's door, started the engine, did a rapid turn-around, and sent the car hurtling away.

Willi got to his feet, angrily brushing himself down. He stared balefully at the departing Turbo.

'They kidnapped the general!' he snarled. 'I want that fat pig, Pappenheim!'

'Willi,' Reindorf said. 'Shut up. They did not kidnap the general. They took your radio, didn't they? Why do you think? Müller is not a man who does anything without purpose.' Then Reindorf appeared to relent. 'You'll get your chance at Pappenheim.'

Müller stopped the car at Wannsee, southwest of Berlin, near the Gllenicke Bridge.

'I think we're far enough, General,' he said, as he cut the engine and climbed out. 'Hope you enjoyed the ride.'

Pappenheim followed suit. 'Cigarette,' he said to Müller in an urgent gasp, stretching briefly. 'Leave you two pals to have a chat, shall I? Need my nicotine input. And you'll need this.' He handed Müller the radio he had taken from Willi. 'Nice piece of kit – a radio as well as a handy. Press to transmit,' he added with a thin smile, then walked a short distance away to thankfully light up a Gauloise.

Müller stood back and watched neutrally as the general began to squirm himself out of the small rear seats. He did not help. When the general was finally out, he shut the door and locked it with the remote.

The general was shorter than Müller, and did indeed look fit, if now slightly crumpled. His balding head was surrounded by a growth of steely grey hair, giving a strong impression that he was wearing a Caesar's laurel. The arrogant, pitiless face and the feral eyes underscored this. Dark and thick arching eyebrows, tufted at the ends, enhanced the look of a bird of prey; the smallish, but sharp, beak of a nose completing the impression of an eagle. All this, combined with the reptilian eyes, encouraged the belief that this was a man who already imagined himself to be at the head of an empire; a man who would let nothing stand in his way, and who would do anything.

'What now, Müller?' the general demanded.

Müller was looking in the direction of the bridge. 'Not so long ago, this was one of the deadliest crossings on the planet. An exchange of spies between East and West. Over there, Potsdam, once a city of enemies. Today, this bridge is just like any other bridge and, in a way, a museum piece.'

'You brought me here to give me a history lesson, *Hauptkommissar*?'

'No, General. Why should I tell you about something you already know?'

'Then why this descent into the past? Why bring me to this bridge?'

'It's as good a place as any,' Müller replied. 'The past, General, is so full of secrets; secrets that many are afraid to look at. As far as I am concerned, it is never another country. All things stem from there.'

'Is this directed at me?'

'You tell me. How many times did my father cross this bridge, General? How many times did *you*?'

The General stared at Müller. 'You are quite mad. Obsessed.'

Müller ignored the remark. 'And here on Wannsee, just last month, I lost a colleague. Blown up in a rigged explosion. The tally against you is mounting, General. Clock's ticking.'

The reptilian eyes gazed at Müller. 'You also suffer under the delusion that you are clever; that you know answers to things you have no understanding of . . .'

'I have the rings.' Müller had removed them, and they were now in his pocket. 'You know I could not have come by them without also coming by some highly sensitive information.'

But the general did not bite.

'I could have your home raided,' Müller goaded.

'If you had wanted to raid my home, you would have come with a swarm of your colleagues, assuming you could have got the authorization in the first place—'

'Friends in high, and low, places?'

'—which I strongly doubt,' the general steamrollered as if Müller had not spoken. 'There are mighty forces ranged against you, Müller; mightier than you can possibly imagine. Everything is global these days. Finance, entertainment, politics . . .'

'Treason?'

Again, the general did not bite.

'Should you decide to initiate a raid now,' the general continued, again pointedly ignoring Müller's remark, 'you know nothing would be found by the time anyone got there. It is therefore obvious you had, and have, no intention of carrying one out.'

The general glanced at the bridge. 'I recognize your kind, Müller. You are of the alpha class, but you have a boy-scout weakness. You are quixotic, complete with your –' the general glanced at Pappenheim, who was deep into his enjoyment of his cigarette – 'Sancho Panza. Who is your Dulcinea, Müller? Miss Carey Bloomfield? Or is it the young and possibly unspoiled Miss Dubois? Remarkable. A fool like Kaltendorf with such a beautiful daughter. But she has her uses.' The eyes of the reptile seemed to catch a brief fire. 'You are understanding me, are you not, Müller?'

Müller said nothing to that. Instead, he called to Pappenheim, 'How much longer, Pappi?'

Pappenheim had been contemplating the lake as he smoked. 'Nearly there.'

The general cocked his head to one side, giving him even more the look of a merciless predator surveying prey. 'You're also a predator, Müller. It takes one to recognize one. But your predatory instincts are slightly blunted. You have vulnerabilities.

18

They could be your undoing. Pity. Such a waste. You would be a perfect candidate—'

'For the Semper? Thanks, but no thanks, General. Time, Pappi!' he called to Pappenheim. He unlocked the car.

'I'm done,' Pappenheim responded.

Müller passed the hybrid mobile phone/radio to the general, as Pappenheim returned and got in. 'You can call your people to come and get you. I've no doubt this little piece of kit has the range. Oh. Almost forgot. I've found the real flight recorders, General. Tick . . . tock.'

The general could not have helped it. The shock hit his features so hard, he paled significantly; and although he was swift to recover, he had not been quick enough.

Müller turned from him, and entered the car without glancing back.

The general was still standing there in shock, radio still unused, as the Porsche accelerated away.

'What *did* you say to him?' Pappenheim asked, turning round from peering back at the fast-receding figure of the general. 'He still hasn't moved. It's as if you've turned him into a pillar of salt.'

Müller glanced in the rear-view mirror. The general could no longer be seen.

'I've told him about the flight recorders.'

'Ah. Was that wise? Or safe? What about the people who really found them?'

'I've already warned them to take a holiday in the mountains. They originally come from a mountain village near Grenoble. It has a reputation for hiding the hunted. Now let us hope the goth is ready to hunt down the frequency being used, when the general finally brings himself to make contact with his pals.'

'What it is to be devious,' Pappenheim remarked with a brief smile.

The general, standing near the bridge, continued to stare in the direction the Porsche had gone. It was hard to tell what he was thinking. The planes of his face were quite still, the reptilian eyes opaque. He stood like that for some time, seemingly oblivious to the world around him.

At last, he raised the hybrid radio, and began to speak in even tones that effectively screened the fierce anger raging within him.

A grim-faced Reindorf was standing alone, outside the general's house.

The limousines had long gone, the general's companions having chosen discretion, and made themselves scarce.

Reindorf spoke into his radio. 'We've got the call,' he said to Willi. 'Take Norstang. Bring the car round to me. We're going to the Glienicke Bridge.' He ended the conversation before Willi could make comment. 'Very pointed, *Hauptkommissar*,' he went on. 'But you're not as clever as you'd like to think.'

A short while later, a big Mercedes saloon with darkened windows crunched to a halt before him.

Two

Müller and Pappenheim were approaching the end of the A115 Autobahn where it merged into the A100 peripheral. They had been travelling at speed, but Müller had begun to slow down.

Müller glanced into the rear-view mirror. 'What's that idiot doing?'

'Which one?' Pappenheim asked with lazy unconcern. 'There are so many.'

'That blue BMW on the right. He either wants to race, or he's about to overtake on the inside. Some people can't see a Porsche without wanting to race it.'

'Then you shouldn't have got one. Just joking.' Pappenheim leaned slightly to the right to peer into the wing mirror. 'You could always frighten him with your hidden blue lights.'

The car had small, but very high-intensity, police flashers, behind retractable panels beneath the nose. Since having them installed, Müller had never used the lights to apprehend anyone. But he had shamelessly used them on occasion to clear traffic, when in a hurry.

Pappenheim was still peering into the mirror. 'Perhaps he's not a racer,' he suggested.

Müller understood. 'If you're thinking of the general, I doubt he would have had anyone organized so quickly. Besides, he has no idea where we are. I'll match speeds with this idiot. Show him your ID when we're close enough. That should frighten him.'

'Such nice things the man says.' Pappenheim fished out his ID as Müller allowed the BMW to catch up, and placed the ID flat against the window. 'Here you are, Mr Undertaker,' he said to the unaware driver of the other car.

They were now close enough for the man to see very clearly what was held against the glass. His eyes popped in shock, and the BMW was suddenly very far behind as the driver rapidly decelerated.

'As I thought,' Müller said. 'You frightened him. So, not the general's man, after all.'

'Sticks and stones. Talking of the general,' Pappenheim went on as he put the ID away. 'You'll notice I haven't asked the question.'

'Ask.'

'As both you and Miss Bloomfield have seen him face-to-face; as you've both described him well enough for even a police cadet to recognize; and as I have had a partial look at him from that goldmine of a minidisc that he passed our way . . .'

'You're thinking of Grogan, who may be Russian, American, a bit of both, or none of the above.'

'I am thinking of Grogan, etcetera, etcetera, etcetera. You two made a good job of seeing each other for the first time. He's with the Semper,' Pappenheim finished with deliberate meaning.

'Perhaps an infiltrator, like my father was.'

'Perhaps.' Pappenheim paused. 'And perhaps not.'

'He certainly has an agenda.'

'Should we trust him?'

'Trust is not the word I would use.'

'Next question.'

'Another?'

'This one has to be asked. What do we do about our lord and master, the Great White? He's also a member of the Semper. We saw him with our own eyes.'

'That we did.'

Pappenheim glanced at Müller. 'Don't tell me you're going soft on him. That little speech you gave him . . .'

'I meant it. I'm thinking back,' Müller went on, 'to the many things we know about this man. Once, an excellent policeman . . .'

'Until he faced the wrong end of a weapon in the hands of your late, and unlamented distaff cousin, Dahlberg. Former

22

colonel of police, DDR, former spy, former leading light of the Romeo Six project –former assassin at large, and Semper all-round hit man.'

'Kaltendorf lost his nerve that day,' Müller said, 'and never got it back. He was made ripe for the Semper. Politically ambitious, he was just the kind of material they wanted. One of the people they could mould to their liking. There are times when I believe the Dahlberg business was more than just one professional enjoying defeating his opposite number. Kaltendorf had been hunting him.

'Given the type of man he was, the humiliation of his adversary was something in which he would have revelled. He had plenty of autonomy; but he was also arrogant, and believed his capabilities made him almost invulnerable. Sooner or later, the Semper would have had to eliminate him. He was a dangerously loose cannon. Their problem was finding someone good enough . . .'

Pappenheim stared at Müller. 'Are you saying they *allowed* him to hunt you out? And that the killings of those shaveheads that started all this—'

'Gave them two birds with one stone. They did plan to create unrest with the killings, of course. It fitted their agenda perfectly. But they also let Dahlberg have his head. If he had succeeded in killing me, the grief I am now giving them would never have occurred. If I killed him in the process, so much the better.'

'They only got half the deal.'

Müller gave a fleeting smile. 'I did have Miss Bloomfield to help me. Little did I know at the time that she was on her own vengeance trail. My – until then – unknown cousin had a way of making enemies.'

'They want the other half of the deal, as well you know.'

'First, they've got to catch me. As for Kaltendorf,' Müller continued, 'I much preferred it when he was just a tick that annoyed me. Arresting my own boss is not something I relish, even if he is Kaltendorf.'

'They've got him hooked through his daughter,' Pappenheim remarked after a long silence.

'Now *you're* feeling sorry for him?'

23

'For the girl,' Pappenheim corrected. 'Kaltendorf is cosy with the general and his cronies; people who wish to subvert the state. Sorry is not what I feel for him.'

Unknown to the general, a zoom lens was trained upon him. This was no ordinary lens. It had a normal max focal length of 800mm; but, with a 2x converter, this was doubled to 1600mm. The general's head was so close to the eye behind the lens, he might have been mere feet away. The lens was zoomed back until the general's entire body, and part of the bridge, came into view.

For a sudden instant the general turned, and seemed to look directly into the lens; an impossibility, since distance and cover gave him no idea of the position, or presence, of the watching lens. Even so, his predator's instincts had caused his sudden jerk of the head, reptilian eyes seeming to zero un-erringly into the eye behind the lens.

'Jesus!' the owner of the watching eye uttered softly, and blinked.

Then the general appeared to relax, as if having convinced himself there was no one studying him.

The unusual lens had been waiting when Müller and Pappenheim had brought him to the bridge. A long, thin tube-like device, looking very much like a scope on a sniper's rifle, was fixed to its upper surface; but this was no sniper's scope. Highly sensitive, it was in fact an acoustic sensor, and slaved to the lens. Whatever the lens was focused upon was also acoustically pinpointed. Manually selectable or automatic filtering could narrow all sounds down to the target within the field of view. As a result, every word spoken by Müller, Pappenheim, and the general, had been recorded.

The lens continued to watch and record, as the big Mercedes drew up to where the outwardly calm general was waiting.

The general went to one of the rear doors before anyone could get out.

'You two remain,' he said to Willi and Norstang, who were in the front.

Reindorf did not wait for the summons, and was already

climbing out of the car, knowing the general did not want to speak within earshot of his subordinates.

The general shut the door, and walked a little distance away. Reindorf followed obediently.

The general went over to the side of the bridge and, standing erect, stared down at the water. He remained like that for some moments, saying nothing while Reindorf waited patiently.

'Müller has found the flight recorders.'

This was so quietly spoken, Reindorf was not certain he'd heard it. It took him a few seconds to assimilate this shocking piece of information.

'Im— impossible!' He could not have helped himself.

He stared at the general, who was now looking back at him, reptilian eyes at their most merciless.

'Do you believe I would say such a thing lightly?' The general's voice was still low, but barely sheathed daggers were in the eyes.

'No! Of course not, General! But . . . but how could Müller possibly . . .'

The general turned again to look at the water. 'I asked myself that question several times as I waited for you to arrive. The world knows only of the flight recorders discovered at the supposed scene of the crash. The real ones were never found. They were gone by the time our people had finished inserting into the area, the ones that *were* found. Months, years of surreptitious searching revealed no sign of their whereabouts. It was assumed that they had somehow been flung into a deep fissure in the mountains, by the force of the blast. Stranger things have happened.'

The general paused. 'We had suspicions of possible culprits.' His mouth turned down briefly. 'A French rag of a newspaper with radical student leanings began asking the wrong questions. It was taken care of. But no recorders surfaced. We closed down that area of investigation. We may have been wrong to do so.'

'*They* found them, and gave them to Müller? Forgive me, General, but I cannot see—'

'I did not say that,' the General interrupted with impatience. 'What I am saying is that, somehow, Müller came by

25

information which led him to the genuine recorders. He was as ignorant of the truth of the matter as anyone else. But he said the *real* recorders. Only someone who had come by factual information would have known that the ones which had been found by the crash investigators were fakes. Who told him, and who led him to the real thing is now our prime concern. We must find the recorders, and eliminate the source of the information. Time to wake our fraternal companion in France from his decades-long sleep; and for Willi to take a flight. Time for a pincer.'

The general paused once more. Reindorf waited.

'Have you noticed Pappenheim's tie?'

Confused by the question, Reindorf frowned. 'Can't say that I've taken much interest . . .'

'You should. Ties can be interesting. They can give you an unexpected insight. Pappenheim's taste is impeccable . . . far superior to Kaltendorf's. And Müller never wears one if he can help it. The crumpled dandy – not quite the ragged trousers – and the rebellious noble. One does, the other doesn't. Interesting pair.'

Reindorf was looking even more confused by the general's apparent rambling.

'Never underestimate them, Reindorf. People like these two have, throughout history, sought to disturb the rightful order of things. In the days when orders like ours wore chainmail, they would have been put to the sword. They shall have their wish.'

Again, the general paused suddenly, and looked out across the water to the far shore. His stance was now of a prey-hungry creature that had scented its next meal.

Reindorf tried to spot what he was looking at. 'What is it, General?'

But the general did not reply for long moments. 'Let's get out of here.' He turned abruptly, and began walking back towards the car.

Following uncertainly, Reindorf began to speak, then hesitated.

'Have you ever sensed an ambush, even when you can see no one, Colonel?' the general asked.

26

'Several times,' Reindorf answered, still uncertain. 'Saved my life on at least two occasions.'

The general gave a brisk nod in agreement. 'This is an ambush. Müller did not bring me here to give me a history lesson about this bridge. If he did, this was only part of it.'

He said nothing more as he entered the car.

While the general was heading back to his home, a man in clothing that seemed to blend with his surroundings carried the big digital SLR camera with the huge lens a short distance to where a black van with darkened windows was parked in some woods.

He went to the back of the van, took a swipe card from a pocket, and passed it through the slot guarding the twin doors. The doors popped open.

There were two other men in the van. One was in the back, the other at the front, in the driver's seat.

It was no ordinary van. Inside was a bank of up-to-the-minute electronic surveillance and recording equipment. Sitting at the console on a chair that slid on rails fixed into the floor was his bespectacled colleague, who glided his chair towards him.

The man handed the camera and its solid tripod over. Neither spoke. The man moved away from the doors, and they hissed shut.

He went to the front, and got in beside the driver. Again, no one spoke, as the van began to move off.

In the back, the bespectacled man had removed the camera from the tripod, and had connected it to the console. The shots and the recording were downloaded, and copied to a CD.

He would be making further copies.

Berlin, at about the same time.
In the glass palace of a building that housed Müller and Pappenheim's special unit on Friedrichstrasse, a mild argument was softly raging. In the sergeants' office of their section, Berger, Reimer and Klemp, were having a go. They were, as was normal, in civilian dress.

'I don't see why you should get promoted before me,'

Klemp was saying to Berger. 'Why should you be made a *Kommissarin*? I've got the seniority. *I'm* the *Hauptmeister* in this section. You're the *Obermeisterin*. In anybody's book, that makes you my subordinate.'

'What are you talking about? Who told you I was being promoted, Klemp?'

'Don't pretend you don't know.'

'Did you miss what I said earlier? I'm *not* pretending. I don't know what foolish rumour you've been hearing, but whatever it is, it's news to me.'

'You would say that.'

Berger sighed with exasperation. 'I give up. Reimer, you take over. I'm going to the toilet.'

Reimer waited for some minutes after Berger had stomped out.

'So where did you hear that story?' he asked Klemp. 'She would have been the first to know. You could see she was surprised when you first brought that up. You've been banging on for ten minutes now. If *she* doesn't know, how do *you*?'

'A little bird told me.'

Reimer glanced at the girlie magazine Klemp was pretending to read in between pretending to write reports.

'Go back to your magazine. Give your brain a rest.'

'You can't talk to me like that. I outrank you!'

'Jesus,' Reimer said, getting to his feet. 'You're in a shitty mood today. What's the matter? No one fancied you at the fitness club?'

'And where do you think you're going?'

'To the toilet. Any objections? Want to hold my hand?'

'You two think you're so special because you work for Müller and Pappenheim.'

'So do you.'

'They never send me on the important jobs.'

'I wonder why,' Reimer delivered as a parting shot.

At that moment Müller and Pappenheim, coming from the lift, turned into the long corridor that led to their individual offices. It was festooned with no-smoking signs, erected at Kaltendorf's behest. Every other corridor was similarly decorated.

Berger was coming towards them, expression thunderous. They stopped.

'*Obermeisterin* Berger,' Pappenheim began as she reached them. 'You look . . . well . . . how shall I put it . . . ?'

'Klemp.'

'Klemp? What about him?'

'He's getting on my nerves.'

'Klemp gets on everyone's nerves. But he's a good policeman, in a brutish sort of way.'

'Well . . .' She began to move away.

'Did you want to see –' Pappenheim paused – 'one of us about something?'

'Changed my mind, Chief.' Berger glanced at Müller. 'Boss.' She walked on past them.

'I'll have to talk to Klemp,' Pappenheim said as they stared after her.

'Won't do much good,' Müller said with an air of experience. 'She'll tell us when she's ready. Let's see what the goth has for us in the rogues' gallery.'

They walked on, heading for the documents room with its solid black, armoured steel door, and keypad-operated locking system. The room was one door down from Pappenheim's office, whose own door was one down from Müller's. There were no other offices at that end of the corridor, which terminated in a tall, triple-glazed window of armoured glass.

They stopped at the door. A clear, green light showed above the numbers on the keypad.

'The goth's still inside,' Müller said. 'Good.'

'Didn't you tell me that Miss Bloomfield once described her as tall, ethereal, fragile-looking – which she suggested was a front – loves to dress in any colour, as long as it's black; paints her fingernails in a way that would make the surrealists weep for joy; can disarm tiny electronically primed bombs attached to people . . . and has a fancy for you. Did I get that right?'

'Close enough.'

'Dangerous woman, Miss Bloomfield.'

'She has her moments,' Müller said as he tapped in the entry code.

Pappenheim gave Müller his most innocent of looks as the massive titanium bolts, deep within the door, slid back with a sigh. It popped itself softly open, then yawned wide.

Müller stood aside for Pappenheim to enter. 'Age before—'

'Don't say it.'

'Alright. I won't.'

Müller kept a straight face and followed as the door began to swing back. It shut with a finality that would frighten, had they no way of getting out again. The hum of the powerful climatization unit, which kept a finely balanced atmosphere within the room, was a subdued presence that was just on the threshold of being heard.

Hedi Meyer, in her mid-twenties and the goth in question, was indeed there, and as palely ethereal as Carey Bloomfield had, in barely veiled acid tones, described her. The fine sculpture of her classic face was, at the very least, a fragile-looking masterpiece; and her dark hair, so rich it seemed unreal but was very much the genuine article, gleamed in the artificial lighting of the vast room. Her eyes were a vivid blue.

Back towards them, she was sitting at a big desk with a computer on it. She had improved the already extremely powerful machine far beyond its original specifications. Hedi Meyer was an electronics genius with a need to continuously upgrade – a serious power junkie with computers. She seemed unable to stop trying to make it even better, and was always messing around with it. Her ministrations had evolved it into the fastest computer possessed by the unit, beating even those in the dedicated communications department to which she really belonged.

She was not dressed in black. On this day, Hedi Meyer had decided to wear a fiery red dress that reached to her ankles. The material walked a fine line between transparency and opacity. More opaque than transparent, it was still a close call. There was blue on her eyelids, and black on her fingernails. Her toenails were unpainted. Her feet were bare, and her flat-soled, stylish trainers were neatly placed to one side. They too were red, with black diagonal side stripes.

She was not flying.

'You didn't tell me she was in red today,' Müller whispered to Pappenheim.

'I heard that!' Hedi Meyer said without turning round. 'I'm in my fiery period. I'm a furnace. My temper is short today. Very short.'

'I promise to tread very carefully, Miss Meyer,' Müller said. 'Pax?'

'We're not at war.'

She swivelled the high-backed leather chair round, to turn the full power of her eyes upon them.

'You're very quiet, sir,' she said to Pappenheim.

'You two were doing so well, *Meisterin* Meyer. I was enjoying it.'

She swung round again, not deigning to respond.

The rogues' gallery was the most secure area in the entire building. Three people had autonomous access: Müller, Pappenheim, and Kaltendorf. Before setting off, uninvited, for the general's home, Pappenheim had let the goth in, while Müller had waited for him in the underground police garage.

Every wall in the room but one was lined from floor to ceiling with wide, steel cabinets, each with its own keypad. A tall, wheeled ladder which hung from a solid rail and had a two-ton breaking limit could be slid to each cabinet in the room. The centrepiece of the room was a wide and solidly built table, with a white top that also served as a photographic lightbox.

The virgin wall was reserved for the computer and its ancillary equipment. Flanking the keyboard were two items that continued to rile Kaltendorf: a joystick and throttle that seemed to have come straight out of an F-16 jet fighter. They belonged to the goth, who enjoyed flying one of the best combat-flight simulators ever created for computer use.

Müller had permitted her to indulge herself, considering it a very small reward for the remarkable work she did. Kaltendorf, wisely knowing when he was beaten, had opted for discretion, deciding after a few abortive tries not to argue further with Müller over it. But he was still unable to prevent himself from scowling at the items, whenever he had reason to enter the room; which was as rarely as possible.

The computer, sporting a large plasma screen, was connected

to a multi-speaker sound system that would do justice to a cinema.

They approached the desk to stand on either side of her.

'So, Miss Meyer?' Müller began. 'Did you manage it?'

'I won't even answer that,' she said, and tapped a key once. 'I've installed a little program to illustrate,' she added.

The desktop screen faded to black and from a tiny pinprick of red, a rose blossomed until it had opened wide, almost filling the screen. Then, very clearly, the general's voice appeared to fill the room. With each modulation, the rose opened and closed, the speed with which it did so depending upon the forcefulness of the words spoken. The rose also changed colour, from a bright red to almost black.

'The rose changes colour,' she went on, 'according to the emotion in the voice. The darker the emotion, the darker it gets.'

'Very . . . er . . .' Müller began.

'Don't worry, sir. I've got an ordinary, boring frequency display for you to show to . . . whoever . . . when you need to.'

'Thank you for the consideration.'

'Shh!' she admonished.

Müller took the censure good-naturedly, and let the general's voice take over.

'Glienicke Bridge,' the general was saying angrily.

The rose shifted colour to a darker hue.

'Yes! Glienicke! Yes. That's where he left me. Wretched, interfering, ponytailed, earringed policeman!'

There was a harsh click as the general cut transmission.

The rose was close to being black, and had closed upon itself.

'"Wretched, interfering, ponytailed, *earringed*",' Pappenheim said without looking at Müller.

'When you're quite finished, Pappi.'

'A lot of rage,' Hedi Meyer said. 'He doesn't seem to like you, sir. What have you been doing to him?'

'Not as much as I intend to,' Müller replied in a hard voice.

'And he seems to like your taste in ties,' she said to Pappenheim.

'Don't forget the crumpled dandy part.' Pappenheim glanced at Müller. 'And the rebellious noble.'

'I'd ignore that if I were you, Miss Meyer,' Müller advised. 'But excellent work. Impressive. I am very grateful.'

She glanced up at him. 'I'll think of a way for you to pay me back.'

'Sounds like a threat.'

She smiled to herself and said nothing.

'Is there more?' Pappenheim asked.

'That was all from the general, sir,' she answered. 'But I've got some more from someone else. Listen to this.'

She tapped another key and this time Reindorf, as clearly as the general, could be heard ordering Willi to bring the car.

'As I said,' Müller remarked when Reindorf had stopped speaking, 'impressive work, Miss Meyer. Are you quite certain they won't suspect you're piggy-backing on their frequency?'

'Not a chance,' she told him. 'And even if they decide to hop as a security measure, I'll be hopping with them. They can't hide from me. Not now that I've got them. Even when the computer's asleep, it will still be tracking.'

'If we can track them, can't they track us?'

'No chance,' Hedi Meyer repeated. 'We've hardened all our systems since the time we found out people were eavesdropping on our communications. If they try, I've got a nasty surprise that will fry *their* systems.'

'You're very frightening, Miss Meyer,' Müller said. 'I'm glad you're on our side.'

'I'm glad I'm on your side,' she responded opaquely.

'Hmm. Well. We'll leave you to it. If *Kommissar* Spyros is not screaming for you, stay as long as you wish. I know you would like to fly that game of yours.'

'I'll have to go back soon, but I've got time for one mission. He's always saying that, although I belong to his section, he has a feeling that I'm on loan to him from you.'

'He would say that,' Müller said with one of his fleeting smiles. 'Make sure the door is shut when you leave.'

'Yes, sir. And what if *Direktor* Kaltendorf comes in?'

Müller glanced at Pappenheim.

'I don't think he'll be troubling you for a while.'

She gave each a searching glance, but did not make comment.

Berlin outskirts.
Willi was in a smaller version of the general's main study. The room was itself nearly as big, and he was standing virtually to attention before the huge inlaid desk at which the general was seated.

The general had two photographs, side by side on the desk.

'Your flight to Washington leaves tomorrow morning,' the general said. 'You will be flying business class. Your genuine passport says you are Willi Helmer, businessman, dealing in communications, which can mean a host of things. You are visiting the States on business for three days. Even with the heightened security over there, you will have no problem.

'You will be met at Dulles, by Paul Böhmen. He is a US citizen, and knows Washington like the back of his hand. He should. He has lived there for over twenty years. He will take you to where you will be staying. Don't let his apparent age fool you. He is one of our best. He did the Semper extremely valuable service over two decades ago, when he carried out a highly efficient operation. If you are remotely as efficient, I shall be very pleased. You will listen to what he says. You will do nothing to compromise his position. He will assist you as he thinks fit; but he is *not* your assistant. He will do nothing to compromise his position. Is that clear?'

'Very, *Herr General*!'

The general tapped at the two photographs. 'Car.' The car in the photograph was an old-model red BMW M3, in superb condition. 'And target.'

Willi went closer to study the face in the photograph minutely, as if soaking up every nuance in the target's expression. He still appeared to be standing to attention.

'I expect you back here at the end of your three days,' the job completed.'

Willi nodded. 'It will be, *Herr General*.'

The reptilian eyes fixed themselves upon Willi. 'Do not fail me.'

Willi did not blink. 'I won't, *Herr General.*' He gave the photograph of the target a final stare.

'An accident on the Little River Turnpike would not arouse suspicion,' the general continued. 'Just another driver losing control. She sometimes uses the Beltway on the return journey to Annandale, where she lives; but, more normally, it's the Little River Turnpike. Böhmen will give you all the details on how to find her, and supply you with any weapon you may need. We have absolute proof that she was the one who killed Mary-Anne. I know you liked Mary-Anne,' the general finished softly, adding some poison.

A pulse twitched in Willi's left cheek.

He was looking at Carey Bloomfield.

'Do you get the impression,' Pappenheim began as they made their way back to their offices, 'that when we're with Miss Meyer, *she's* the *Kommissarin* and we're the sergeants?'

'You too?'

'Me too.'

'But she's worth it.'

'Oh yes,' Pappenheim agreed as they paused by his office.

'Who would have thought it?' Müller said. 'When she first came to us, she was so shy . . .'

'She,' Pappenheim interrupted, 'was never shy.'

'Do I hear other meanings hiding in there?'

'I never speak in allusions. About the Great White,' Pappenheim hurried on, changing tack quickly. 'I suppose we won't be hearing from him any time soon, as Miss Bloomfield would say.'

'He'll be keeping out of my way, which, for now, is a blessing. It gives me freedom of movement without his interference. He has got some serious thinking to do. We've got his career in our hands, and he knows it.'

'That could make him worse. Not better.'

'It could. We'll just have to wait and see.'

Pappenheim glanced down the corridor. No one else was about. 'You'll be heading to France, I assume.'

Müller nodded. 'Tomorrow, or the day after. Warm up your contacts.'

35

'Already done. Grenoble, and the south. Cap Ferrat, to be precise.'

Müller stared at him. 'The south?'

'I have a feeling you'll be checking on the Great White's daughter. Making sure she's OK. The general might be entertaining some ideas.'

'Sometimes, Pappi, you frighten me more than Miss Meyer.'

'I should hope so. Now I'd better get into my smoke pit. I'm gasping.'

'Enjoy.'

'Oh I will. I will.' Pappenheim sounded as if he were on the verge of fainting.

They parted, Müller shaking his head slowly.

About half an hour later, Pappenheim was deep into smoker's nirvana, having started on his third cigarette to make up for his enforced abstinence. He had described his office accurately. It was indeed a smoke pit; and despairingly messy.

His big desk seemed to overflow with paper, some piles balancing precariously and seeming in danger of launching themselves off the desk. An overfull ashtray, dead butts sticking out of it like the horns of a small mine, was encircled by a fine rim of ash. The only other chair in the room, apart from the large example he was sitting on, was similarly overburdened. Files and loose sheets of paper appeared in equally imminent danger of covering it completely and, like their counterparts on the overburdened desk, threatened to spill on to the floor; and yet, miraculously, he could find any item he needed, in an instant. It was as if each file, each scrap of paper, resided in neat storage within his mind. Give him the date of a letter, a report, a memo, and he would find it in that clone of a rubbish dump.

Yet if someone were there to watch him, he would feign absentmindedness, and mumble to himself while he made hard work of retrieving whatever he was looking for. It was one of his chameleon poses that fooled many an unsuspecting victim.

Had there been wooden beams in the room, they would, by now – despite the newness of the building – have taken on the look of rich mahogany. August notwithstanding, the single, wide and already stained window was firmly closed, and the air conditioning was turned sufficiently far down to make habitation just bearable; to others. To Pappenheim, this was his haven.

He was following the antics of a perfect smoke ring with singular interest as it floated towards the tobacco ceiling, when one of his two phones rang.

'A little present coming your way,' a voice said as soon as he had picked it up, and before he had even spoken.

'I like presents. Especially good ones.'

'You'll like this one. That's a promise. Warn whoever's on the front desk to take it without asking questions that won't be answered.'

'I will. You're so nice to me.'

'That makes us even now, Pappenheim.'

'No it doesn't.'

There was a pointed silence. 'When you leave the police – if you live that long – take up usury.' The line went dead.

Pappenheim put the phone down slowly, then blew another smoke ring at the ceiling.

'No sense of humour, some people.'

He picked up the second phone, and tapped in an extension. 'Ah, Rüdi,' he began when the sergeant on duty had answered. 'Glad you're on the desk. A package will be coming in for me any time now . . .'

'And you don't want me to ask questions.'

'Rüdi, you're a champion.'

'Keep telling me that. Now, take my wife . . .'

'No, Rüdi. Not now. Busy.' Pappenheim put the phone down. 'Now, some people do have a sense of humour.'

He had barely finished the cigarette when the same phone rang. It was Rüdi.

'Your package is here. I can get Paul Lohberg to stand in. Shall I bring it up?'

'No need. *Don't* put it through the scanner. I'll be down. Need the exercise, anyway.'

'You? Exercise?'

'Rüdi?'

'Yes . . . ?'

'Watch the line.'

37

'Ah. Yes, Chief.'

'See you soon.'

Pappenheim put down the phone. 'Yep. Some people do have a sense of humour.'

He finished the cigarette, and went out.

The front desk was a solid counter that effectively blocked any entry into the building, beyond the lightly armoured revolving doors. Between the doors and the desk was a large waiting area, scrutinized by hidden micro cameras, and listened to by equally unseen microphones. Despite its being already comprehensively rigged with unobtrusive security systems, they had been added to the building after the failed attempt on Pappenheim's life in May, mere metres from its entrance.

Actual entry was possible from behind the desk, or through side doors, operated by swipe card, or by the officer on duty. In an emergency, the door behind the desk could be electronically locked. In all cases, each door could withstand rounds up to 23mm calibre, and close-proximity blasts.

Pappenheim came through the rear door and into the horseshoe area of the front desk. *Obermeister* Rüdi Schneider was sitting at a bank of security monitors that displayed images of the building's environs.

He turned as Pappenheim entered, and handed over a small package with just Pappenheim's surname upon it.

'Looks like a CD,' he suggested.

'Got x-ray eyes, have you, Rüdi?'

'Well, it looks like one.'

'You didn't put it through the scanner, did you?'

'I'm not suicidal.'

'Good.'

'What if it's a bomb?'

'Sometime later, you'll hear a big noise.'

'I wouldn't joke about things like that, Chief.'

'Who's joking? What did the person who brought this look like?'

'Weird. Not a smiler. See for yourself.'

Schneider ran a replay on one of the monitors. An unsmiling man in a neat suit looked straight into the camera.

'How did he know where that camera was?' Schneider asked.
'Even some colleagues in here don't know where it is.'

'I know his type,' Pappenheim said. 'He's had lots of practice. You're right. He is weird-looking. Thanks, Rüdi.'

'No problem, Chief.'

Pappenheim went out, leaving a puzzled Schneider to stare after the closing door.

As soon as he got back to his office, Pappenheim called Müller. He had opened up the package on the way. It was indeed a CD.

'We should meet in the rogues' gallery. Something to see. A humourless bird delivered a little parcel.'

'On my way.'

When they got there, Hedi Meyer was still at the computer. She stood up guiltily as they entered.

'I was just about to leave . . .' she began.

'Relax, Miss Meyer,' Müller told her. 'In fact, we're rather glad you haven't gone. Saves us having to give Hermann Spyros any more grey hairs.' He handed her the disk that Pappenheim had passed on to him. 'Let's see what we've got on there. No need to ask you to first check that it's clean.'

'Sir, I won't even answer that.'

'My humble apologies, Miss Meyer.'

'I should think so, too.'

Pappenheim found something of interest on the toe of a shoe as the goth sat down again, put the disk in, and checked it.

'Clean,' she announced.

'Before you start, Miss Meyer . . .' Müller said.

She paused, and swivelled the chair to face him.

'You have worked with us on many occasions,' he continued, 'and I will never forget the courage you displayed when disarming that bomb around Miss Dubois' waist . . .'

'I was scared,' she said.

'So were we. But you were the one dealing with the bomb. That, Miss Meyer, was a display of exceptional courage. The disk I have given you contains information that you cannot, and must not, discuss with anyone not here in this room. I know that, during the times you have helped us, it was

39

inevitable that you would see some material that could be considered sensitive. However, there is much that you do not know, and won't know.

'But on this disk may be information that is not only highly sensitive, but could also put your life in extreme danger, should the people on there have any suspicion that you know of it. The bomb was a danger you faced, and overcame. This is very different. The dangers you may face will be far more inimical. What I mean by this speech is that you are free to go if you wish. I want you to understand exactly what you're getting into, if you stay.'

'Are these the same people responsible for that bomb, and the colleagues who were killed?' She looked at Pappenheim. 'And the ones who tried to kill you?'

Pappenheim nodded.

She swivelled back to the computer. 'Can we start?'

'Alright,' Müller said after a slight pause. 'Let's see what we really have got.'

The goth hit a key, and the CD began to whirr. The screen turned black, then went straight into the recording. The Porsche was seen approaching the Glienicke Bridge and pulling to a stop. The recording, both visually and aurally, was exceptionally clear.

'The wonders of technology,' Pappenheim murmured. 'Your Porsche looks good, by the way,' he added to Müller slyly.

'You wait,' Müller countered.

They watched as all three in the car got out. The ensuing conversation had been recorded with sharp clarity. It filled the room.

Hedi Meyer did not quite manage to stifle a giggle when it came to the part where Pappenheim announced he needed a smoke.

'Watch it, Miss Meyer,' he admonished.

'Yes, sir.' Despite this, the giggle broke through.

Pappenheim gave her a resigned look.

The recording showed Pappenheim in close-up, taking his grateful drag.

'I'll have him for that,' Pappenheim vowed. 'He did it on purpose.'

Then he fell silent when the general called him Sancho Panza, glaring at the image of the man.

When Müller dropped the bombshell on the general about the flight recorders, the hidden camera mercilessly recorded the appalled expression on the general's face.

'Got him!' Pappenheim hissed.

Müller said nothing.

The recording briefly switched to the departing Porsche, before again zeroing on the general. They heard the general call Reindorf. Then the scene switched to the arrival of his limousine and Reindorf getting out, and continued to record the entire conversation between the two men.

Müller's face went very still as the general condemned himself out of his own mouth, when mentioning the flight recorders.

When the recording at last ended, the silence in the room was so profound, the subdued hum of the climate-control unit sounded like thunder. It was as if they had all been frozen in a moment in time.

It was the goth who first spoke.

'They used a very advanced digital SLR,' she said. 'Like a handy with a camera, it can create a video clone; but usually you can see the slightest of stop-starts. But this is very smooth. I'd love to get my hands on one of those.'

Pappenheim appeared to rouse himself with some effort. 'You won't find one on the open market. But no reason why we can't find a way of getting one for 'official' use. I'll talk to a man who knows a man. See what I can do.' He glanced at Müller, whose expression remained perfectly still. 'You've got him, Jens. He's admitted it.'

Müller took his time. 'It's just the beginning,' he said at last. 'There were, and are, many people involved. I want them all. Not just the general. But he's as good a start as any. More to the point, we know at least one tactic he plans to employ.'

'The pincer.'

Müller nodded. 'You've seen his house. He sees the Semper as a great martial order; a modern version of the Templars. He also admires the great generals in history. The question is whether he sees himself as a Sun Tzu, a Clausewitz, a Hannibal, or a Rommel. Whichever of those, the tactic he intends to use found favour with all of them. He's after what he sees as my vulnerable flanks, hoping to weaken, and demoralize me . . . a repeat, he hopes, of what happened to Mrs Jackson.'

'And your "vulnerable" flanks?'

'You, Miss Meyer, Berger, Reimer, Aunt Isolde, Greville . . . and Kaltendorf's daughter, Miss Dubois. Even he would not be crazy enough to attack every one of us in this place; but he will make attempts on those he feels are close enough to me. That means our little group, my family, and, as for Miss Dubois, he believes the "quixotic" element he sees in me will force me to respond. The Semper managed it with Colonel Jackson's wife,' Müller continued heavily. 'My flank was exposed, and she died because of it.'

'That was not your fault, Jens,' Pappenheim remarked in support. 'You did everything correctly. The man who actually carried out the kidnapping was a psycho. He abused her, then killed her. He even killed one of his own team. Our assault-team colleagues were perhaps just seconds too late.'

'That does not make me feel better. Those seconds cost Mrs Jackson her life.'

'None of us feel good about it. But we're not time travellers. We can't change what happened.'

Müller fell into a thoughtful silence.

'One name is conspicuous by its absence.' Pappenheim said this tentatively.

'You mean Miss Bloomfield.'

'I do mean Miss Bloomfield. Remember, it was she who killed that other homicidal psycho, Mary-Anne. The general will want his revenge. Mary-Anne was his pet killer.'

'Miss Bloomfield is quite capable of looking after herself. She is also at the Pentagon. Hardly out in the open.'

'She does not *live* at the Pentagon,' Pappenheim said. 'And besides, the world now knows the Pentagon is not invulnerable.'

'Annandale,' Müller remarked softly. 'She travels to and from work, not necessarily at regular times, and it usually takes between twenty and thirty minutes.'

'Plenty of time for someone to strike. All they've got to do is check out her routine.'

42

'The general may not go that far,' Müller said, 'but I'll warn her, just in case. Miss Meyer,' he went on to the goth. 'Now do you understand?'

'Yes, sir. But, from what we've just seen, whether I know anything or not does not matter. If he decides to go for me, he'll go for me.'

'We won't allow him to do so. I know you don't like taking your weapon home with you. From now on, you take it. That is not open to interpretation. It is an order.'

She nodded. 'Yes, sir.'

'The worst might not happen; but just in case, better safe.'

The goth nodded again, but said nothing as she looked at him, slightly wide-eyed, but not obviously afraid.

'Pappi,' Müller said, 'I'll leave you to warn the others.'

'Consider them warned.'

'And I'll call Aunt Isolde and Greville. Let them know, just in case. Greville is still a prize he wants. But the general should also appreciate the value of Intelligence. He should know that if your enemy is aware of your tactic, that makes you vulnerable to counter-attack. In our case, we now know his tactic. This gives us the upper hand. If he is following Sun Tzu, he should heed the modern version of his warning . . .'

'"*If you know yourself,*"' Pappenheim began to quote, '"*and know others, you will win a hundred times in a hundred battles.*"'

'Exactly,' Müller said. 'I know myself. He does not know me, even if he thinks he does. And I will ensure that I know him more than he thinks possible. I don't intend to lose this fight. He called me a predator. He's about to find out just how much of one I am.'

Three

B ack in his office, Müller got out his mobile phone and searched out a page that held secure numbers, protected by coded entry. He opened the page, selected the number, and called it.

It was answered immediately.

'It's six in the morning over here, Müller. You saw me last month. Missing me already?'

'Good morning, Miss Bloomfield. Sorry to wake you.'

'I was already awake. And it's Carey, damn it. I'm assuming you would not call this number, at this time, without good reason.'

'I hoped to catch you before you went to work.'

'I'm picking up something here. Should I worry?'

'You should be careful. Extra careful.'

'You know something?'

'I know something. Anything that appears wrong to you, no matter how trivial, take seriously.'

'OK. Anything else?'

'It's enough.'

'That serious?'

'Very.'

'OK,' Carey Bloomfield repeated. 'Sounds like things have shifted some gears.'

'A few.'

'I'll watch my back.'

'Please do.'

'You OK, Müller? That was some bad stuff last month.'

'It was. And I am fine. Thank you for asking.'

'I know you, Müller. Getting you to admit you're feeling lousy is like pulling teeth without anaesthetic. Hard, and painful.'

'How well you know me.'

There was a slight pause, as both of them sought to say the right thing.

'Even though this is secure,' she began, 'we should not stay too long on here.'

'No.'

'If you want me to come over, I can find a way . . .' She let the words hang.

'See if anything happens on your side within the next few days. We'll take it from there.'

'Got it. Still got that Venet hanging in your office?'

'Yes.'

'Life still indeterminate lines for you?'

'It is for all of us.'

'Müller?'

'Yes?'

'Thanks for the warning. And *you* watch your step. Say hi to Pappi.'

'I will.'

There was another pause as both seemed reluctant to end the call. Then there was an emptiness in his ear, and Müller knew she had cut the connection.

He put the phone away, hoping he had warned her in time.

Müller's office was as different from Pappenheim's as it could possibly be. Large, and sparklingly clean, Carey Bloomfield had once said that if dirt got in there it would die of fright, and that if she licked the gleaming surface of the desk, she would poison it.

The furniture, Müller's personal choice and definitely not standard issue, had been kept to a bare minimum, the storage units and the single narrow wardrobe almost disappearing into the walls. This gave the strong impression of vast space.

Müller was an accomplished organist, and Hammond fanatic. In pride of place was a pristine model of the B3. He had two of the real items at home. Compared to Pappenheim's over-crowded desk, Müller's was a polished desert. The only other items with the seeming audacity to mar its surface were two telephones: one red, one black.

Beyond the desk was a wide window that gave Müller an

almost panoramic view of the city. On the wall next to the window was the Venet that Carey Bloomfield had mentioned. As the mood took him, the works of art tended to be changed. A Monet, a Mondrian, and a Matisse had previously resided there.

Müller smiled to himself as he remembered how he had surprised her, while she'd been waiting for him. Unaware he had come into the room, she had been standing, feet close together, hands in the back pockets of her jeans, behind slightly stuck out, as she had stretched briefly. It was a memory he cherished.

Then a frown fleetingly creased his forehead as he remembered something. He picked up the black phone.

'She says hi, Pappi,' he began as soon as Pappenheim had answered.

'And reciprocated,' Pappenheim responded warmly. 'So she's duly warned?'

'Took it like the lieutenant-colonel she is.'

'That's our Miss Bloomfield. Anything else on your mind?'

'Why would there be?'

'There always is.'

'Since you mention it. Do you still have copies of the reports from the individual members of the assault team who attempted that rescue of Mrs Jackson?'

'That's funny.'

'What's funny?'

'I was thinking of rechecking them myself.'

'Great minds, as you would say. Why?'

'Mention of the incident earlier triggered something, I had a feeling there was something we might have missed in all the trauma of the time.'

'How odd. I had the same feeling.'

'Which could mean,' Pappenheim said, 'we might have subconsciously spotted an anomaly. What it might have been, I can't tell at this very moment.'

'As we appear to have had the same thought, why don't you dig them out? See if you can find whatever it is that's nagging. If you come up with nothing, I'll have a look. There could well be nothing . . .'

46

'But there could be.'

'Exactly.'

'I'll start digging. It was a local team closest to the crime scene; not one of ours, as you know . . .'

'I remember. Ten in the team. So we should have ten individual copies of the reports.'

'We should indeed.'

'Alright, Pappi. Let me know what you find, if anything.'

'Will do.'

Pappenheim finished the cigarette he had been smoking as he put the phone down. He stubbed the dying weed out in the full ashtray, creating a small eruption that floated down to add to the encircling ring of ash.

He studied his handiwork briefly. 'My own Saturn.' He rose from behind the desk and went across to the overladen chair. 'Assault-team reports.' Within a fleeting second, he'd spotted the pale orange file. 'There you are.'

He pulled it out without disturbing the precariously balanced pile, and returned to his desk. He sat down, and began to read.

When he had finished, he read through the entire file a second time. He paused, tapped at it, opened it again, and thumbed through.

'No matter how many times I do it,' he muttered to himself, 'there are only nine reports. Who removed the tenth?'

He lit a cigarette, and took his time about smoking it. He did not call Müller.

He finished the cigarette, stubbed it out with deliberation, then picked up a phone to dial an outside number.

'Lorenz,' he heard when the person at the other end answered.

'Ollie,' Pappenheim began.

'Pappi! Pleasant surprise. Still trying to make things right in the world?'

'And failing miserably.'

'Our lot.'

'Indeed,' Pappenheim said. 'And how's life treating you?'

'As always. Like shit.'

'I like to hear a man who's happy in his job.'

They both made snorting noises.

'What a pair of cynics we are,' *Oberkommissar* Lorenz remarked.

'We've seen too much, done too much.'

'You said it. So, Pappi . . . what can I do for you?'

'The Jackson kidnap.' Pleasantries over, Pappenheim got straight to the point.

'Ah. That one. Nasty, nasty business. One of the bastards raped her, then killed her. I can only regret he could be shot just the once.'

'That's what I want to talk to you about. Remember you sent us copies of the assault team's individual reports?'

'I do indeed. The team, as you know, was commanded by one of our best . . . Ulrich Mainauer. *Kommissar*. Plenty of experience. He worked with other teams before coming to us. Fantastic record. Good man.'

'I don't doubt it. I seem to remember you mentioned there were ten in the team.'

'That's correct. Ulrich, plus nine colleagues, two of them women. Tough cookies, those two.'

Pappenheim chuckled. 'Every woman I've ever known has been a tough cookie, my late wife included. I think we men like to think of them as wilting flowers, to protect our supposed machismo.'

Lorenz gave a bark of a laugh. 'No truer thing.'

'Can you run off those names for me?'

'Of course.' Lorenz sounded curious, but did not probe. 'Ulrich, of course . . . then Swartau, Maier, Sarrach, Hoventhaler, Lehrmann, Beyer, Siepen, Fernberg, Hirsch. Our female colleagues are—'

Pappenheim had been thumbing through the file. 'Trudi Sarrach, and Lotti Beyer.'

'That's them. I'm very curious, Pappi. Anything wrong? And what brought this up?'

'The last question first. The incident came up in discussion, and we decided to check the reports again. As for anything being wrong . . . at this stage, I don't know. But there's an anomaly.'

'Oh?'

'I've only got nine reports.'

'Ah. Now, that is strange.'

'Do you still have the original file to hand?'

'Not directly to hand. But I can get it. Give me fifteen minutes.'

'OK. There may be nothing wrong, Ollie. I've probably lost the tenth somewhere in this mess I call an office . . .'

'Which one's missing?'

'Hang on.' Pappenheim had also written the names down as Lorenz had reeled them off. He looked at the one against which he had placed a question mark. 'Here we are. Hoventhaler.'

'Johann.'

The way Lorenz had spoken the name made Pappenheim ask more sharply than intended, 'What's wrong, Ollie?'

'Johann Hoventhaler is dead.'

'*What?* When?'

'A week after the event. You didn't hear about it because it happened after the inquiry. He was a motorcycle freak. He had a powerful bike. Accident on the way home. No witnesses.'

'Evidence of another vehicle involved?'

'None. We checked that scene with a fine-toothed comb. Nothing. It's a mystery. Johann was an excellent biker.'

'And the bike?'

'We checked that too. Apart from the expected damage, there was a rip in the rear tyre. Could have been anything. A nail, even a broken bottle. There are enough morons about who think throwing empty beer bottles on to the road is fun . . .'

'And a smashed bottle leaves plenty of sharp spikes just waiting for a tyre.'

'Exactly. They even do it at bottle banks. My wife went to drop some off recently, and stumbled. As she fell, she put out a hand to break the fall. Just in time, she was able to shift the hand from something that looked sharp. It was a short piece of the upturned neck of a bottle, stopper still on, nasty jagged edge just waiting for her hand to fall on it. Luckily, she managed to miss it. So, even at a bottle bank . . .'

'Nice people. And were any bits of glass found at the scene?'

'None.'

Pappenheim digested this. 'Where exactly did the accident happen?'

'On a sharp bend. But Johann could take that bend in his sleep. Not like him to lose control.'

'We all can, at times.'

'True, but I have to admit I find it hard to think Johann just lost control of a bike he was at one with. I'll go get that file. Do I call you? Or you call me?'

'I'll call you in fifteen minutes or so.'

'OK.'

'And Ollie . . .'

'Yes?'

'Was Johann married?'

'Yes. Only just. Last May, to one of our colleagues. She's administrative, not an investigator.'

'Bad,' Pappenheim said in sympathy.

'Very. The only good thing about this – if you can call it good – is that they had not had the time to have kids. But, given the way this hit her, I think she wishes they'd had a chance for at least one.'

'I can understand that.'

'She's on extended leave. Staying with the parents. Strange thing, though. Some of our colleagues wanted to visit her, but she said she wanted to be alone. Understandable, I suppose.'

'Indeed.'

'I'd better get that file.'

'Thanks, Ollie.' Pappenheim replaced the receiver very slowly. 'If that report is missing, Johann Hoventhaler did not die in an accident. Which brings up several questions.'

He lit himself a fresh Gauloise, leaned back in his chair, and calmly blew smoke rings at the ceiling.

He decided not to call Müller as yet.

Promptly after fifteen minutes had passed, he again called Lorenz.

'Well, Ollie? What do we have?'

Lorenz did not beat about the bush. 'A missing report.'

Pappenheim remained silent.

'Pappi? You still there?'

'Right here.'

'I can't understand it. I well remember seeing one by Johann.'

'I can only assume that the copy that came to us had just the nine. With the uproar going on at the time, we missed the discrepancy. Easily done.'

'But why take Johann's report? There was nothing special about it. Just a normal duty report. And, at the inquiry, he said nothing unusual.'

'Don't worry about it,' Pappenheim said. 'It could be a simple thing . . . like whoever bound the reports into files put nine together in error, and missed the fact that one was left out. Desk cleared, report goes into the bin; or filed in the wrong place. Very easily done, believe you me. Look . . . why not hunt around for it when you can, see if you find anything, then give me a call? No hurry.'

'Are you sure that will be OK?'

'Quite sure,' Pappenheim lied.

'Thanks, Pappi. I'll see what I can do.'

'Thank *you*, Ollie. And please don't worry about it. No rush.'

When they had ended the call, Pappenheim again put the phone down slowly. 'So what did you see, Johann Hoventhaler, that cost you your life? What did you put in that short report that Ollie Lorenz missed, but was enough to worry somebody?'

He picked up the phone once more, and dialled another number. 'I need a favour,' he said, as soon as the person at the other end answered.

'You're always needing favours. What is it this time?'

'I'll give you some names,' Pappenheim said. 'I need backgrounds, and addresses.' He passed on the names.

'I'll do what I can.'

'You're an angel,' Pappenheim said to the woman at the other end.

'And you're a shameless flatterer, but I won't hold that against you. You can't help it.'

'She loves me, really.'

'More likely, she's crazy.' The woman hung up.

Pappenheim put the phone down, and smiled. He decided it was time for another smoke, after which he would update Müller.

But by the time he had finished the cigarette, his contact rang.

'That was quick,' he said, 'even by your standards.'

'I'm a busy person. With this out of the way, I can get on with my real work.'

'I love your efficiency.'

'You take advantage of me, Pappi.'

'No, I don't. You just love telling me.'

'Whatever. You're going to have to do this the hard way, and write it all down. This is not a good time to fax, or mail you anything.'

'Someone's always snooping around me.'

'It's not you.'

'Oh.'

'We've got our own mole to hunt out.'

'They get everywhere, moles. Alright. Fire away.'

When he had taken it all down, the contact said, 'You do realize one of these is dead.'

'I'm well aware.'

'Why would you be interested in a dead man?'

'Sometimes, dead men do tell tales.'

'You're crazy, Pappi.'

'I thought that was you.'

The line went dead.

'Hmm,' Pappenheim said as he hung up. He studied the information he had been given. 'Hmm,' he repeated.

'Some people should never get behind the wheel of a car,' Müller said.

They were in Müller's office. Müller was standing by the window, looking down upon the Friedrichstrasse traffic. A small car had nosed out too soon at an intersection, and was causing a minor jam. He shook his head slowly, and turned to face Pappenheim, who was leaning against the desk. Pappenheim had brought him fully up to date.

'So what do you think happened?' Müller asked.

'Hoventhaler saw something that didn't quite seem right,' Pappenheim suggested, 'during the assault.'

'But if he had put it down in his now missing report, Lorenz would, or should, have spotted it.'

'That's what I thought. Unless . . .'

'Unless Lorenz is the one who sent the report "missing".'

'I've considered that too. And Hoventhaler said nothing at the inquiry to arouse suspicion. But Mainauer led the team, not Lorenz. If Lorenz is dirty, it means two dirty people; at least.'

'Lorenz, and the member of the team who perhaps aroused Hoventhaler's suspicions . . . assuming he did see anything unusual.'

Pappenheim nodded. 'I'm making a lot of assumptions. We have no idea what he put into that report. It may just be an ordinary report, and his death really was an accident.'

Müller looked sceptical. 'His report is the only one missing – both in the original file, and our copy. One week later, he's dead, killed on a bend even Lorenz said he could take in his sleep. How does that smell to you?'

'Not sweet.'

'There is another possibility. Assuming the person interested in that report is *not* Lorenz . . .'

'Such as any other member of the assault team not wanting to risk being exposed . . . He, or she, would have somehow managed to see the entire file, and checked each individual report to see if anyone had spotted whatever was causing the worry.'

'And Hoventhaler's was the only one to cause alarm.'

'Candidate for disposal,' Pappenheim finished.

'Alright, Pappi. I know something is burning in your mind.'

'Göttingen.'

'Göttingen?'

'The list of addresses I got for all the team members. I'm only really interested in one. A village outside Göttingen. That's where Hoventhaler and his brand new wife lived. They had just bought the house.'

'You would like to talk to the wife.'

'She doesn't want to see her husband's colleagues. Strange attitude from the wife of a colleague at a time of bereavement . . . especially as she is herself a colleague. Lorenz thinks she just wants to be alone. Understandable, but I have my suspicions.'

Müller gave him a sideways look. 'Hoventhaler might have said something to her.'

'Yes. If he did – and I have a strong feeling about that – she could be in danger, if the colleagues know about it. One or more of them is dirty. That's the real reason she's keeping them away. She can't trust herself to face them.'

Müller again turned to the window. He looked down upon the street. The traffic was again moving smoothly.

'I agree,' he said. 'You believe she's at her home, and not at her parents?'

'It's a guess. She's on extended leave. She said she was going to her parents. She will have done so . . . in the beginning. But I believe she will also have gone to her own home. All those memories. Their first house. Something like that is important. Perhaps she does not go often, or even stay the night; but I think she definitely visits the place. Who knows? She might even have been there all along.'

'Well, you've got the addresses of both sets of parents if she isn't there. Do you want to go over there now?'

'No time like the present. Besides, if someone does stink in that team, sooner or later he or she might decide to risk forcing an entry into that house – or worse, threaten the wife. We should be ahead of that.'

'I agree.'

'It's only a three-hour drive,' Pappenheim said. 'I'll take the BMW. Berger can accompany me. Having a female colleague from outside might help in getting her to talk; if she has anything to tell. We should be back this evening.'

Müller nodded. 'Alright. If the hunch is right, it would mean that the Semper has someone in that assault team.'

'Not good.'

'Not good at all. Watch your back, Pappi.'

'I've got eyes there.'

'Why don't you just keep this car, Chief?' Berger suggested. 'It's not as if the owners are ever going to come for it.'

'On the grounds that it might implicate them in murder,' Pappenheim intoned.

'And none of our colleagues dare touch it without your permission.'

The big, gunmetal grey BMW 645csi coupé was hurtling

towards Göttingen, Berger driving, Pappenheim reclined in the passenger seat, eyes closed.

'Quite right too. And anyway, are you crazy?' Pappenheim went on, keeping his eyes closed. 'Have you any idea how much it costs to maintain something like this? As an "official" car, it gets maintained. Plus, its acquisition cost the taxpayer absolutely nothing.'

'What if the taxpayer decides to sell it?'

'For a start, it's evidence. For another, if the *Direktor* entertained the idea of officially selling it in the name of the taxpayer, there are many ways to dissuade him.'

'Speaking of the *Direktor*, he hasn't been on his normal prowl today.'

Pappenheim continued to keep his eyes closed. 'He's a busy man.'

'You've called him a lot of things, Chief. I've never heard you call him busy. I'm saying this respectfully.'

Pappenheim cocked his left eye open. 'Are you trying to tell me something, *Obermeisterin*?'

'Not me, sir.'

Pappenheim closed the eye. 'Hmm.'

'So where are we going?'

Pappenheim again cocked the eye open. 'Are you going to talk all the way, Berger?'

'I'm driving. I want to know where we're going. Sir. You might still be asleep when we get to wherever we're going . . . wherever that is.'

'For your information, I am not asleep. I am not even trying to sleep. I'm thinking. We're going to a village to the east of Göttingen. We're going to talk to a dead man's wife. Will that do?'

'It's a start.'

Pappenheim closed the eye. 'I'm very relieved.'

They had stopped just the once for Pappenheim to have his obligatory smoke, and were making such good time along the A2 Autobahn that, half an hour later, he decided to call a halt for fuel, and to have something to eat.

'We'll top up the tank,' he said, 'but not eat at the *Rastätte*. Let's find a nice country place on the way.'

After the refuelling stop, they left the A2 northeast of Göttingen, and headed southwards on country roads.

'You've only smoked once,' Berger said. 'I don't mind, if you want to.'

'I thought you hated smoking.'

'Well . . . yes, but this is your car . . . well . . . it's the car you use . . .'

'My office is a smoke pit. My home is a smoke pit. It's refreshing to have one place I spend time in that isn't.'

'Is this your way of saying you're trying to give up?'

Pappenheim stared at her. 'Are you crazy?'

'Not crazy enough to try and stop you,' she said, unperturbed.

Not far from Seeburger See, they found a small family run hotel-restaurant. It was less than half an hour from there to Hoventhaler's house.

The little hotel was appropriately called Seewald, in a quiet location with a fine view of the lake.

Berger stopped the car in a parking area of smooth gravel. There were tables outside, but the few guests they could see had decided to remain indoors.

'This looks good,' Pappenheim said, as they climbed out. 'And I swear I can smell *Schweinebraten*. Jens loves it, and so do I. You?'

'I'm not on a diet, anyway.'

He glanced at her. 'You don't need a diet, Berger.' He looked about him, and spotted a table that was positioned a little distance from the others. 'Here . . . that table over there. Let's take it. It has a nice view of the lake.'

They went to the table and sat down opposite each other.

Almost immediately a tall, friendly woman in a long summer dress and sandals on her otherwise bare feet came to their table. Her silver-grey hair was tied in a bun.

She smiled at them. 'Something to eat? Or a drink?'

Pappenheim gave her the full benefit of his baby-blue eyes. 'Is that *Schweinebraten* I smell?'

She beamed. 'With onion and mustard crust.'

'You have a customer.'

She turned to Berger. 'And for you?'

'The same, please.'

56

'A good choice. And to drink?' the woman added.

'No alcohol for me,' Berger said. 'I'm driving.'

'We have fresh orange juice.'

'That will be fine,' Berger said.

'And sir?'

'I'll stay with the orange as well.'

'Very well.' She gave them another smile, and left.

The food was as excellent as the aroma had promised.

'That,' Pappenheim announced when they had finished, 'was good stuff.' He looked at Berger's plate. 'I can see you thought so as well.'

'It was good,' she agreed. She stood up. 'If you'll excuse me. I need to, umm . . .'

'Of course,' Pappenheim said, getting to his feet.

'Sir!' Berger whispered, astonished. 'What are you doing? You don't have to do that . . .'

'Oh.' He looked momentarily confused. 'Well. We are eating out . . .' He sat down.

She gave a tiny smile, and went into the building.

A little later, the woman came out and made for his table. 'Did you enjoy it?'

'It was perfect.'

'Thank you. My son will be pleased. He's the chef.'

'Then you can certainly tell him from me.'

'I will. Anything else?'

'I would love a coffee, but we must be going. Perhaps we'll stop by again. I have this place in memory now.'

The ready smile came on. 'We would be very happy to see you both again.' She began to clear the table, just as Pappenheim looked up and saw Berger coming out of the hotel.

The woman looked at him, then glanced back at Berger. 'She is very lovely, your wife.'

Taken completely off guard, Pappenheim heard himself say, 'Yes. She is.' It was hard to tell whether he was thinking of his dead wife, or of Berger.

The woman saw something in his eyes and gave a little nod, as if confirming something she already knew. 'I'll get the bill,' she said.

'Yes. Yes. Thank you.'

Pappenheim looked at Berger as the woman left.

'Are you OK, sir?' Berger said as she sat down.

'Ah yes. I'm fine.'

'What did she say? You looked a little . . . well . . . as if you couldn't quite understand something.'

'Don't worry, Lene. I understood perfectly.'

She gave him a quizzical look. 'Are you sure you're OK, Chief?'

He smiled at her. 'Never better.'

Four

'There!' Pappenheim said. 'That's the one. At the end.'

The BMW was cruising down a recently laid road that bordered a small stream. The area spoke of newness, with a small clutch of houses at different stages of construction. Hoventhaler's house was one of the few so far completed. The signs of building were everywhere: dusty trucks, concrete mixers, piles of earth, all the detritus of a house-building programme.

The road went past the house, and on into the distance, through open country.

'It must have been a building site when they first bought,' Berger said.

'It still is,' Pappenheim remarked, looking about him.

'Should look good when it's all done, though.'

'But not much help to Johann Hoventhaler's wife, having to live with seeing her dream vanish.'

Pappenheim was staring past the house.

'What is it?' Berger asked.

'Look at the road beyond this development . . . where it goes into open country. What do you see?'

'A house, a road going past it, open country . . .'

'Look again,' Pappenheim insisted. 'Far ahead.'

'I still see a road . . .' Berger paused, as the car moved closer. 'The road disappears into woods . . .'

'Sharply,' Pappenheim said. 'It bends sharply. Let's go there first. See where it leads.'

Half a kilometre later, they discovered that the road was a sharply curving triple bend, following the route of the stream. The bends were themselves deep within a thickly wooded area, before the road once more emerged into open countryside.

Some flowers were just off the side of the road, between the first and second bend.

'Stop where you can,' Pappenheim ordered.

At the end of the last bend, the road straightened, and Berger found enough space to park the car off the road.

Pappenheim got out, and looked in each direction. The road was deserted.

'Not exactly busy,' he said, mainly to himself. He lit a cigarette, and drew deeply upon it, exhaling a stream of smoke into the warm air. 'Not even a hint of approaching traffic . . . and plenty of cover for anyone wanting to hide. Plenty of cover to make an escape across country. No witnesses. And it rained like hell last month . . . just about everywhere, from Schleswig-Holstein to Baden-Württemberg. Triple bend, wet road, powerful bike. Lethal combination, if you suddenly lost control. If what happened here was no accident, a silenced shot from a good marksman would have had the same effect. All assault-team members are excellent shots. They have to be. Hoventhaler may have been shot off his bike.'

Berger had got out of the car, and had heard most of it. 'The dead colleague whose wife lives in that house we passed?'

'The dead colleague.'

'If what you say really happened, Chief. The person who did it would not leave any clues behind to be found. He would know the routine.'

'I'm certain he, or she, didn't leave a single thing behind that would be incriminating. As you've said, such a person would never be so incompetent. And anyway, we had one of the wettest months ever, last July. Everything washed away. Nothing left to find, even if the shooter had been careless; which I doubt. Let's go to the house and see if I'm right, or just having a wild guess that will prove to be just that.'

He did not walk back to the car. He finished the cigarette, pinched it dead, and put it into his pocket.

Berger watched as he did so. 'Why didn't you just chuck it into the stream?'

'I'm a smoker, not a vandal, Berger.'

They got back into the car. Berger turned it round, and they headed back towards Hoventhaler's house.

As they re-entered the bends, Pappenheim said, 'Did you see that?'

'See what, sir? I'm busy taking these corners.'

Pappenheim had craned round, staring through the rear window.

'Gone,' he said, turning round again to face forwards.

'What's gone?'

'A gap in the trees, just by the flowers. Couldn't be seen coming from the other direction.'

'Could that be important?'

'It might be interesting to check out the line of sight . . . see where that leads. We'll check back after we've been to the house.'

'You're the boss.'

There was a short driveway that stopped at a garage door, and Berger pulled off the road and on to it. There were only two other houses nearby, but none oppressively close.

Pappenheim checked for curtain-twitchers, but no one seemed to be peering at them.

'They're either not very nosy around here,' he grunted as he got out, 'or they really do mind their own business.'

'That would be a first,' Berger remarked drily as she too climbed out 'Where I live, people will even stare into your living room without embarrassment. They're looking. They're just hiding it well.'

'Well, let's give them something to talk about.'

'But if you're right, Chief . . . anyone coming here to check will only have to ask . . .'

'Which is what I want them to do. If I am right, Hoventhaler's wife will be coming back with us; for her own safety.'

'You want them to know.'

'Oh yes. Which is exactly what Jens would want me to do.'

They went up to the door of the house, and Pappenheim pressed the doorbell. A distant chime sounded.

They waited. The minutes ticked by.

'Perhaps she really doesn't come here . . .' Berger began.

'She's here,' Pappenheim said.

'There's no movement in the house.'

'Car in the garage.'

Berger stared at him. 'How . . . ?'

'Come on, Berger. Forgotten what I've taught you? Sniff. What do you smell?'

Slightly sceptical, she did so. 'Oil,' she said. 'Diesel.'

'There you are. As it's not our BMW, it must be hers. She either has an oil problem with her car, or it's an older diesel.' He pressed the bellpush once more. 'We've got to convince her we're on her side. Talk to her, Berger.'

'What do I say?'

'Use your intuition.'

'What's that?'

'If you don't know, I certainly don't.'

Berger looked up, hoping to see an open window on such a warm, bright day. None were open; even slightly.

'Mrs Hoventhaler?' she called softly; but her voice carried sufficiently, without alerting the invisible curtain-twitchers. 'We are colleagues from Berlin. We are here to help. We know about what happened to your husband.'

They waited some more, but nothing happened.

'Perhaps she really isn't here, sir,' Berger said. 'The car may just be parked in there and she's not using it. Her family may be driving her around. She's probably not in a fit state to get behind the wheel.'

'She's a grieving police officer, not a porcelain doll. Try again.'

Berger repeated her message to the unseen and unheard person who might, or might not be in the house.

There was still no response.

'What's her name?' Berger asked.

'Elke.'

'I feel stupid talking to an empty house, but . . .' She began a third try. 'We've come a long way, Elke. We're really here to help. We know what they did to Johann.' She sighed in exasperation. 'It's no use . . .'

'Wait!' Pappenheim whispered sharply. 'Listen!'

They listened. There were definitely soft footfalls.

Berger stared at Pappenheim. 'How could you—?'

'Hunch,' he said, and smiled at her. 'If you had any idea what that woman said to me back there . . .'

'What did she say?'

'For me to know, and for you to wonder.'

A turning key cut back whatever response she had been about to make.

The door opened a crack. A haunted eye peered out at them.

Pappenheim took over. He gave his most beatific of smiles, blue eyes dispensing trustworthiness.

'I am Pappenheim, *Oberkommissar*, and this is my colleague *Obermeisterin* Lene Berger. As she said, we are from Berlin.'

'Why would Berlin colleagues want to see me?'

'We are here to help. We belong to a special unit. We know about Johann's report. Look. May we come in? The neighbours are bound to talk.'

'You could be anybody. IDs.'

Pappenheim took his out, as did Berger. They handed them through the crack. Elke Hoventhaler took them, and closed the door.

'At least there's enough of the police officer still in her,' Berger said.

'Are you being dry?'

'I'm being something.'

The door suddenly opened. 'Come in,' Elke Hoventhaler said.

She handed back the IDs when they had entered, then shut and locked the door.

'The place is a mess,' she said as she led them into the living room. 'Sit where you can.'

Berger shot a glance at Pappenheim. The place was scrupulously clean and tidy. They sat down in pristine armchairs.

Elke took a seat on an upright chair facing them, knees pressed together, back straight. 'What special unit?'

'Let's just say,' Pappenheim replied, 'we work in grey areas.'

The incident had taken its toll on Elke Hoventhaler. The haunted darkness of her eyes appeared to look at nothing. Lines had appeared on her young face. Her hair, loosely bunched, was straggly. Of average height, she seemed thinner than she normally would be. Yet, for all this, her clothes were scrupulously neat and clean. She bit her lips frequently.

63

Berger watched her closely.

'Grey areas,' Elke Hoventhaler repeated. 'That could mean anything.'

'It does,' Pappenheim said.

'Well, you're in here. What do you want?'

'To help. As I've said, we know what happened to Johann. We know something was bothering him. Did he mention anything to you?'

'Pappenheim,' she said abruptly, as if suddenly remembering. 'I've heard about you. From *Oberkommissar* Lorenz.'

'Probably all bad.'

She darted him a look of uncertainty. 'What?'

'Don't mind me. Warped humour. Please continue.'

She retreated into a world of her own. 'Müller and Pappenheim. That's what I remember him saying. The Berlin boys . . .'

'That's us. Now you see? We are what we've said we are; not people who have come to frighten or hurt you.'

'I wouldn't have let you in if I'd thought that. And I've got my gun here.'

'Good thinking.' He shot Berger a glance that could have meant anything. 'So tell me, Elke . . . No, I'll tell you. We received copies of the individual reports from the assault team that went in to rescue a kidnap victim . . .'

'The American colonel's wife.'

'Yes.'

'Terrible thing.'

'Yes. It was.'

'Johann was very upset that they were too late.'

'I can imagine.'

'He put that in his report . . . but . . . but not everything. Did you see what he said?'

'I'm afraid I did not. His report was not with the others.'

Elke Hoventhaler fell silent for long moments.

'I removed it,' she said at last.

This astonished Pappenheim. Berger stared at her.

'*You* took it out?' Pappenheim asked. 'But you just asked whether I'd seen it.'

She nodded. 'I know. I know.' She paused, again seemingly

uncertain. 'I'm responsible for collating them. I saw what Johann had written. Even though he had left out nearly all of what he'd told me, I still felt it put him in danger. I took it out to protect him. It didn't help.' She seemed about to cry.

Berger stood up, intending to go to her.

'No,' she said, raising a hand briefly. 'I'm . . . I'm OK.'

Berger sat down again.

'He must have seen what Johann had written,' Elke Hoventhaler continued, 'before it got to me. All Johann put down was that he felt that something was not quite right. It was enough to get him killed.'

'You're certain he was killed?' Pappenheim asked. 'It was not an accident?'

'Of course he was killed!' she replied with a sudden fury. Then, just as suddenly, it vanished. 'Johann could ride that bike as if glued to it. I've been on the pillion many, many times. We used to enjoy taking those bends. Johann was a brilliant rider. He used to practise skids on the bends when there was no traffic about. Even in the wet. He never came off. It was *not* an accident.'

'What exactly did he tell you, Elke?' Pappenheim posed the question very carefully, not wanting to frighten her into renewed silence.

She seemed to consider whether she wanted to answer or not, then made her decision.

'He was the second man on the stairs,' she began, 'going up to where the woman was being held. A man came out of the room, and stopped at the top. He had a gun, but it was pointing down. He made no move to shoot. It was as if he did not expect to be shot. He was smiling, recognizing someone. Then he was shot by the colleague ahead of Johann. No warning to put down the weapon. Just one killing shot. The man looked surprised as he died.'

'Did the other colleagues see this?'

'No. They were going through the rest of the house.'

'Who was the colleague ahead of Johann, Elke?' Pappenheim asked softly.

'*Kommissar* Mainauer.'

Pappenheim forced himself to remain calm. He did not

glance at Berger, but kept his eyes firmly upon Elke Hoventhaler.

'Are you quite, quite certain?'

'Of course I'm certain! You should have seen poor Johann. He was so . . . disappointed, and shocked. He admired Mainauer, you see. Whenever the team split to go in, Mainauer always took him as back-up. Johann was proud of that. It showed Mainauer respected him. Anyone who knew of Mainauer's record with ready groups or assault groups knew of his reputation for tough entries and fast, clean results. If he respected you enough to guard his back, this was almost like a decoration.'

Elke Hoventhaler paused, and looked into a great distance.

Pappenheim did no prompting, letting her choose her own pace.

'Johann,' she continued, rousing herself from wherever she had been, 'was dependable. Mainauer knew Johann would always watch his back. But he didn't watch Johann's. Instead . . . instead . . .' The words died, and a tremor went through her.

Again, Berger began to rise; and again was stopped by Hoventhaler's widow.

'Don't worry, I'm not going to cry. I've done . . . a lot of crying since July.'

'Let me ask something of you, Elke,' Pappenheim began with gentleness. 'Try, if you can, to shift, just for a moment, from grieving widow to police officer. In your opinion, what do you believe happened to Johann?'

'That's easy. I . . . I don't mean it's easy to shift, just that it's easy to say what happened. He was shot off his bike. No other way for it to have happened. Mainauer is a champion shooter with a rifle. The very best. I've seen him. Johann has . . . had . . . and so have the rest of the team. At shooting practice, only Johann came close . . . although he was still far behind. I used to think Mainauer was grooming him . . .'

'Perhaps he was,' Pappenheim said, seemingly deep in thought.

'Then *why*? Why kill him?'

'Perhaps he hoped Johann would watch his back, no matter what.'

66

'Are you saying . . . are you saying he killed Johann because Johann would not cover up what he had seen?'

'I'm only guessing. I don't know.'

'That man used to come to *my* house! He ate *my* food . . .'

Fearing she would break down, Pappenheim stepped in quickly. 'You said "he". Doesn't he have a family?'

Pappenheim already knew something of all the team members from the background notes he had received from his contact; but only mere snapshots had been supplied within the available time. He wanted to see whether Elke Hoventhaler could add some flesh to the bones.

'He was married,' she said. 'But the wife died in an accident somewhere abroad. No children. As he seemed to like Johann from the day he took over the team, they became friends outside the job. So he came here quite often when we got the house.' She gave a sudden, bitter laugh. 'One of the reasons we bought in this location was because he lives not far from here.'

'Oh?'

'His house is only six kilometres away by road, on higher ground; but it's even closer across country. Just one and a half kilometres.'

Pappenheim looked at her keenly. 'Really? How do you know that?'

'He's very fit. He likes cross-country running. We used to joke he would run for his breakfast. He used to do that, you see, Get up early, have a fast run to here, have a light breakfast with us – an orange juice, sometimes with a croissant as well – then run back to have his full breakfast. He never took coffee, or butter, on that first section of the run. Sometimes, for the fun of it, Johann would run back with him and eat there, and they'd go off to work together. It was almost a routine.'

Pappenheim nodded slowly, and waited.

'Would you like to know how I think he did it?' she asked.

'Tell me.'

'I think he shot Johann from his home.'

'*What?*' Pappenheim exclaimed.

'From one and a half kilometres away?' a stunned Berger asked.

Elke Hoventhaler made a scoffing noise. 'That would be nothing for him. He has a rifle that can do that easily.'

Pappenheim's baby blues were fixed upon her. 'He has a *sniper* rifle in his home?'

She nodded. 'I've seen it. Johann saw it. Mainauer said it was a trophy he'd won in a shooting competition. He's a police *Kommissar,* isn't he? A colleague, and Johann's boss. Why would we think anything about it?'

'Why indeed. And what make is this wonder weapon?'

'A Dragunov. He called it an SVDS. It has a folding stock.'

'A Dragunov SVDS,' Pappenheim repeated softly. 'Some trophy. Very nice toy. Killing range three thousand eight hundred metres. More than twice the distance from his home to the bends. Well within range. But it still takes an exceptional shot to hit the rear tyre of a moving motorbike going through those bends, *through* those woods.'

'He is an exceptional shot, and there is one place through the woods where you can get a good sighting, from a top-floor window. You can't really see the gap from the road . . .'

'That opening you saw, Chief,' Berger reminded Pappenheim.

He nodded. 'You can only spot it – very briefly – from one direction.'

'That's the one,' Elke Hoventhaler confirmed. 'It's at a sharp angle. The three bends are like an M, with the whole middle section and part of the first bend, if you're coming in this direction, in full view of the window. A car or bike taking those bends seems to stand still for long enough; because, although it may be moving fast, the route the road takes makes it look as if it's taking a lot of time to go out of sight. On a straight section, the car, or bike, would just flash past.'

'He didn't even have to leave his house,' Berger said in wonder. 'Still a fantastic shot, though.'

'For someone like Mainauer, it was easy.'

Pappenheim looked hard at Elke Hoventhaler. 'Elke, you are very sure about this? If we are to take Mainauer down, we *must* tie him up so tightly he can't wriggle away.'

'I am very sure.'

Before either Berger or Pappenheim realized what she was doing, she stood up abruptly and left the room. They stared at each other questioningly.

She was soon back. 'Hold out your hand,' she said to Pappenheim.

Frowning, he did so.

She placed a small, unsealed envelope on his opened palm. There was something solid in it.

Pappenheim carefully opened the flap of the envelope and peered in. It was very recognizably a bullet, only partially deformed.

Pappenheim stared at it. Berger leaned forward to look, astonished.

'Where did you find that?' Pappenheim asked, still staring at the spent bullet.

Elke Hoventhaler went back to her seat. 'I'm not an investigator, but I'm still a police officer. When I got the news, I wanted to see where it had happened. Mainauer was very caring, and supportive. Of course he would be! Despite the fact that people were crawling all over the scene, no one was looking for a bullet. Mainauer would be, of course, but he had to wait for everything to die down. I kept going there, just to remember how Johann and I used to play at skidding, and to put some fresh flowers. People still put a lot down. Even now. Kind of them. Did you see the flowers?'

'Yes. But we did not stop there. We stopped just after the bends, in case of traffic.'

'It's never really busy, which is why Johann always took that route. No houses for at least three kilometres when he started the straight, until he arrived here. He could use the bike to the full. Mainauer knew that, of course,' she added bitterly. 'So I kept going back. He accompanied me at least twice. I didn't know then that he was trying to pinpoint where the bullet had ended up after going through the tyre, so he could come back later to get it out.

'Once, when I went there alone, he was on duty. I was just standing there, thinking about Johann, when I saw something giving off a dull shine on the far bank of the stream. It was easy to miss, and when I tried to find it again, it took me a while. The rain in July had made the stream rise a little, but it had already sunk back. I saw the thing again. I really can't tell you why I did it. I just felt I had to. I went into the stream and dug whatever it was out of the mud. That's it in your hand.'

Pappenheim was staring at her. 'There's a job for you in Berlin, if you want it.'

This forced a weak smile out of her. 'I wasn't looking for anything. It just happened.'

'Sometimes, the hardest cases are solved by things we are not looking for; and, for the perpetrator, the most unseen of circumstances can ruin the best-laid plans. Mainauer must be wondering what happened to his bullet. And he would not dare ask you if you had seen anything during your visits to the flowers. He would not expect you to.'

'He did try,' she said, 'in the beginning. He was trying to find out if Johann had said anything to me. Nothing obvious. Just little questions about whether Johann had liked his job. I always said yes. I also told him how much Johann had admired him. That seemed to please him. He twice invited me to his home, after it happened. I went. Once before the bullet, and once after . . .'

'Why after?'

'I wanted to be sure. The window where the shot would have come from is in the bedroom Johann and I had used when we had stayed the night after a party for the team. It's the one he used to shoot Johann off his bike. I am certain. There is no other that gives such a good, clear shot. As I said, it's the position from where the bends are in perfect view. Johann and I have used binoculars from there to see if we could spot our house. That gap in the woods is right where Johann came off the bike.'

'You have done your homework. I'm impressed. Now tell me, Elke,' Pappenheim continued, 'did Mainauer ever mention whether he did time in the military as a conscript, or as a professional soldier?'

'He never really talked about that side of his life. Perhaps to Johann, but I never heard anything about that from either Mainauer, or Johann.'

70

'Hmm,' Pappenheim said. He closed his fist around the small envelope. 'Can I keep this?'

She nodded. Then, as if giving up the spent bullet had released something within her, she suddenly began to cry. She let go completely, and did not resist when Berger rushed up to hold her.

'Take her upstairs, Lene,' Pappenheim said quietly. 'Help her pack. We're taking her out of here. No need now to double-check that place by the flowers. I'll call Jens.'

Berger nodded, and led Elke Hoventhaler out of the room.

Müller picked up the phone at the first ring.

'I was wondering when you would call. How did the search go?'

'Found her.'

'That is very good news.'

'Wait till you hear the bad.'

'Which is?'

'Mainauer is dirty.'

'How dirty?'

'Very. He's the accident maker.'

'Evidence?'

'Oh yes.'

Müller stared at the painting on his wall. 'So he's with the Semper.'

'Considering what I do know . . . it certainly looks like it. He lives in the area. I'd love to take him down.'

'In due course, Pappi. Not today. But I promise you the pleasure of doing so. They won't know we've uncovered one of theirs. Let them continue to think they're safe. Gives us another edge. We'll carry out our own pincer movement, without the enemy spotting it. What say you?'

'I say OK. The longer the wait, the sweeter the bait. Let's dangle him.'

'My thoughts exactly.'

'The widow will be coming back with us. Safer for her, the way things are. By the time the neighbours get round to gossiping, she'll be well out of danger. We should be back by twenty-one hundred hours, at the latest. Much to tell.'

'I'll be here,' Müller said. Call ended, he put the phone down. 'Tick . . . tock, General,' he added.

In the main bedroom of the Hoventhaler home, Elke was no longer crying, but her eyes were red-rimmed, and still full of tears. Every so often, one would spill down a cheek. Sometimes, she would wipe at it with the back of a hand; sometimes, she simply allowed it to run down the cheek and on to her blouse.

Berger looked at her anxiously as she moved about the room in a seeming daze, packing haphazardly. She saw Berger's look.

'Don't worry,' she said. 'I get these rushes of tears, and then they stop.'

'Till the next time.'

She gave a low sniff, and nodded. 'It's been like this since the day we . . . buried him. How . . . how did you know I was here?' she went on, shifting the conversation away from the burial.

'We didn't,' Berger replied. 'Well . . . I didn't, but the chief had a hunch; and when he has a hunch . . .'

'. . . he plays it,' they said together.

'There,' Berger said. 'A little smile. That's better already. It was your car that did it.'

'My car?'

'Yes. He smelled the diesel. Said that meant you were in.'

Elke Hoventhaler actually gave a soft giggle. 'That old thing? It's been smelling like that for . . . oh . . . months. We had to tow it here. It hasn't moved by itself for , , , God knows. Johann is good with cars and planned to work on it . . . but he . . . never did . . . have . . . the . . .' The tears began to flow again. 'Oh God, oh God . . .'

Berger put an arm about her shoulders. 'It's OK. It's OK.'

'I'm a police officer and I'm behaving like a baby.'

'Not from where I'm standing.'

'Well, you don't look like someone who would cry so easily . . .'

'I'd probably shoot Mainauer first and ask questions later; but I do cry when the fancy takes me.'

'Over someone?'

'That would be telling, wouldn't it? Now let's finish the packing before the chief bellows from downstairs. Let's get you out of here, eh? Leave the ghosts for now. And I promise not to tell him about the car. Spoil his lunch.'

That brought a new, hesitant smile from Elke Hoventhaler. 'I'm nearly finished, anyway. Ah. Which reminds me.' Wiping at her tears, she went to a drawer, took out her police-issue pistol and its ammunition, and put that into a small bag.

'Didn't Mainauer suspect you could be here all this time?' Berger asked.

'I saw him drive by once – probably while he was looking for that bullet – but he had no reason to think I'd be here. My parents, and Johann's, told everyone who asked I'd gone abroad to be by myself. And if they wanted to know where, they said I'd told them not to say.'

'And all the time you were here, but nobody bothered to check. Why would they?' Berger added. 'Smart.'

'Your boss found me.'

'Ah well . . . Pappi is . . . different. Müller too. Very . . . unusual, those two.'

'*Pappi*? You call him *Pappi*?'

'Not to his face, I don't. It's "Chief", or "sir".'

Elke Hoventhaler peered at her. 'He . . . he's not the "someone", is he?'

'Don't be crazy. Never go for the boss.'

'That denial was a bit quick.'

'I . . .'

'Up there!' came Pappenheim's mild bellow. 'Time to go!'

'I told you,' Berger whispered. 'We're ready, Chief!' she called down.

'We've got a long way to go,' he said. 'I'll drive.'

'Yes, Chief.'

Mainauer had decided to leave his office early.

At that time of day, he did not expect any traffic to speak of; and the reality proved he had judged correctly. There was no other car on that particular stretch of road, either in front of him or behind.

Wearing the uniform of a police *Kommissar*, he drove his

73

Volvo estate at an easy pace along the same road on which Hoventhaler had met his untimely death.

Mainauer came to the triple bends and drew to a halt, almost exactly where, earlier, Berger had parked the BMW. He had arrived at precisely half an hour after Pappenheim and Berger had taken Elke Hoventhaler with them.

He got out of the car, and began to walk slowly towards the first bend, taking his time about it, turning his head this way and that, calculating angles at which he thought the rico-cheting bullet might have gone.

He walked right through to the last bend, then began to work back. He stopped by the flowers, looked to the gap in the trees, traced an imaginary line from where the shot had come from to a possible point on the opposite bank of the stream. As with all the other times he had done so, he saw nothing to excite his interest.

In all the time since he had arrived, no vehicle had passed. But he was not worried. If anyone still remembered – or cared about – what had happened at that spot, they would simply think he was a conscientious policeman, still trying to find out what had really happened.

He made his way back to the car, without a successful find. He got in, and drove on.

The road eventually took him past the Hoventhaler house. He slowed down perceptibly, glanced at it, but kept going.

He did not glance back.

Berlin at the same time.
Müller was looking at an A5 envelope that had just been brought in to him. The name on the back was Jack Dales, Lieutenant-Colonel; sender address given as CAFA Base.

Müller opened it to find a written note on headed paper, and another envelope inside. He took out the note, and began to read.

'Dear Mr Müller,
The enclosed was sent to you via myself, from Bill Jackson. I know he has the greatest of respect for you. He sent this letter with one to me, and has

74

asked me to forward it on to you. All of us at CAFA thank you for what you did for Bill and Elisabeth.

My very best regards,
Jack Dales'

'I did nothing,' Müller said. 'I failed.'

He put the note to one side and fished out the second envelope, with the sweepingly bold hand of Jackson's writing upon it.

He opened it, and began to read silently:

'Dear Jens,

It has occurred to me that you may believe – wrongly – that I hold you responsible for what happened to Elisabeth. Nothing can be further from the truth. The people I hold responsible are the animals who did what they did to her, and the movers and shakers who pulled their strings. I know and understand your fight, and I know that you did everything in your power to save her. I also thank you for preventing me from being killed by my own side! I thank you for having the guts to tell me straight what had happened when the rescue failed, and for not even attempting to evade responsibility. I must stress – you are *not* responsible.

As a commander, I pride myself on knowing the measure of a man. I feel no hesitation in telling you that I see in you a man who could be my friend. Therefore, it is as a friend that I say to you that you must appreciate those whom you hold in special regard every minute of every day, for you never know when they may be taken from you.

My superiors, in their wisdom (or unwisdom!), have seen fit to return my command to me. However, I'm taking some time out to be with my children at this difficult time for them. My superiors have reasoned that I was affected by the "understandable, extreme stress" of the situation. Their way of saying I went nuts!

At first, I will admit, I blamed Germany for taking

Elisabeth from me, and in such a terrible manner. But reason tells me that it is the people involved – the people you are fighting – who are responsible, and they are the ones I should (and do) hate. In any case, I cannot deny my children their German heritage. Germany gave me something beyond beauty: the love of the woman who became their mother. For that, I shall be eternally grateful.

I would like to sit down and have a drink with you one day soon, Jens Müller.

May you conquer the demons. (Perhaps, one day, I can help!)

Your friend,
Bill'

Müller folded the letter slowly, and put it back into the envelope. He put that into Dales's envelope, followed by the note from Dales. He then unlocked a drawer in his desk, put the envelope into it, then shut and relocked the drawer.

'You may have given me absolution, Bill,' he said quietly, 'but can I absolve myself?'

East of Göttingen.
Less than five minutes after he arrived home, Mainauer's mobile phone began to ring.

'Mainauer.'

'Any problems?'

Mainauer recognized the familiar voice. 'None.'

'And the grieving widow?'

'Still away.'

'Good.'

The call was ended.

Müller picked up a phone and dialled Hermann Spyros's extension.

'I'll bet I know who that is,' Spyros said in a long-suffering voice.

'Don't panic, Hermann. I'm not poaching her . . .'

'Yet, you mean.'

76

'Hermann, Hermann.'

'Before you break my heart, here she is.'

'Sir?' came Hedi Meyer's voice.

'Miss Meyer, if I asked you to stay a little later tonight, what would you say?'

'How late?'

'You won't have to do anything in the gallery before nine. And you'll be driven home later. I know your car is in for its Transport Ministry tests.'

'Can I fly till then, after I'm finished here?'

'Of course. I'll let you in. When would you like to be there?'

'Let me just check with *Kommissar* Spyros.'

The sounds of whispering came through. Müller stared at the Venet with a tiny smile, while Spyros and Hedi Meyer bargained.

'Sir? Will six thirty do?'

'That will be fine. I'll wait for you at six thirty. Thank you, Miss Meyer.'

'A pleasure.'

'And the flying game,' Müller said with some amusement after he had put the phone down.

She was waiting for him, punctually at six thirty.

'You're late, sir,' she greeted. 'Thirty seconds.'

'Miss Meyer,' Müller said as he tapped in the code, 'enjoy your flying.' He stood back to let her enter as the door popped open.

'I will.'

A blazing glory in red, she went past, giving him a sideways glance beneath blue eyelids.

As the door shut behind her, Müller returned to his office, shaking his head slowly in wonder.

Less than half an hour later the internal phone rang.

It was Hedi Meyer. 'Sir, I think you should come and see this.'

The urgency in her voice made him say, 'On my way.'

When he got there, she was staring at the computer screen. She did not turn round. 'Take a look,' she said.

She had been flying the F-16 simulation and on the left multi-function display of the aircraft cockpit was a message: SOMETHING YOU NEED TO KNOW?

Beneath that was a narrow rectangular panel, waiting cursor blinking.

'From our friendly informant, do you think?' Müller asked.

'It's his code. I checked.'

'Seems he wants to talk. Ask . . . *what do you have?*'

Her fingers flew over the keys. The question filled the panel. Then both panels blinked out; but were soon back. The top one had a new dialogue: WHAT DO YOU WANT?

'Alright,' Müller said. 'Give him this: Mainauer, Ulrich.'

THIRTY MINUTES, came the reply.

Both panels blinked out, and did not return.

'We wait,' Müller said. 'Might as well finish your mission. I'll be back in time.'

She nodded, and rejoined the friend she'd been flying with online.

Müller returned five minutes early. Hedi Meyer had stopped flying, in anticipation of the message coming through.

At exactly thirty minutes, the panels returned.

DOC COMING. ENCRYPTED. YOU HAVE KEY.

'Thank him,' Müller said. 'Then let's see what we've got.'

She did so, and the panels blinked out.

'Shall I convert and print out?' she asked. 'Or convert and leave it on the server?'

'Convert, and print me a copy. Then secure the original on the server.'

'Being done as you speak.'

The document was just five A4 pages long; but its information was devastating.

Müller did a quick scan through. 'My God!' he exclaimed softly. 'How the hell did he manage to get hold of this?'

'I haven't really seen it properly while I worked on it,' Hedi Meyer said. 'But what little I have seen . . .'

'You forget.'

'Already forgotten.'

'Don't even talk about it in your sleep.'

Hedi Meyer saw the look in Müller's eyes, and took his advice very seriously. 'Not even in my sleep.'

He glanced at his watch. 'Pappi should be here in just over

an hour. You can go back to your game if you'd like to, until he gets here.'

She shook her head. 'I think I'll make a few adjustments to the machine instead. Get some more speed out of it. Still plenty of room for improvement.'

'Keep up like this and one day you'll make the computer itself fly.'

'It's the challenge. I enjoy it.'

'All yours, Miss Meyer. And I must say that, despite your comments earlier today, your temper appears to be—'

'Don't let that fool you. Deep down, a fire burns.'

'Something wrong?'

She kept her attention on the computer. 'Nothing you would recognize.'

'Too cryptic for me.'

'Goodbye, sir.'

'See you later, Miss Meyer.'

Müller returned to his office, taking the sheets of paper with him. He sat down at his desk, and began to study them closely. When he had finished, he put them neatly together to one side, got to his feet, and went over to the window.

He looked out over the city that he loved; a city of sometimes terrible history. But it was also a reawakening city; vibrant, alive. Full sundown was not until 21.00 but already a few lights, sparks within a creeping twilight, were beginning to show.

A phoenix, his city; with invisible shadows.

'What do you know?' he asked his city of shadows.

Berlin, 20.55.

Pappenheim brought the BMW to a halt outside the main entrance.

He got out, and said to Berger, 'Here. You take the wheel.'

Berger swapped the passenger seat for the driver's. Elke Hoventhaler was in the back. She began to move, as if to get into the front with Berger.

'No,' Pappenheim said to her, leaning into the car. 'You stay there. Just in case anyone's watching. Unlikely, but you never know.'

She nodded and remained in her seat.

'Are you two OK with the arrrangements?' he continued, glancing at each in turn.

Both women nodded.

'Thanks for helping out, Lene,' he said to Berger.

'No problem, Chief. I've got room to spare. Should I bring the car back, and pick up my Beetle?'

'No. You stay with Elke. Bring the car back in the morning. But don't you dare scratch it.'

'I'll guard it with my life.'

'I wouldn't go that far.'

'I was joking.'

So saying, she sent the BMW rushing down the street.

'You could have let me get my head out of there first,' Pappenheim said without rancour. He watched as the BMW turned a corner. 'Be careful, Lene.'

It was not worry for the car.

He lit up a cigarette, taking his time about it, and continued to look in the direction in which the car had gone. He smoked the Gauloise to the end, pinched it out and, as usual, put the dead stub into his pocket, before entering the building.

The single knock on the door told Müller it was Pappenheim, who entered almost immediately.

'Home is the successful hunter,' Müller greeted. He was back at his desk, and stood up as Pappenheim came in.

'Have I got something for you!' Pappenheim said.

'And I have a few things for you too. You first.'

Pappenheim leaned on the desk, while Müller went over to the window and glanced out. More lights were coming on.

Müller turned to face Pappenheim.

Pappenheim began to recount all that had happened, omitting the part about his late lunch with Berger. Müller listened with a grim expression as Pappenheim detailed his talk with Elke Hoventhaler, and her certainty about Mainauer's involvement in her husband's death.

When Pappenheim had finished, he took out the small envelope with Manauer's bullet, and put in on the desk.

'In that little paper pocket,' he said, 'is the evidence.'

Müller went across to the desk and picked up the envelope.

He lifted the flap carefully, and peered in. He did not touch the spent round. His mouth tightened briefly as he closed the flap once more and put the envelope back down.

'Another for the rogues' gallery.'

'This one comes from a particularly nasty rogue. If Elke's right, he's still looking for that thing.'

'Which,' Müller said, 'is where this comes in.' He leaned over to pick up the thin sheaf of paper, and handed it to Pappenheim. 'Read, and weep. I'll look at this city of ours while you digest it. Don't vomit on my floor.'

Pappenheim gave Müller a questioning frown, before turning his attention to the thin document.

'*What?*' Pappenheim began.

'Read it all first, Pappi. Then you can explode.'

Pappenheim fell silent. The only sound in the room was the sibilant noise of the sheets of paper as he passed them from top to bottom. Finally, he slammed them down on the desk.

'Jesus!'

Müller turned to face him. 'I said that . . . three, or four times, I think.'

'Is there anywhere the Semper have not infiltrated?'

'Remember they planted Hammersfeldt, even here. Remember *Direktor* Neubauer, deceased former pal of our wonder boss, Kaltendorf . . . who, by the way, has not been in at all today. Perhaps he has a headache,' Müller added with a cold savagery.

Pappenheim heaved himself off the desk to join Müller at the window. 'When we talked on the phone, I suggested that Mainauer may have been Semper; but I never expected . . .' He glanced back at the thin document. 'I never expected this, even in my craziest moments.'

'A second skeleton, forming about the original so that, by the time you try to remove it, you damage the host, perhaps irreparably. My father wrote an approximation of that in the documents he left me. He was right.'

Pappenheim went back and again picked up the document. He leaned against the desk, and began to sift through.

'Joined the Heer as a conscript,' he began, 'but stayed on as a professional. Showed aptitude for sniper training. What a surprise. Was so good, passed with flying colours and was an instructor by *twenty*. Expert at camouflage and selecting optimal firing positions. Accelerated promotion to sergeant. Recruited by the Semper while still doing military service. Selected for a commission, for which highly recommended by the then colonel, now General a. D. Armin Sternbach.' Pappenheim paused, looked up. 'Our general with the taste for medieval orders doing his work long years ago. Mainauer completed his service with the rank of captain,' he continued, finishing sourly, 'The general certainly looked after his own.'

He selected another sheet. 'And now the part that makes me want to vomit. Joined the police, but carried out several private contract killings both nationally, and internationally. Names of the victims, and dates of the killings. Jesus. Some of these names are—'

'Known,' Müller said. 'A few unexplained ones our colleagues, nationally, are still wondering about, and others that police in other countries will never clear up. That wife of his who supposedly "died" in an accident is there too. She must have been surplus to requirements. One wonders whether he was ordered to kill her by the Semper, or whether it was on his own initiative; which hardly matters now, all things considered.'

Pappenheim again put the papers back on the desk. 'Our informant is well up to date with his list of victims.'

'Yes. Johann Hoventhaler is there. Final confirmation, if we ever needed it.'

'How did this get to you?'

'Grogan. I'm assuming it *is* Grogan. Same code, according to the goth. She was in there – still is – when a message came on, asking if we wanted to know anything. On impulse, I asked about Mainauer. Those five sheets of paper were the result. Almost as if he knew what we wanted.'

'So the entire kidnap of Colonel Jackson's wife was even more than it seemed,' Pappenheim said. 'We knew they wanted to drag you down, but in a way that left them clean. A psycho leads the kidnap. They knew what he would do to her. They wanted to make a point; but they also organized it so that the house where they would take her would be in Mainauer's area.

82

We organize an assault team. Who leads it? Why, Mainauer, whose job it is to silence *all* the kidnappers. No one left alive to talk.

'But something goes wrong. The leading kidnapper comes out, *knowing* it would be Mainauer in charge. He lowers his weapon, not expecting to be killed. Probably thought he would "manage" to escape at some stage; and certainly not expecting betrayal . . . How am I doing?'

'Following my own thoughts.'

'But poor Johann Hoventhaler is there,' Pappenheim continued. 'He sees the strange behaviour, and wonders. He makes the mistake of hinting at it in his report. Not much, but enough to seal his fate. But even that would have been it. Another successful kill by the master sniper.'

'Then along comes the widow,' Müller said. 'On such small things. Where is she now?' he added.

'Berger was kind enough to offer a spare room. I accepted. Practical. Both of them are colleagues . . . both armed. And no one will expect it. Elke is supposedly somewhere abroad. But if Mainauer starts asking the neighbours, the nosy gossips will talk.'

'Let them. Let him worry for a change.'

'Strange thing about this,' Pappenheim said, pointing to the document. 'I planned to ask my contact to dig up more on him. No need now.'

'There is always a need. Ask your contact as soon as is practical. You never know. We might get something to add to the picture.'

'I'll do that first thing in the morning. When do we hit Mainauer?'

'When he least expects it.'

'Always the best time. I like. I want that piece of shit. The Dragunov seems to be the Semper's favourite tool,' Pappenheim went on. 'We've got the one from Rügen in the gallery. Now it will soon have a partner: Mainauer's. I wonder how many more of those things there are out there, in their hands.'

'Certainly more than we would like. One more would be too many. I would be very surprised if one or two are not at the general's. He is the sniper overlord, after all. And given the trail leading back to the DDR days, I would think Dragunovs were not, and are not, difficult for him to come by.'

'Well, he's not going to be sniper overlord for much longer,' Pappenheim vowed.

'We'll get him,' Müller promised. 'Now we'd better release the goth. I kept her back until you got here. I had planned to ask her to hack into the military personnel archives to see if we could find something about Mainauer. As it is, Grogan pre-empted us.'

Pappenheim gave him a slightly amused stare. '*You* would have asked *her* to hack into military archives? Oh, we are breaking the rules today. Now, *I* do that all the time . . . but *you*? Have you forgotten all that I taught you?'

'No. You taught me how to break the rules.'

'Now that you mention it, so I did. We'd better see to the goth.'

Five

'You're in luck, Miss Meyer,' Müller announced as he and Pappenheim entered the rogues' gallery. 'We won't be keeping you late, after all.'

He was carrying the document on Mainauer. He went over to the cabinet where they stored all the pieces of information directly, or indirectly, concerning the Semper, tapped in the entry code, and pulled out a drawer. He put the loose sheets in a hanging file. He had long changed the code to the cabinet, and only two people could now independently gain access to it. He was one, Pappenheim the other.

The cabinet contained a small gold mine of information about the Semper, and he did not want Kaltendorf having access to it. Now that they had actually seen their superior with members of the Semper, Müller was prepared to resist any attempt by Kaltendorf to get in there, to the point of blatant insubordination. Kaltendorf, in the current circumstances, would not dare threaten him with a disciplinary board.

Hedi Meyer had been so engrossed in her tinkering with the computer, she only decided to turn round to look at them after Müller had put the document away.

'Ah,' she said to Pappenheim. 'You're back.'

'I'm back.'

She looked at Müller. 'Really nothing for me to do?'

'Not unless there's been a new message.'

'Nothing new. Not even transmissions from the general's radio units.'

'In that case, I'll arrange for someone to take you home.'

'Perhaps . . .' Pappenheim began. They both looked at him. 'Perhaps I can steal a march. Miss Meyer, an encrypted email to an address I shall give you. Content: Anything you've got on Ulrich Mainauer, including military service, and photographs, if any. Appreciative thanks, Pappi.'

She repeated the message to him, then set about preparing it. 'Ready to go,' she said.

'That was quick.'

'I've speeded things up. Lots more to do, though.'

'I believe you,' Pappenheim said. 'OK. Send it.'

She clicked the mouse once. 'Gone.'

'We should have a reply by morning,' Pappenheim said to Müller. 'Will you be coming in? Or are you heading south?'

'I'll be in, but I might start off later in the day.'

Pappenheim nodded. 'OK. Well, I'm off to my pit for a smoke. See you tomorrow, Miss Meyer.'

'Good night, sir.'

'You can shut down,' Müller said, after Pappenheim had gone. 'Then—'

A burst of transmission interrupted him.

'When are you leaving?' a female voice asked.

'Tomorrow morning.'

'That's Willi's voice!' Müller exclaimed softly. 'I would know it anywhere.'

'Why didn't you tell me before?' The question was petulant.

'I only found out today.'

'His *girlfriend* has a radio handy?' Müller asked rhetorically. 'Does the general know?'

'Where to?' the female voice demanded.

'Washington.'

'What for?'

'Look, that's all I can tell you. I've probably said too much already.'

'You certainly have,' Müller said. 'This classes as pillow talk, Willi. Bad for your security, but good for me.'

'When will you be back?' The petulance was even more pronounced.

'I'll not be gone long. I'll be back in three days.'

'Why not come over . . . ?'

'I can't. Things to prepare.'

The transmission came to an abrupt end.

'Was that us?' Müller asked Hedi Meyer.

'No, sir. I think he just cut her off. He didn't want an argument.'

'I'm not surprised. But I am surprised Willi gave her that radio handy. He must have done it against orders. He's got his weak flank, after all. You finish up here. I've got something to attend to. I'll arrange that transport.'

The goth swivelled her chair round to face him. Blue-lidded eyes studied him boldly. 'Why don't you take me home, sir? I've never been in your Porsche. I've never been in any Porsche. I'd like the experience.'

Taken completely by surprise, he said with distinct wariness, 'Not many people have been in my car.'

'Don't worry. I'm not making a play for you. I just want a ride in your car. And I know all the things going on in your mind right now. You're my superior, I'm your subordinate, we're colleagues, bad idea for colleagues to get involved . . . but, as I'm not planning to get involved, there's nothing to worry about. Is there?'

Müller stared at her. 'Payback.'

'What?'

'You told me you would find a way to—'

'Oh that. I wouldn't worry about it. So, it's a deal, sir? I'll see you in the garage.' She smiled at him.

'I wish I did not feel as if I had just lost an arm-wrestling match.'

'What a strange thing to say,' she said.

'Very well. In the garage. An hour. You've got time for another mission, if you feel like it.'

The smile was still on her face when he went out.

Müller knocked on Pappenheim's door, opened it, put his head through and coughed as the smoke hit him.

'It's not that bad,' Pappenheim said.

'Speak for yourself. You just missed a transmission from Willi . . . to his girlfriend.'

'*She* has one of those things?'

'I don't think Willi was authorized.'

'He's taking a chance – as if I should worry. The general is not the kind of man who loves anything but total obedience.'

'But good for us, if one of the chosen, like Willi, is prepared to disobey from time to time . . .'

'At least where women are concerned. So, what was the transmission about? And are you going to stand there creating a draught?'

'Yes. Unless you want to hear it in my office.'

'I'm only halfway through this.' Pappenheim pointed to the cigarette in his mouth.

'Finish it, I'll wait for you.'

Pappenheim sighed. 'I knew it. You've whetted my appetite, damn it.' He killed the cigarette, and stood up. 'You win.'

'Willi is flying to Washington,' Müller said as soon as they had entered his office. He went to his favourite spot by the window. The lights of the city were fully on now. 'I love looking at this.'

'*Washington?*' Pappenheim repeated.

'And only for three days. What does that tell you?'

'He could be going after Miss Bloomfield.'

'Or he may not. But . . .'

'You're going to warn her . . .'

'And give her his description, just in case.'

'It's what I'd do,' Pappenheim said.

'It was worth it, having the goth wait, after all. If we had not been in there, we would not have known about this till we checked . . . perhaps not until too late. Certainly, not before tomorrow. I'll call Miss Bloomfield, then take the goth home.'

Pappenheim stared at him. '*You're* . . . taking the goth home?'

'It's not funny. She wants a ride in the car . . . so she said.'

Pappenheim gave a huge smile. 'Payback.'

'Thank you, Pappi. I've gone down that route already.'

Pappenheim went to the door, opened it, and glanced back. 'Have fun.'

The door closed on the sound of a chuckle.

'Who needs enemies?' Müller grumbled at the closed door. He walked over to the desk and picked up a phone. 'It's still afternoon over there,' he said to himself as he began to dial.

'*Twice* in one day?' came Carey Bloomfield's voice. 'You're really missing me that badly, Müller?'

'Someone you should look out for.'

'That's a serious tone you've got on.' Carey Bloomfield said. 'How urgent?'

'He'll be on your patch some time tomorrow.'

'Description?' She was now the brisk colonel.

Müller gave her a detailed word picture of Willi. 'Don't underestimate him.'

'I never underestimate.'

'He's dangerous.'

'So am I.'

'Be careful,' Müller said.

'Of course. You too,' she added.

As before, when they hung up, they left many things unsaid.

'And Miss Meyer awaits,' Müller said, looking at the phone.

The hour gone, she was indeed waiting.

A vision in red, black bag slung from her shoulder, she stood near the gleaming Porsche in the underground garage.

Müller opened it with the remote, from a distance.

'In you get, Miss Meyer,' he said to her as he approached.

She had made herself comfortable by the time he had got in behind the wheel. 'This smells good,' she remarked, looking about her. 'I never realized how low down you really sit in one of these. Lots of room for the legs. That's a surprise. Big difference from my old Beetle.'

'Why don't you get one like Lene Berger's? Not so many visits to the testers.'

'Oh no. My Beetle's a classic. It's like the one in the film, where it races to Monte Carlo. Not exactly like it, of course; more like the original model they changed to suit. Anyway, it suits me.'

'And it's black.'

'Of course.'

'Of course,' Müller said as he started the car.

'I love that sound,' she said.

'So do I.'

He drove out towards the armoured, roll-up gate, and waited just long enough for the right amount of clearance before driving up the shallow ramp and into the street. He turned right, as the gate began to lower.

'Have you had dinner, sir?' the goth asked.

'Dinner?' Müller said, as if hearing the word for the first time. 'I knew there was something I had to do. I'll get something together when I get home.'

'There's a nice little place near Potsdamer Platz. My invite, for driving me home.'

'You don't have to . . .'

'I know I don't have to.'

He knew she was looking at him, but he did not glance at her. Instead, he glanced in the rear-view mirror. A slight frown briefly creased his forehead.

He turned left into Mauerstrasse, then right into Leipziger Strasse. They were now headed towards Potsdamer Platz.

'Was that a no?' the goth asked.

For reply, Müller again glanced into the mirror. The frown made another brief appearance. He reached the communications unit in the central console and selected hands-off telephone. A single button push got Pappenheim.

'Yes, master,' Pappenheim answered drolly.

'I want two people from the Ready Group duty shift. Not in assault gear. Ordinary clothes, but well armed, in a chaser.'

Pappenheim's manner underwent an instant change. 'Trouble?'

'Early to tell. This is just in case. We've got company. Following since we left the garage.'

'I'll get it done. Where are you?'

'Heading towards Potsdamer Platz. I'll lead them a dance. Tell the unit to contact me when they're in pursuit. We stopped at some lights and I was able to identify the car. It's a BMW like yours, but paler.'

'Got it. I'll pass that on. Hope it's nothing.'

'So do I.'

When the conversation had ended, Müller said to the goth, 'Being with me can be dangerous, Miss Meyer. Did you bring your weapon as I advised?'

She swallowed, and nodded. 'In my bag.'

'Have it ready.'

She fished in the bag, and brought it out. It was a big Beretta 92R.

Müller glanced at it. 'What's this? An epidemic of Berettas? This is non-issue, Miss Meyer.'

'Just like yours, and *Oberkommissar* Pappenhcim's, sir.'

'I'll ignore that. Can you fire that thing?'

'I can.'

'Where did you get it?'

'Mmm . . . should I really tell?'

'Yes.'

After a while, she said, 'Someone from the Ready Group. I . . . I think he thinks he likes me . . .'

'You "think he thinks"?'

'He says he likes intellectual women. I thought it was an interesting line. So I asked him to get me a Beretta like yours.'

'That makes . . . sense. Well, he certainly succeeded . . . legally, or illegally.'

'Do you want me to tell you who?'

'I think I would rather you did not.'

A loud double click told him she had cocked the weapon. 'Well, I'm ready for whatever happens.'

They had passed Potsdamer Platz and were now in Stresemannstrasse, heading southwards, prior to turning right into Schöneberger Strasse. The BMW was still with them.

Müller kept the pace steady, giving all the appearance of being oblivious to being followed.

'Are they still there?' the goth asked.

'As if they're feeling lonely.'

Müller turned right into the one-way system of the Reichpietschufer, along the right bank of the Landwehrkanal, heading northwest, and towards Tiergarten.

The BMW followed.

Then the communications system pinged. 'We're in position,' a male voice announced. 'Keeping distance.'

There was no need to respond.

The small convoy kept going, branching off to the right on Köbisstrasse, crossed Klingelhofer Strasse and into Rauchstrasse.

The BMW was still there.

The two members of the Ready Group kept on station, but maintained distance, allowing two cars to fill the gap.

Müller glanced in the mirror. 'Whoever they are, the surprise is about to come.'

He came to a T-junction and turned right. They were now on the borders of the park and its many small lakes. The road ended in a sharply angled turn to the left. They had entered Lichtensteinallee.

Müller drove a little way down, allowing the BMW to follow far enough, then slowly drew to a halt. The two cars that had been behind the BMW were no longer in the convoy.

'The people in the BMW probably think we're stopping for a private view of the park . . .'

'Private?'

'I think you know what I mean, Miss Meyer. When I say get out, you get out with your weapon. Fast. Follow my lead. And don't get in my line of fire.'

She swallowed again. 'Yes, sir.'

'Don't worry. The trap is about to be closed. They'll have too much to worry about to concentrate on you. Ready?'

She nodded quickly.

At that moment, the Ready Group chaser came fast round the corner, headlights blazing, detachable blue light flashing. It pulled to a stop almost on the BMW's bumper; effectively blocking it.

Two men sprang out, fanning behind, Heckler and Koch sub-machine guns held ready.

At about the same time, Müller said, 'Alright, Miss Meyer. Out now!'

She had already released her seat belt in preparation. She opened the door and was out of the car faster than she imagined she could be. She saw Müller running towards the BMW, but in a sideways manner that took him into shadow, gun pointing at the driver of the car.

She copied him, so that her own gun would cover the passenger.

But there was no passenger.

'Keep your hands on the wheel!' she heard Müller order.

The driver obeyed. He looked towards Müller, a slight smile on his face.

The goth had taken up a position that gave her a clear shot

into the car. The driver turned from Müller to look directly at her. For a man covered by four guns, he seemed strangely calm.

'All pretty in red,' he said to her softly. 'Going to a party? Can I come? My, my, what a big gun you've got. Do you know how to use that?'

Perhaps it was uncertainty that made her say, 'Shut the fuck up!' But her gun did not waver. '*Arschloch!*'

'Such words from such a pretty mouth.'

Müller was now at the car, his 92R close to the man's head. 'If you're quite finished.'

The man again turned to look at him. 'The noble *Hauptkommissar.*'

'Why are you following me?'

'Interesting question. Perhaps I like your car. Perhaps I've taken a fancy to the pretty lady in the red dress. Perhaps you simply happen to be going my way.'

'Perhaps you will talk more sense when those gentlemen over there invite you to their car for a ride back to our offices.'

'Thank you, but no. I have an aversion to police buildings.'

'Then you have got a problem. Please get out of the car.'

'Really, Mr Müller, you should be saying thank you to me, instead of pointing that cannon at my head.'

'And why should I be doing that?'

'Because I have something you need.'

'What could that possibly be?'

'May I move my hand? I promise you I won't give you the slightest excuse to shoot me. And please ensure the pretty lady does nothing hasty.'

'She won't.'

'I admire your confidence. Now, may I move that hand?'

'Do it. Very, very carefully.'

The man made a great show with his right hand, while Müller moved back slightly, keeping him covered. The man picked up something from the shadows of the passenger seat: a brown envelope for A4-sized contents. He held it out of the window.

'I think Pappenheim requested this. Fast work, don't you think? Don't worry. It's not a bomb.'

93

'If it is, you'll be dead just as quickly.'

'Exactly. And I have a very strong survival instinct.'

Despite himself, Müller could not hide his astonishment. Motioning to the others to hold fire, he reached forward to take the envelope.

'Watch him,' he said to them.

The goth kept her gun unerringly trained on the man in the car.

Keeping his gun in one hand, Müller braced the envelope against his body, and opened it. He put an exploratory hand inside, and felt sheets of paper.

And photographs.

'Now will you say, thank you, uncle?' the man said with a smile that reeked smugness.

'How long have you got?'

The man shook his head slowly. 'Not a nice thing to say to someone who has just given you gold dust.'

'People have died hungering after gold dust.'

'The person in there certainly is a killer. Psychotic. I know him.'

'You *know* him?'

'Let us say we have an interest in him, which coincides with yours.'

'And now you're just giving him to me.'

'The time has come.'

'If you knew about him, why did you not take him down?'

'There are many things at work, Mr Müller. The man in there is a very small part of the big picture.'

'The big picture. I see.'

'We are on the same side. If I am not mistaken, you have your own big picture.'

'A colleague lost his life . . .'

'Inevitably, in a war, there will be collateral damage . . .'

'Get out of here,' Müller said in a low, tight voice.

The man smiled. 'I'm amazed Pappenheim doesn't come here for walks, soak up the atmosphere. Reeks of smoking history, if you get my meaning. All the world's a zoo, Müller.' He turned to peer at the goth. 'I know you, don't I?'

'I very much doubt it,' she replied.

'I'm certain I do,' he insisted. 'We tried to recruit you. You turned us down. Quite amazing. Pity. I suppose we're not as dashing as the *Hauptkommissar.*'

The man started the BMW.

Müller indicated to the two members of the Ready Group to let it go. One of them got into their car and reversed. The flashing blue light was turned off.

Müller stood back to allow the BMW to turn round.

The man had to reverse twice. When he was facing the way he had come, he stopped, and looked the goth up and down, then shook his head in regret.

'Stunning,' he said, and drove on.

The blue shadows on Hedi Meyer's eyelids were made dark by the night, and her look was venomous as she stared after the departing car. Slowly, she at last lowered the gun.

'You look as if you feel cheated,' Müller said to her.

'If you mean I wish I could have shot him . . . yes. Condescending shit.'

'Miss Meyer, I never imagined you used such language. "Shut the fuck up"? "*Arschloch*"?'

'I did tell you about the state of my temper today.'

'I remember. Fiery. So, smiling boy belongs to that bunch you turned down before you came to us.'

'Yes, sir. If they are all like him . . . ugh! I made the right decision.'

'They won't all be like him; but I do get your point. And Miss Meyer . . .'

'Sir?'

'You did well.'

She beamed at him. 'Thank you!'

He gave her a quick smile, then went over to the men from the Ready Group. 'Nice work. Thanks for the back-up. Quick reaction.'

'Was it a false alarm, sir?' the one outside the car asked.

'No. It was good to have you as back-up, in case it went any other way.'

'Glad we could help.'

Müller shook hands with them, and waited until they had turned their car around and driven away.

He went back to the Porsche. The goth was already back in.

He got behind the wheel, but called Pappenheim before starting the car.

'Not what I'd feared, Pappi,' he said when Pappenheim answered. 'But good to have them, just in case. And you've got a response to your mail.'

'That was quick.'

'Tell you about it when I see you.'

'So, you're coming back here?'

'Yes. I haven't looked at it. We'll do that later . . . after I've taken Miss Meyer home.'

'Have fun,' Pappenheim said, repeating his earlier parting shot.

'Thank you, Pappi,' Müller said drily. 'Miss Meyer,' Müller continued to the goth when he had finished speaking to Pappenheim, 'after this, I now feel hungry. Will that place you mentioned still be open?'

She glanced at the digital clock on the central display. 'If we hurry, we'll have just over half an hour when we get there, before they close.'

'Then we hurry. Here.' He passed her the envelope the smiling man had brought. 'Put that into your bag. Will it fit?' He started the car.

The envelope went into the bag easily. 'It does.'

Müller turned the car round, and they headed for Potsdamer Platz.

'It's very popular,' she said as they left the car and walked the short distance to the bistro, 'and sometimes it gets very crowded; usually when there's a film festival. But we should be fine tonight, even this late.' She was carrying her bag – with weapon and envelope inside – slung from a shoulder.

They arrived at the entrance of the Italian-flavoured bistro, to find it full. People were crowded at the small bar, some on stools, laden plates on the counter before them. Further in, every chair and bankette was taken. A staircase, beginning near the bar, curved upwards.

'Oh no!' the goth cried in a soft wail. But she refused to

be defeated. 'Let's try upstairs. People come and go all the time. We could be lucky.'

Without waiting for Müller to react, she entered, and was already making her way up the stairs by the time he decided to follow.

'Do I have a choice?' he mumbled.

Several eyes followed the goth in her red dress. Many were male.

When Müller arrived at the top, he discovered it was also packed. Then he looked round to his right and saw that Hedi Meyer had commandeered a table in a far corner, which was just being vacated. She was making urgent motions at him.

'She certainly has the luck,' he admitted, going to the table.

The departing customers, a couple in business suits, smiled at him as they went past. The man glanced at the goth.

'See?' the goth said triumphantly. 'Luck. We can see everything from here – a great view outside, and most of downstairs – even the bar. All sorts of people come here.'

'Even police,' he said, quietly enough not to be heard beyond their table. Müller's jacket hid his gun completely. 'And yes, Miss Meyer,' he added. 'You do have the luck. Getting seats in a place like this must be a lottery.'

'Not always. But tonight, as you can see . . .'

They sat down next to each other, so that each had a full view of the place.

'Do you think we'll have more surprise visitors tonight?' she asked.

'I doubt it. But you never know.'

'Was I really good out there?'

'You were,' he assured her.

'I was frightened.'

'You certainly did not look it.'

Conversation was interrupted when a waitress approached.

'Hello,' she greeted the goth, clearly recognizing her. She smiled at Müller, then glanced back at the goth with a raised eyebrow of approval. She placed a menu before each of them.

'Hi,' the goth responded. 'Are we too late to order?'

'Well normally, last orders for food have just gone. No

problem with drinks. But if you want to eat, I'm sure I can do something.'

'Oh thanks,' the goth said gratefully.

The waitress stood patiently by as they opened their menus.

Hedi Meyer leaned across to tap a finger on Müller's menu. Her shoulder touched his briefly. 'I'd recommend this. It's really good.'

'Then I'll go with your recommendation.'

'I'll have the same,' she said to the waitress. 'Can we have that?'

The waitress looked. 'No problem. Drinks?'

'I'll have the Pinot,' the goth replied. 'He won't. He's driving.'

The waitress gave Müller a sympathetic, enquiring smile.

'What can I say?' he said. 'I'll have water.'

'Still? Or . . .'

'Still will be fine, thanks.'

'Did you mind my sort of taking over?' the goth asked when the waitress had gone away with their order. 'I don't want you to think . . .'

'Be my guest,' he said. He felt under scrutiny, and turned to look. A man across the room was staring at them.

'That man's staring,' she said.

'I know. But not at us. At you. Many men in here are.'

'Don't make me blush,' she hissed.

'Not guilty,' he said. 'So this is one of your favourite places?' he went on.

'I've been here once or twice.' She did not elaborate.

'Does your waitress friend know what you do?'

'No. I think she'd probably die of shock . . . but perhaps not.' The goth gave Müller an appraising look. 'She'd never imagine it of you, either.'

'Touché. How did you feel when smiling boy claimed he knew you?' he continued.

'Annoyed. He was obviously one of those people watching from somewhere I couldn't see, while I had that interview.'

'You turned them down. Why?'

'I didn't feel comfortable. Too shadowy. And I certainly would not have liked working with that . . . that man.'

'Why did you decide on us? It can be dangerous, as you already know only too well. And, as I told you when we first spoke about this months ago, you could make a fortune in industry. Definitely be driving your own Porsche.'

She smiled. 'I heard about two crazy people called Müller and Pappenheim. You have reputations, you two. You give people headaches. That appealed to something a little crazy in me. When I heard about the unit, I thought, OK. That's where I'm going.' She lowered her voice. 'Just look at this thing we're dealing with. So many strands. So many levels. I could not get that working in an ordinary office.' She grinned. 'Anyway, which industry boss would let me fly my jet?'

'Miss Meyer,' Müller began, responding to her grin, 'I've given up trying to understand how your mind works. But thank God you're with us. I'll try to ensure that danger does not get too close to you again.'

'I knew what I was buying into,' she said, 'as the Americans would say.'

At that moment, the waitress arrived with their drinks.

'Thank you for that, Hedi,' Müller said as they left the bistro. 'It was excellent.'

'You didn't mind my paying? Some men hate that, even if it is the woman who has done the inviting. They seem to think it takes something away from them.'

'Then they have a problem. It was very kind of you to invite me, and I enjoyed it very much.'

She smiled to herself in the warmth of the evening, as they reached the car.

'Now I'll take you home to Prenzlberg, and then I'll go back to the office with smiling boy's little present.'

She paused as she was about to get in. 'Can't we go to the office first?'

'You would like to see.'

'I would like to see, sir.'

'You're going to be very late home tonight, Miss Meyer.'

'Then I'm going to be late.'

Müller shook his head slowly. 'Alright. Get in.'

Traffic was considerably thinner, and it took them very little time to get back. They walked along the corridor to Pappenheim's office. Müller knocked, opened the door, and put his head through.

Pappenheim, for once not smoking, looked up. 'Ah. You're back. Lady safely tucked in?'

'Come and see for yourself. We're going into the gallery.'

Pappenheim got to his feet. *"We"*?'

'As I said. Come and see.'

Pappenheim came to the door, and stared at Hedi Meyer as he emerged into the corridor. 'Miss Meyer, you're either very late for work, or very early.'

'Or both.'

'Don't get her going, Pappi,' Müller said. 'She's had two glasses of Pinot.'

'Oh ho!'

'But she has earned them.' Müller told Pappenheim about the incident with the smiling man as they walked to the gallery. He left nothing out.

'"Shut the fuck up"?' Pappenheim said to the goth as Müller tapped in the entry code.

'It was the best I could do,' she said in explanation.

'Wonders indeed,' Pappenheim said as they entered.

They went over to the light table, and the goth took the envelope out of her bag to hand to Müller. He opened it, and spread its contents on the table. There were four, full-colour photographs, and two sheets of printed paper.

Müller laid the photographs side by side. They were of Mainauer. One showed him in recruit fatigues. Another in the uniform of a sergeant, instructing trainee snipers who were all in full camouflage gear. The third showed a high rock face. The fourth was of Mainauer in police *Kommissar*'s uniform.

Müller briefly flipped each photo over. Captions were printed on the backs. 'Mainauer at nineteen', 'Mainauer instructing specialist sniper unit', 'Mainauer in cover', 'Mainauer, police *Kommissar*'.

Hedi Meyer studied the photographs. 'He looks so pleasant,' she said of the one showing Mainauer at nineteen. 'Friendly, too.'

In that photograph, Mainauer was smiling shyly at the

camera. Slim, of average height, he looked like the cleancut boy next door. A ready-to-smile mouth, and an easy-going expression, completed the picture: that of a young man uncertain of his future, but prepared to go for it. The brownish hair, with its severe military cut, emphasized this. The eyes, however, seemed a little strange. They were a milky grey; like fog on a cold day.

The sergeant in the next photograph was a changed man. The body was still lean, but looked much tougher. The boy next door had vanished. In his place had come a hardened veteran. The foggy eyes now looked menacing.

The third of the photos showed the rock face.

'Nothing but rock,' Müller said. 'See anything, Pappi?'

Pappenheim shook his head. 'Nothing.'

'Miss Meyer?'

The goth was peering keenly at the photograph. The rock was needle-like, its summit high above the surrounding landscape. It was scoured by deep fissures, and scrub vegetation sprawled across it in untidy patterns. The angle of the shot gave an almost three-dimensional impression of great distance from the landscape below.

She shook her head. 'Nothing there. Perhaps they made a mistake with this one.'

'No mistake,' Müller said. 'The caption says "Mainauer in cover". But I can't see where he could be. Not even a mountain goat could stand up there.'

'A lupe might help,' she said, and pulled out a drawer. There were several lupes in it. She got two out, and handed one to Müller.

'You try first,' he said. 'Younger eyes.'

'Hmm,' she said.

She placed the lupe on the photograph, and began to move it slowly, searching for a tell-tale sign. She had almost given up, when she paused.

'My God!' she breathed. 'I can't believe it!'

She straightened, blinking. 'You have a look, sir,' she said to Müller. 'Tell me what you see.' She left the lupe in position.

Müller bent down to peer at the photo. 'Nothing . . .' he

began. 'Nothing at all . . . Wait . . . wait. No. It can't be.' He sounded uncertain. He straightened. 'Pappi, you try.'

Frowning slightly, Pappenheim had a look. It took him a little longer. 'Rifle muzzle,' he said at last, putting a hand to his back as he too straightened once more. 'Oh, my aging body. Definitely the muzzle of a rifle,' he added.

Müller moved the lupe, and stared at the photograph. 'Although I *know* where it is, I can't even see it now. Well spotted, Hedi. Your eyes are certainly excellent.' He traced a hand along a fissure. 'He's *inside* that thing,' he remarked in wonder, 'and you can barely see the muzzle . . . even with the lupe.'

'Do you have the feeling,' Pappenheim began drily, 'that the people who sent smiling boy with this are telling us something?'

'If they wanted to tell us how dangerous he is, they've succeeded.'

Müller turned to the last photograph. Mainauer looked up at them, in his police uniform.

'Those eyes,' the goth said. 'They look as if the soul left a long time ago.'

Müller looked at her. 'That's a very perceptive observation, Miss Meyer. You are quite right.' He turned back to the photograph. 'This man died a long, long time ago.'

'Then I'd like to send the eyes where the soul went,' Pappenheim said in a hard voice.

'You'll get the chance, Pappi. Sooner, rather than later. The people who sent this to us want Mainauer taken, but, for reasons of their own, they don't want to do it themselves.'

'I think they made use of him, sir,' Hedi Meyer said.

Pappenheim stared at her. 'What makes you say that?'

'I'm remembering something from my interview. Something one of the interviewers asked. She asked whether I had any objections to actions that may or may not be strictly within the law, but were in the interests of national security. I said there were possibly occasions when such things might be contemplated. It pleased them.'

'You're saying that even though they knew he was with the Semper, they still used him for their own ends.'

102

'Yes, sir.'

'I agree,' Müller said. 'Now they want him neutralized, without warning the Semper.'

'Which is where we come in,' Pappenheim said.

'Johann Hoventhaler's killing gives us cause.'

'So the Semper concentrate on us, and not the smiling boy's people.'

'Your contacts, Pappi. We use them, they use us.'

'Ah yes,' Pappenheim said. '*Sed quis custodiet ipsos custodes?*'

'"But who will guard the guardians,"' the goth translated.

'I see you've had a misspent youth, Miss Meyer,' Müller said to her.

'One of the interviewers quoted this to me, and asked me if I knew what it meant.'

'And?'

'When I answered, they looked impressed.'

'So they've got a sense of humour too . . . if warped.'

Müller picked up the sheets of paper.

'And look at this,' he said after a few seconds of silent study. 'Another list of his killings. It almost mirrors the one from Grogan; but there are exceptions. Some names and locations are not among those we got from Grogan. But one particular name does appear on both.' He handed the papers to Pappenheim.

'Kill confirmed, kill confirmed, kill confirmed.' Pappenheim read on silently, then paused. 'Kill . . . confirmed.' He handed the sheets of paper to the goth. 'Johann Hoventhaler,' he said to Müller heavily.

'No doubt at all now,' Müller said, 'even if we still had any.'

The goth had put the papers down without reading them. She was looking towards the computer. A tiny red light was blinking.

Müller saw her look. 'What is it, Miss Meyer?'

'Message waiting.'

'Then power up. See what it is.'

She quickly went to the machine and started it. She launched the flying game, and when the cockpit had come on, there was indeed a message blinking on the left-hand

MFD. DEFINITIVE INFO ON CRASH. JACK AND MAGGIE HARGREAVES. WOONNALLA STATION. Then followed a set of co-ordinates. That was all.

'What does that mean, sir?' Hedi Meyer enquired of Müller. '"Definitive info on crash".'

'If you wouldn't mind, Miss Meyer, I'd rather keep this one from you. For your own safety.'

'Yes, sir.'

Müller glanced at Pappenheim. 'You do know what it means, don't you?'

'Oh yes.'

'Can you find where those co-ordinates belong?' Müller asked the goth.

'Easily,' she replied.

She called up a global map, and went to work. First, it changed to the image of the world as a spinning globe, with crosshairs within a targeting square shifting across it. The marker went south, and east. It zeroed on Australia. Australia expanded past the width of the screen, and continued expanding until Western Australia came up. The expansion continued at speed until, finally, it stopped near Broome.

'*Broome?*' Müller exclaimed. 'In *Australia*? Has he gone mad? And what is Woonnalla Station?'

'A sheep farm?' Pappenheim suggested. 'I once knew someone whose parents owned an Australian sheep farm. They called it a station.'

Müller nodded. 'I know they do, but this does not necessarily have to be one. Miss Meyer, could you please see if you can find out anything about a Woonnalla Station?'

Fifteen minutes later, she had found nothing.

'Sorry, sir. I tried a really fast search engine. One that finds just about anything that's in the Net database. Woonnalla Station is not there.'

'For a very good reason,' Pappenheim said. 'Otherwise he would not have sent co-ordinates. The Hargreaves, whoever they are, don't want to be found. I don't blame them, sitting on something like that.'

'But how did he find them?' Müller wondered.

'As you've said,' Pappenheim told him, 'Grogan has many

104

facets, and God knows how many sources of information. It wouldn't surprise me if he also worked with the smiling boy's people, and any others that suit his agenda.'

'It would not surprise me, either. Two sources of information, with disturbingly similar material. Try something else, Miss Meyer,' Müller went on to the goth. 'Call up a road map of the area. See where those co-ordinates get us.'

She did so, getting a very detailed, colour map that showed main as well as secondary roads, and even tracks.

'Sir, the nearest *track* is sixty kilometres from where the co-ordinates say that place is supposed to be. As for the roads . . . Let me see if a satellite map can do better . . .'

'Try it.'

The satmap yielded empty outback space.

'Sorry,' the goth said. 'But that map could be out of date.'

'No matter. It was a long shot. Can you print me a colour copy of the road map, with the co-ordinates marked on it?'

'Easily done.'

When it was ready, Müller took the printed map and put it on the table. He leaned over to stare at the co-ordinates marker for long moments.

'Alright, Hedi,' he said as he straightened. 'Time I really took you home. Give me half an hour, then I'll come for you here. Have another flight, or tinker, if you wish. I'll not be long.'

She nodded. 'I'll be here.'

Müller turned to Pappenheim. 'Take Mainauer down. When you want to. How you want to take him.'

'Tomorrow will do for me. Strike before he knows what's hit him.'

'He's all yours.'

Müller put all the information from the smiling boy into the cabinet, but kept the map the goth had printed out; then he and Pappenheim left the gallery.

'Amazing woman,' Müller said as he and Pappenheim walked back to his office. 'It's already tomorrow, and she's got to be back here in a few hours, but she's not complaining.'

'I'll talk to Hermann,' Pappenheim said. 'Make sure he does not give her any grief in case she's a little late in the morning.'

'I'd appreciate that.'

'So?' Pappenheim began when they had entered Müller's office. 'Are you thinking of going to Australia?'

Müller did not answer immediately. He put the map on his desk, then went over to the window and looked out.

'Am I letting this get to me, Pappi? Am I becoming obsessed?'

'How do you want me to answer you?'

'As you always have. Honestly.'

'Then I'll do so,' Pappenheim said. 'When you were a boy of twelve, your parents died in a mysterious plane crash. Stories were put out about sordid affairs and marital breakdown. Not something pleasant for a boy to hear. School friends were less than kind. It was not until more than *twenty* years later that you discover, almost accidentally, that it had all been a lie; that your parents had in fact been murdered. All the character assassination had been part of the deal. You discover that some family friends had also colluded in the betrayal.

'People began to seek to destroy you for reasons you could not quite understand. A cousin you never knew about, who turned out to be part of the organization we now know as the Semper, sought to kill you, and your aunt. Your aunt's long-lost husband Greville – believed long dead – turns up with a DNA timebomb in his body, created by pyscho scientists for even greater psychos. His body is a gold mine for them; but they don't know for certain he is the one.

'You discover from Greville and other sources that your father was in fact a very brave man who had infiltrated the Semper. When they found out, they killed him and your mother all those years ago, to prevent him from disclosing their agenda, which has been years in the making. You discover that the flight recorders found at the time were planted fakes; but you have also found the *real* ones. Your father left you some highly incriminating and dangerous evidence that can be used against them. They have infiltrated many levels of society, and have international affiliations. The DNA weapon is part of this.

'So, to cut it all short, are you obsessed? No. You are

106

fighting a war and, so far, you are doing well. And . . . you cannot walk away from all those who have already died: your parents, our colleagues, the colonel's wife . . .' Pappenheim paused. 'If this were me, I would go to the Antarctic itself, if there was the slightest chance that someone out there had information that would help seriously damage, and perhaps destroy, the Semper.' As if stunned by his own eloquence, Pappenheim gave a sudden grin. 'So when do you go to Australia?'

'As soon as is practical.'

'When you suddenly vanish, I won't know where you are . . . if the Great White asks, which I doubt.'

'He'll be too busy watching his back. Interesting to see if he turns up in the morning.'

'He won't.'

Müller went to his desk, and opened the drawer in which he had put Colonel Jackson's letter. He put the printout of the map in there, paused, then took out the letter to hand it to Pappenheim.

'Got this from Colonel Bill.'

Pappenheim took it, and read it through. He pursed his lips, nodded slightly, then handed it back.

'Good man,' he said. 'Another reason why you can't turn your back on this, after all that has happened.'

Müller put the letter away. 'You're right as usual, Pappi. I suppose I just wanted to convince myself that what we're doing is the right thing.'

'We don't have a choice.'

'That we do not,' Müller agreed. 'Now that my brief wobble is over, I'd better take poor Miss Meyer home at long last.'

'You should.'

They went out together.

Pappenheim stood by the door of his office and watched as Müller entered the gallery. A short while later, the goth preceded him into the corridor. They turned, and saw Pappenheim.

Hedi Meyer smiled at him. 'You should get some sleep, sir.'

'Plenty of time for that when I'm dead.'

'See you later,' Müller said to him.

Pappenheim nodded, watching as the goth walked next to him with light steps.

'Don't fall for him, Miss Meyer,' Pappenheim cautioned softly, as they turned a corner. 'There lies heartbreak.'

Six

Getting to where the goth lived in Prenzlberg did not take long. Müller turned left up Friedrichstrasse, and right into Unter den Linden. After that, it was virtually a straight run all the way.

Her spacious apartment was in one of the many renovated and modernized buildings from the days of the DDR, close to the café nirvana of Kollwitzstrasse. There were parking spaces next to the building, and he pulled into one.

'Bit late to ask you up for a coffee, I suppose?' she said to him.

'I think it is.'

'Yes.'

She opened the door, climbed out, and slung her bag from her shoulder.

'I'll wait till you're safely inside,' he said, climbing out.

'I've made it home many times before, you know.'

'Even so.'

Impulsively, she came round the car to kiss him softly near the mouth. 'Thank you.'

She hurried to the entrance of the building, dug into her bag for her keys, opened the door, turned to give him a quick wave, then went in.

Müller waited, looking up.

Eventually, lights on the top floor came on. A window opened. The goth looked out, and waved to him again, before shutting the window once more.

He got back into the car, feeling better. Perhaps the Semper would leave her alone.

Perhaps.

*   *   *

In his office, Pappenheim made a call to Berger's home number. Not wanting to wake her, he knew she would have the answering machine on her main phone switched on.

'We're going on a trip, Lene,' he said into the machine. 'Bring your guest. She'll want to be in on this. Be bright and early. Seven o'clock will do.'

He also called Reimer, and gave the same time.

The next morning, 07.00.

Mainauer, in uniform, got into his car and set off for work. He decided to use the route that would take him past Johann Hoventhaler's house. When he came to the triple bend, he did not pause. He did not even glance at the flowers.

He entered the bend that led into the straight run past the house. When he got there, he slowed down, then stopped.

Normally, he would have simply driven on. But that morning he chose to get out of the car, and to go up to the house. He pressed the doorbell. He heard the faint chime, but no one came. He tried again, then a third time. The result was the same.

'She's gone, *Kommissar* Mainauer,' a voice said behind him.

He turned. A middle-aged woman with over-curious eyes was looking at him with interest.

An uncertain frown briefly appeared. 'It's Frau . . . Kreschke, isn't it? I remember you from when my colleague was killed.'

'Terrible thing, that,' she said, nodding, glad that she had been recognized.

'Yes. It was. The hazards of being a policeman. What was that you just said about her being gone? When did she get back?'

'I'm not sure if she ever went away, poor thing.'

'But I thought . . . well, her family said she had gone away.'

'Perhaps. Perhaps not, Anyway, she's definitely gone now.'

Mainauer kept his cool, and pretended to look puzzled. 'I don't quite understand, Frau Kreschke.'

'Well, yesterday a BMW with a Berlin licence came here. A big man and a young woman – pretty thing, in a . . . bossy way – stopped by the house. They put the car in the drive.

110

The man tried the doorbell many times. Then the woman began to talk at the house, talking to someone inside. I couldn't hear what she said.'

'Someone *inside*? Are you sure?'

Frau Kreschke gave him a look that was close to being haughty. 'Of course I'm sure!'

'Sorry, Frau Kreschke. Policeman's habit. We've got to get everything straight.'

This served to mollify her. 'I'm sure you do. I think the people who came were not sure anyone was there,' she went on, 'but after some more talking, the door opened slightly. Was I surprised.'

'I'm certain you were.' Mainauer kept the irony he felt out of his voice.

'She must have asked them for something,' Frau Kreschke said, well into her stride now. 'They each handed whatever it was to her . . .'

'IDs perhaps?'

'Perhaps. Anyway, she took them, and closed the door. A little later the door opened, and she let them in. They stayed in there for some time, then all three came out. She was carrying a suitcase, and a bag. They all got into the car and left.'

'So she went away with them?'

'That's what I just said.'

'Sorry. Policeman's habit again. Facts are important in our work.'

'I can understand that.'

'Thank you, Frau Kreschke. You've been a great help.'

'She will be alright, won't she? I mean, those people . . .'

'That's just what I'm going to find out. Thanks again.'

Mainauer got into his Volvo, and turned it round. He headed back the way he had come, leaving a bemused Frau Kreschke staring after him.

The narrow road to Mainauer's house rose steeply in parts, with wide bends. About a hundred metres or so from the house itself, the road levelled and widened sufficiently to allow two vehicles to pass without pulling over. It was thickly wooded on either side. The roofs of a few houses could just be seen.

Paved tracks led off on either side, clearly access routes to the part-hidden buildings.

Then the road narrowed again, disappearing behind a screen of trees for the final bend that led to the house. The road ended there, levelling into a wide parking apron before it.

The spacious two-storey house was perched in splendid isolation upon its low hill. Its nearest neighbour was a hundred metres away, where the road widened.

Mainauer's Volvo charged up the road, taking the bends with barely a reduction in speed. When he reached his home, he brought the car to a halt with a squeal of tyres.

He leapt out, and almost ran to the house. He hurriedly unlocked the door, switched off the alarm, and rushed to his study. He unlocked a drawer in his desk, and took out a black phone. This was connected to a secure line.

He dialled a number. It was answered immediately.

'Yes?'

'I must speak to the general.'

'"Must"?'

'Listen, Reindorf, don't give me that you-captain-me-colonel bullshit. If you don't want to look in the mirror one day and see a hole where your brains should be, connect me with the general. *Now!*'

There was a pause, then Reindorf said stiffly, 'Hold on.'

'What is it, Ulli?' came the general's voice after a brief delay.

'There's a problem, General.'

Mainauer then gave the general the full details of what Frau Kreschke had told him.

'It was quite obviously Pappenheim,' Mainauer continued. 'The description, the Berlin plates, and the IDs. Hoventhaler must have told his wife, and she will have told Pappenheim. No other reason why he has taken her to Berlin. Protection. My career as a policeman is effectively over. I'll have to leave quickly. Today.'

The general was very quiet for some time. Mainauer waited, curbing his impatience.

'I agree with you,' the general said at last. 'Even if the people the woman described were not Pappenheim and one

112

of his colleagues, the risk is too great. Arrangements will be made. Start preparing for your departure. You know the rendezvous point. You will be sent where you can lie low in safety. You will be contacted when you are needed.'

'Thank you, General.'

A sharp click ended the conversation.

Mainauer did not put the phone back into the drawer. Instead, he pressed a button under the base. That button had a once-only operation. It permanently switched the line to a normal one. He left the phone on the desk, then hurried through the house, and began packing. The first item he took was the Dragunov.

He changed into civilian clothes, and hung the uniform in a wardrobe. When he had packed everything he felt he needed, it came to one large suitcase, and the Dragunov.

He then spent another half hour in the house before going out to load the Volvo. He went back to pull the door shut, but did not lock it.

He got into the Volvo, and drove off.

Berlin, 07.20.

'Last chance to change your mind, Elke,' Pappenheim said.

'I'm not changing it,' Elke Hoventhaler said firmly. 'I want this.'

The four of them were in the garage. Berger was already at the wheel of the BMW, Reimer in the driving seat of a black Mercedes.

Pappenheim nodded. 'Alright. Let's go.'

He got into the BMW, while she joined Reimer. The two cars headed out of the garage, and set off for Mainauer's home near Göttingen.

In twenty minutes, Willi would be in the air, bound for Washington.

The goth, in tight black jeans and loose shirt, and the red trainers with their black stripes, arrived in her department at precisely 08.00. Her eyelids were black, her eyes shining.

Hermann Spyros stared at her. 'I thought you'd be later. Pappenheim said you were here till well after midnight.'

'Slept like a baby,' she said. 'I'm quite refreshed.'

Spyros, no ancient, commented, 'What it must be like to be young.'

'And pure of mind.'

'You've lost me,' he said.

'Don't worry about it,' the goth said, and began to tinker with the nearest computer.

At nine o'clock, Kaltendorf proved both Müller and Pappenheim wrong, by putting in an appearance.

He strode along the corridor to their offices, and first knocked on Müller's door. He opened it and marched in, without waiting for a response. He paused when he saw that the place was empty and strode out again, face expressionless.

He went to Pappenheim's door, and repeated the routine. He went in, astonished to find he could breathe without coughing. He soon saw why. He retreated and stomped off, making his way to the sergeants' office.

He found Klemp, who just managed to hide the usual, picture-rich newspaper he was reading and jump to his feet in time.

'*Herr Direktor!*'

Kaltendorf did not waste time with niceties. 'Where are Reimer and Berger?' he demanded.

'Gone, Herr *Direktor.*'

'I can see they're gone! Where?'

'They didn't say, Herr *Direktor.*'

'You're the senior sergeant, and you don't know where they are?'

Klemp swallowed.

'Thank you, *Hauptmeister* Klemp,' Kaltendorf said acidly. And went out.

'Herr . . . Herr *Direktor,*' Klemp said weakly, but Kaltendorf was long out of earshot.

It took Klemp a while to get back to his paper.

All of two minutes.

About five minutes after Kaltendorf had returned to his office, one of his phones rang.

'Ah, Heinz,' the familiar voice said in his ear. 'Where are Müller and Pappenheim?'

'Neither is in his office. Their favourite sergeants are gone as well.'

'I believe I know where to. Thank you, Heinz.'

The line went dead.

The general put down his own phone and looked at Reindorf.

'We moved none too soon. Müller and Pappenheim are certainly on their way to Mainauer's place. They opted for the element of surprise. No warning was given to Mainauer's superior. Thank God for gossips, or he would have been caught in the trap.'

'But how did they find out?' Reindorf asked. 'They showed no previous interest then, suddenly, a flurry of action.'

'It is quite possible that they did not come by the information until now. But those two never work as expected. They could just as easily have been sitting on the knowledge, biding their time. It is immaterial now, thanks to the gossiping Frau Kreschke. Society despises the gossip, with good reason. But there are times, Reindorf, when they have proven to be invaluable assets in exerting control. Many before us have made good use of them throughout history. Gossips are very useful tools.'

Near Göttingen, 10.10.
The BMW led the Mercedes along the road to Mainauer's house. They had made very good time, and Pappenheim felt pleased.

From the driver's seat, Berger glanced at him as he checked his Beretta.

'I know he's supposed to be at work,' Pappenheim said, noting the look. He put the gun away. 'But you never know. Better safe than sorry. We'll stop where Elke says the road widens. Walk up from there.'

'What if he is in?'

'Then let's hope he won't be pointing that Dragunov at us.'

'That makes me feel really safe.'

They came to the level, wider section of road. She pulled

115

to one side, and stopped. The Mercedes pulled up behind, in perfect formation.

'No weapons showing,' Pappenheim ordered as they all climbed out. He waited for the cars to be locked. 'Time for our walk.'

They made their way up the final stretch of road in single file, Pappenheim leading. When they reached the bend, they continued in that manner until they reached the apron. They spread out, Elke Hoventhaler moving ahead.

Then she stopped.

'What is it?' Pappenheim asked in a low voice.

'I'm not sure.'

'Uneasy?'

'Yes. His car is gone, so he must be on duty. But . . .'

'You stay here.'

Motioning to the others to stand back, he went up to the door, looked at it closely, then pressed the doorbell. A buzzer sounded. He waited. Nothing happened. He tried the button again. Again nothing happened.

'Anyone home?' he called.

When silence continued to greet him, he again indicated that the others remain where they were.

Very slowly, he reached for the doorknob, and twisted. It moved. The door was open.

Pappenheim took some steps back. He looked at Elke Hoventhaler. 'Didn't you say this place was alarmed?'

'It is.'

'The door is open. No alarm.'

She was very surprised. 'He's not here, and the door is *open*? That's definitely not like him. He was always going on about security, and telling us how we could improve our home.'

'Could he be in there, waiting for us? Pehaps the car's in the garage.'

She shook her head. 'The garage is full of stuff. No room in there for a car.'

Pappenheim drew his gun. 'All of you stay back . . .'

'Chief—!' Berger began.

'That means you as well, Berger.'

116

'Reimer?'

'Chief?'

'If she moves, shoot her.'

'*Chief!*'

'You know what I mean, Reimer.'

'Yes, Chief.'

'Touch me, Reimer,' Berger said, 'and you lose a hand.'

Pappenheim raised his. 'Quiet!'

They shut up.

He moved back to the door, and took his time about opening it, gun ready for instant use.

He pushed the door wide, staying in cover. Nothing happened.

He looked about him, paying close attention to the floor. He could see nothing to cause alarm.

He sensed the others were moving forward and turned to look at them. He raised a finger to his lips briefly, then again held up a restraining hand. His expression left no one in doubt.

He entered the house and stood there in the hallway, again looking about him. He looked for telltale signs of tripwires or pinpricks of light. He saw none.

He moved further in. Again, he paused. Again he looked about him, searching. He kept his breathing even, as if fearing even its noise might trigger something. Again nothing.

He moved further in, this time stopping at the door to the living room, remaining outside. He did another slow scan, looking for an anomaly.

Pappenheim inched his way just inside the living room, and stopped once more.

Mainauer was a man schooled in the art of subterfuge. Anything was possible. He would not go to work and leave his normally alarmed house open.

Unless . . .

Unless he had no intention of returning.

As the thought hit him, something made Pappenheim look behind and up. There, just above the inside of the door jamb, was the tiniest of pinpricks of light; an almost invisible, twinkling red star.

Pappenheim did not pause to wonder. With a speed that

belied his bulk, he made for the door. He rushed outside, to the startled looks of the others.

'*Move!*' he bawled at them.

After a moment's hesitation, they turned and ran, heading back down the road as fast as they could. They rounded the bend, putting the screen of trees between them and the house.

They kept going, and did not stop until they came to the cars, looking sheepish and uncertain as they turned to look at Pappenheim questioningly.

'Wait,' he said.

Even though he expected it, the massive explosion still made Pappenheim jump. A boiling mass of flame and dark smoke rose upwards, spreading as it did so.

They ducked, even though the thickness of the trees near them afforded cover. Solid pieces of objects flew through the air, a few slamming on to the roofs of houses. Sudden shouts of alarm, made faint by the trees, could be heard.

'Into the cars!' Pappenheim commanded. 'Let's get out of here before the gawkers arrive. Come on. Move!'

They bundled into the cars, which Berger and Reimer rapidly turned round, to head back down the road at speed.

Pappenheim made a call to Ollie Lorenz, Mainauer's superior.

'Ollie.'

'Pappi! Another call so soon? You'll start worrying me.'

'Sorry to be the bearer of bad tidings . . .'

'You are worrying me.'

'Has Mainauer come in today?'

'Funny you should ask. No one's seen him. He was due here at least three hours ago. Calls to his home have not been answered, and as there are no reports of accidents . . .'

'There'll be a report soon . . . of an explosion . . .'

'*Explosion?* Where?'

'His house.'

'*What?* Is he alright?'

'I am most certain he is.'

'Thank God for that!'

'I don't think you'll be thanking God, Ollie.'

'What do you mean? And how do you know what happened to his house? You're in Berlin!'

'I'm afraid not, Ollie. I'm very close to his house. I saw it explode.'

Lorenz fell silent. 'What the hell's this, Pappi?'

'Something you don't want to know about. You won't be seeing Mainauer in police uniform again. That's all I can tell you, except that *he* killed Johann Hoventhaler.'

'That's impossible!'

'I wish it were, Ollie. But I'm afraid it's a fact. I can't tell you more. You'll have to wait for the official report, whenever that comes. Better organize your local team to go up to the scene.'

'Jesus!' Lorenz muttered.

'Sorry, Ollie.'

Pappenheim hung up.

When they were a reasonable distance away, Pappenheim said to Berger, 'Stop here.'

She pulled to the side, and waited for the Mercedes to stop behind them. They all got out to look back. A dark cloud was rising from the hill where Mainauer's house once stood. Rolling explosions could still be heard.

'He's not dead, is he?' Elke Hoventhaler asked Pappenheim. Her face looked pinched. It was clear she felt cheated.

He shook his head slowly. 'Sorry, Elke. I think he's a long way from here. He wired the place. Anyone could have opened that door. A child, someone from the post, colleagues checking to see if he was alright . . .'

'The bastard.'

'Not a strong enough word.' He lit a cigarette with a steady hand. 'I almost missed it,' he continued, blowing the smoke away from her. 'I think the trigger was the opening of the door.' He paused. 'Bastard is too good a word. We'll get him. One way or another . . . one day, somewhere. I promise you that.'

'If you hadn't stopped us . . .' she said, words fading as she imagined all four of them being caught inside the house.

'You could have died in there,' Berger said, not looking at him.

'But I didn't.' He looked at her. 'Can you drive back?'

'I can drive back.' She still did not look at him.

When they returned, Berger lingered in the garage, pretending she had left something in the car. Pappenheim, Reimer, and Elke Hoventhaler went on.

Berger was leaning on the car when she realized she had company. Reimer had come back.

He peered at her. 'Are you alright, Lene?'

'I'm fine.'

He continued to peer at her. 'You look like you've been . . .' He stopped, glanced back to where Pappenheim had gone, comprehension dawning. 'Jesus, Lene. Stop wrecking yourself over Papp—'

She rounded on him. '*Shut it*, Reimer! You don't know what you're talking about. Do I give you advice about your anorexic girlfriend?'

'Er . . . well . . . yes.'

Berger glared at him. 'Shut it, anyway. And if you mention one word to anyone . . .'

'I'm many things, but not that crazy. It's your life.'

'Exactly.'

'Coming?'

'In a few minutes.'

Reimer shrugged. 'Fine.'

He left her to her solitude.

It was precisely 13.45. In exactly six hours, Willi Helmer would be landing at Dulles International.

Schlosshotel Derrenberg, near Saalfeld, Thüringen.

The Honourable Timothy Charles Wilton-Greville, former major, who long ago had consigned both the 'honourable' and the 'major' to the dustbin, was sitting in the breakfast room of the owner's residence with Aunt Isolde, having lunch. Suddenly, he gasped.

Aunt Isolde stared at him, an unnamed fear in her eyes. 'Are you alright, Timmy?' she asked in a perfect English that had more than a tinge of Sandhurst.

120

Greville nodded. 'Don't look so worried, my dear. I'm quite alright.' Whatever it had been, had passed quickly.

'That thing inside of you . . .'

'My own, bespoke DNA poison, you mean? Still working its way through, and taking its own devilish time of it, as usual. Damned fiendish thing they created, what?' Greville tended to speak in a mixture of outmoded rhythms and styles, and modern idioms; a legacy of many years away from the UK.

'You mustn't joke.'

'That's just it, my dear. I must joke. Spirits up, and all that.'

'Was that . . . was that . . . it? That pain?'

'Not so much of a pain, as a discomfort. To be frank, I believe it was a bit of trapped wind. Sort of thing babies get.' He smiled. 'Perhaps I am a baby, and this thing reverses aging.' He reached out a hand to touch hers. 'There, there, my dear. A little joke, hmm?'

She forced a quick smile. 'I have a nightmare that one morning I'll wake up, look at you, knowing you won't be waking up with me.'

'This could also happen to me. There is no guarantee that this devil's invention will take me before you, old girl. Then where will I be? The makers of this potion planned to make it a DNA-specific weapon; a truly bespoke biological monstrosity. Its real horror is in the destruction of the repro-ductive capability, the passing on of this via sexual contact, and the infinitely slow degradation of the host person . . . *all in one.*

'This gives an individual an incredible length of time to pass the infection on. Target the group you wish to eliminate over time, and one day, zero population growth goes steeply into the minus. One day, no more group. And it is completely undetectable, unless you know what you're looking for. Despite its undoubted sophistication, what I've got in me is the only, and relatively crude, prototype in existence; plenty of room for improvement. Fortunately, my team and I destroyed the lab totally, all those years ago. I am, you might say, the formula. When I die, it dies with me. As I've said, damned fiendish. Trouble with weapons like that, is keeping control of it. Like gas in war, you don't always know whether the wind will take it back to you. You could even say I am carrying the first seeds of the effective annihilation of mankind. More effective than any conventional bomb. People survive bombs. This is slower and less explosive, but no one survives in the end.'

'It sounds perfectly horrible.'

'It is. That is why no one will ever get my body to experiment on.' He smiled at her once more, making light of it.

Aunt Isolde looked at him with deep fondness. 'You don't have to explain all this to me, Timmy. It's enough to know you're not dead after all these years, and to have you back with me.'

'I promised your nephew, young Jens, that I'd tell you everything, over such time as we've . . . er . . . got together. He did not force me to. Left it entirely to me. But he's quite right. Quite right.' Greville looked into a great distance. 'You know, while I was out there for those decades in the Middle East, doing my bit for monarch and country, I kept asking myself how many young 'uns you'd have by the time I saw you again . . . if I ever did see you again. Perfectly understandable, your having them, given my strange absence.'

'I never wanted any child but yours, Timmy, despite my marrying Helmut. Had he not died before this place was finished, I'm not sure I would have seen you again.'

'Perfectly understandable. And I would not have come. But thank you, my dear, for saying that about the kiddies. Humbles a man.' He sighed. 'How life takes strange turns. When that monster in a vial broke and emptied its contents all over me in that lab, it put paid to any paternal ambitions. Permanently. At the time, thought I was doing the right thing: stealing it for our side, so forth. Got shot at, vial shatters. Stuff soaks into me. Thus is born my DNA time bomb. No one must have it. Not "our" side . . . not anyone's side. Still, not life's fault. Life goes on its merry way. It is we, the people, who keep putting the spanners in.'

'Well,' she said, 'reproduction is not our worry.'

He gave her a roguish grin that reminded her of the first time they had ever met. She felt as if her heart would swell to bursting point.

'At least there is one thing this wretched monster does not affect.'

'Eat your lunch, Timmy,' she said, smiling.

'Yes, my Red Baroness.'

'My God!' she said. 'You remember that? I've not heard it in years and years.'

'I can still see the headlines in the society papers, both here and in dear old Blighty. "Red Baroness gives party for rebellious youth." Quite funny, actually.'

She gave a giggle that was reminiscent of younger days. '"Red" because my politics were left of centre, and, of course, an easy nickname because of the German connection. Wooo!'

'Wooo, indeed. How about the one at our wedding? "Red Baroness marries Sandhurst."' He burst out laughing. 'Sounded like you'd married the entire college intake. Where do they get their headlines?'

She joined in the laughter, and a fit of giggles hit her. 'That . . . that part hasn't changed. Remember this one? "Red Baroness seen in Prague." Then it turned out they had faked the picture, just for the headline, because, on the same day, another magazine had a real picture of me at a concert in Paris, on the very date they had put me in Prague.'

'Did you ever sue?'

'No. Hardly worth it. And, in those days, the culture of suing for such things had not yet taken root.'

Greville was still smiling hugely. 'I used to remember those too . . . out there. Kept me sane at times.' He became thoughtful once more, and squeezed her hand. 'So very good to be with you, my dear.'

The phone rang.

'Get it, shall I?'

She nodded.

Greville stood up, and went over to take the receiver off the wall-mounted phone.

'Derrenberg residence. Jens, old boy! Talk of the devil. Yes. We were just discussing you. Well . . . in passing. You're coming down? Good show! Is that lovely gel with you? Ah. Shame. Get Isolde, shall I? Alright. Understood. When you get here. Looking forward, old boy.'

Greville hung up, and went back to the table.

'Something's up,' he said to Aunt Isolde.

Müller put down the phone just as Pappenheim knocked and entered.

He looked at Pappenheim's expression, and said, 'Bad?'

'Not good. You could say . . . explosively not good.'

Pappenheim told him what had happened to Mainauer's house.

'You could have been killed, Pappi.'

'But I wasn't, and someone else has already been there before you.'

'Berger.'

'What instincts you've got. The bastard wired the entire place,' Pappenheim went on, 'and very cunningly.'

'It wasn't in the material we got, but no prizes for assuming that, somewhere in his records, his skill with explosives is mentioned.'

'Nice omission.'

'Probably not intentional.'

'Probably. I hate that word.'

'Well, you spotted that light in time, which is why you're standing here instead of queueing for your wings. But you were very close to it this time.'

'I'd better watch those lives then. First, that hit on me in May; now this. The chill hand is getting too close.'

'You've been closer.'

'Am I supposed to feel better?'

'No,' Müller said with a straight face. 'But now,' he went on, 'we've got a highly skilled, dead-souled killer running loose with one of the best sniper rifles on the planet.'

'Should we do the full "wanted" circus with blanket media coverage?'

'Counterproductive. Last thing we want. The general will have got him tucked safely away somewhere, by now. A full media circus would hinder, not help us. Best to keep the general and his pals guessing. They already know we're on to their boy. Let them wonder why we're not raising a hue and cry.'

Pappenheim nodded. 'I'll go with that.'

'Warn Lorenz to keep it quiet for now, which should relieve him. Can't be fun finding out that one of your top colleagues is in fact a cop killer, among many other things.'

'If he only knew the half of it . . . Mainauer knew we were coming,' Pappenheim continued, 'or more likely he expected a visit, and assumed it would be sooner, rather than later . . .'

'And immediately went into a long-planned routine for escape.'

'Leaving us his going-away present to brighten our lives . . . permanently. I don't expect Ollie Lorenz's forensics people to find anything of use. Mainauer will have taken anything likely to lead to him, or his masters; or destroyed them completely in that blast.'

Müller nodded. 'I am certain of it. He must have talked to one of the gossips,' he added.

'Could have been accidental. Elke said he tended to pass the house on occasion. Perhaps he stopped to check at the house, and someone who had seen us talked to him. It could have been as easy as that. One of those things. A spur of the moment decision to take that route. You've done things like that; and so have I. Many times, it's the difference between finding a solution, and not doing so . . . like deciding to double-check those reports from the assault team. Or Elke Hoventhaler's decision to leave out her husband's own report.'

'I know,' Müller agreed. 'But did he have to do it this morning?'

'A creature like that . . . instinct is all. And life, as Miss Bloomfield would say, is a bitch.'

'So they tell me.' Müller glanced at his watch. 'And Willi . . . will be in Washington in a few hours.'

'She can take care of herself. She was doing that before she met you.'

'She was indeed. Even so.'

'Talking of surprises,' Pappenheim said. 'I saw Klemp on the way up. He said the Great White is in, and looking for us.'

'Was in. He'd been and gone by the time I got here. And as for looking . . . I think he is more interested in finding out what we're up to.'

'To tell his friends.'

'Probably.'

'That word again. Elke Hoventhaler's with Berger and the others, by the way,' Pappenheim went on. 'She seems keen to get back into things. I thought we could use an extra sergeant, considering Berger will soon be going up to *Kommissarin*. She was ready to go for Mainauer. You should have seen her. Gun out . . . ready for anything . . .'

'I know that code, Pappi,' Müller said. 'Why not just say you're going to poach her from Lorenz?'

'Do her good, leaving that place.'

'I'll let you handle the transfer bureaucracy.'

'Oh good. Can I go have my smoke now?'

'You can go have your smoke now.'

Müller went to the window after Pappenheim had gone, and looked out across the city.

'Well, General,' he said. 'You got your man away. For now. But the pressure's still on. And there'll be more of it. Lots more.'

Seven

The general was thinking of Müller, even as Müller was thinking of him. Strolling with Reindorf in his extensive landscaped gardens, his face bore a thoughtful, but not unduly worried, expression.

He glanced up at the bright blue of the cloudless sky. 'So near, but so far.'

'Meaning, General?' Reindorf asked.

'Meaning, my dear Reindorf, that Müller believes he is close to dismantling our order. A few blows against us do not add up to much. How little he knows.'

'You cautioned against underestimating him . . .'

'And I still caution against it. I am not sanguine about the blows we have taken. Far from it. My point is that we should not allow his minor successes to cloud our judgement, or affect our faith in what we have set out to achieve. But there are things we must do, to neutralize his effect.'

'So the pincer still applies?'

'Very much so. And where he least expects it.'

Reindorf said nothing.

The general looked at him. 'You seem uncertain.'

'Not uncertain, General. Just considering possibilities. He was able to unearth Mainauer. How he managed this should be of concern.'

'And it is, my dear Reindorf. Do not mistake my equanimity for complacency. Let me show you what I mean.'

They had paused before a large and deep ornamental pond. In it swam a great number of koi, some very big, of which at least four were nudging ninety-five centimetres in length.

'See these koi? Horrendously expensive, fat, complacent, merrily going about their business. Just half of them would

127

buy you a decent car, loaded with accessories.' The general began to point to the larger ones. 'My beauties. See that glorious golden beauty; or this magnificent black and white jewel; or the red crest with its pure white body. All beautiful. But do you know my favourite?' The general pointed to the largest of the lot, an example that looked as if made of metal. Its skin was a mixture of gold streaks, steel-blue, black patches, and a silver mantle-like pattern directly behind the head. 'Magnificent. Proud. Unique. There is not another like it. Anywhere. This one alone would buy you that car.

'Now imagine a great ferocious pike being introduced in there. How long would they last? But, in with the hunting pike, is another; smaller, but equally ferocious. It knows it cannot win in a head-to-head fight against the bigger pike. However, it is not after the koi. It is after the pike. So what does it do? It nips at its bigger adversary, taking bites here and there, and vanishing into the reeds. The big pike has two options: continue attacking the koi and risk being whittled down and weakened by these nipping attacks; or, it leaves the koi for the time being, and concentrates all its fury upon the smaller attacker.

'The problem with that strategy is that it allows the koi to recover while valuable time is spent on eliminating the smaller pike. Unless it can defeat the smaller pike completely, it risks being weakened, defeated, and ends up losing the koi. What then, is the solution? More big pike. And therein lies Müller's problem. There are more pike than he can handle.'

Reindorf considered this analogy. 'So Müller is the smaller pike.'

He was still unsure, but chose discretion, and did not voice his misgivings. He thought that Müller was more than just a little pike 'nipping' at a big one. Müller had his own extra pike, one or more of which was giving him valuable information.

'It's a good analogy, General,' he said.

'Knew you would see it, Reindorf. Come, let us walk on, and leave the koi to their lotus-eating. We, the pike, have work to do.'

* * *

128

Müller was thinking about Australia when one of his phones rang.

'Yes, Pappi?'

'As you're going to Australia . . .'

'I'm going to Australia?'

A pointed silence followed.

Müller sighed. 'Alright, Pappi. Let us suppose I do take it into my head to go down under.'

'There are three ways of going . . . with decreasing levels of advantages. One with none at all, depending on your point of view.'

'I'm listening.'

'The first, you go unoffically. In a private, touristy sort of way. No advantages whatsoever. In fact, many disadvantages: travel bureaucracy for one, and even worse if you do anything down there to annoy the local constabulary. Then there's the official way. Not really to be recommended. The wrong people might get to know, and take an interest in your travels.'

'I know you have a third way.'

'They best way. Semi-officially. You avoid the bureaucratic nightmare, you will have some co-operation, and you avoid the attentions of those you wish to avoid. You get down there, do whatever it is you wish to do, and get out. No fuss, No one even knows you've been.'

'And how do we work this magic?'

'As I knew you'd agree with the third way, I've put things in motion.'

'Don't tell me. You have a contact down there.'

'Sort of.'

'*Sort of?*'

'In my younger days, before I made the insane decision to become a policeman, I made friends with an Aussie who was doing the camper-van pilgrimage of Europe. His father was something in the diplomatic service. Now *he's* something in the diplomatic service down there.'

'Covers a lot of sins.'

'But it's helpful. You'll have some co-operation, not total . . .'

'Can't have everything, I suppose.'

129

'Taking weapons in is strictly forbidden, of course . . .'

'But there's a way . . .'

'You'll be supplied with one if you need it. Believe it or not, a 92R.'

'Why am I not surprised?'

'If you hand in your 92R, it will be handed back to you on arrival. You'll be met. Paperwork for two is in hand, date of travel open.'

'*Two?*'

'In case Miss Bloomfield survives and decides she would like to see Oz, to get over the trauma of having to survive Willi's attentions.'

'I hope she realizes you've been thinking of her.'

'Such nice things, the man says.'

Müller looked out at the city and smiled. 'Pappi, if I told you I wanted to go to . . . oh . . . Terra del Fuego . . .'

'I'm certain I could find a contact who knows a contact who . . .'

'Got the message.'

'So . . . where to in the immediate future?'

'My aunt's.'

'If the Great White shows his face, I haven't even seen you today.'

'Good thing you never go to confession.'

'Good thing you don't.'

In the communications department, Hermann Spyros cast surreptitious glances in Hedi Meyer's direction. She was so totally engrossed in what she was doing, she was oblivious of them.

Then she looked round to pick up a diskette, and caught him. He tried to look away, but it was too late.

'What?' she said, waiting for him to reply.

'I hear,' Spyros began after some hesitation, 'that you were quite the tough cop last night. Gun in both hands, pointing at that guy. Did you really say "shut the fuck up"?'

'Some people talk too much,' she said, turning back to the computer she'd been upgrading. 'Our colleagues from the Ready Group, was it? Are they laughing at me?'

'On the contrary. They were quite impressed, it seems.'

She stopped, and turned to look at him. 'Is this leading somewhere, sir?'

Spyros cleared his throat. 'You were with *Hauptkommissar* Müller.'

'That's obvious. If those two told you about the incident, I must have been with the *Hauptkommissar*. I was there. He was there. He was taking me home. He thought we were being followed. We were. He led the man in the car to Lichtensteinallee. End of story.'

She turned back to the computer, but could sense he was still looking at her. She stopped once more, with a loud sigh.

'Look, sir,' she said, just short of irritation. 'You're my boss, but you're not the boss of my private life. For your information, nothing's going on. OK?'

'Don't rip my throat out, Hedi. I thought yesterday was your bad-temper day.'

'Today too, if some people continue.'

The phone rang. A flash of expectation came into her eyes. Spyros picked up the phone. It was not Müller.

Though the goth was quick to hide her disappointment and went back to her work, it did not escape Spyros's notice.

He turned away to speak to the caller, with a slightly worried expression. A happily married man, he tended to look upon the goth as the younger sister he never had.

At exactly 17.00, Müller decided to leave. Kaltendorf had not put in a reappearance, for which he was grateful. He was not in the mood for one of his superior's rants, and was even less inclined to see how Kaltendorf would react, given what had happened at the general's house. The time was not yet right.

He picked up the direct phone, and called Pappenheim. 'I'm off, Pappi. I'm assuming nothing earth-shaking has happened.'

'The earth's still here. The GW has not pounded on your door?'

'Not yet.'

'Nor mine. He must be hibernating . . . but wait a minute, it's summer. Wrong time . . .'

'Pappi!'

'You could at least let me ramble on for a bit,' Pappenheim complained in an aggrieved tone.

'If I let you, I'll regret it.'

'You know me too well. To your aunt's?'

'Yes.'

'And after?'

'Brushing up on my French.'

'What about the Australian jaunt?'

'I'll call you.'

'If you see Mainauer on the way – wherever he may be – tell him I want a word.'

'There's a queue, and I'm ahead.'

'Just leave some for me. And, Jens . . .'

'Yes.'

'Watch your back. Don't get any Dragunov bullets in it.'

'Same goes for you, Pappi, and the others.'

'They already know.'

'Alright.'

They hung up together. Müller rose to his feet, glanced out of the window, and went out.

As he walked to a lift, Müller thought about how others saw his unit. Its admirers – a substantial few – held it to be staffed by high-calibre, extremely motivated people of a police unit whose status was indefinable, inhabiting a fluid niche somewhere between the intelligence services and the police.

'We handle the "oh-so-sensitive" cases no one will touch even with a barge pole,' he said to himself.

The detractors – too many – looked upon them as yet another tier of politically created bureaucrats with guns, upon whom tax-payers' money was lavished – squandered, according to some – to buy them expensive, high-tech toys to play with. The ongoing hostility had a life of its own; even among some of their colleagues from other forces. Because of this, they hated the perceived autonomy. The irony was, few would want the responsibility of working there.

'But I would not want anyone else handling this one,' Müller went on grimly. '*No* one gets the Semper, but me.'

The lift, a large, stainless-steel cage with a control panel that would make NASA weep with joy, was about to hiss its doors shut just as Müller got there. Half-fearing that Kaltendorf might round a corner and spot him, he ran the last few metres and got in just as the doors closed.

'Got you!' he said in triumph.

The goth was already inside.

'Miss Meyer!' he said, surprised, and feeling a little foolish.

Blue eyes studied him as she pushed the touchscreen to select garage level. The lift shot downwards with the barest sibilance, as if trying to break the sound barrier.

'One of these days,' he said, 'this thing will hit like a jet crashing. There ought to be a speed limit for lifts. So,' he went on, 'off early?'

She nodded. '*Kommissar* Spyros thought, as I didn't get home till very late last night, I should catch up on some sleep.' The blue eyes seemed to swim at him.

'Were you dozing in there?'

'No. I think he was just being kind.' She paused. 'Thank you for taking me home.'

'My pleasure.'

'Those two from the Ready Group have been talking.'

'What about?'

'What I said to the man in the car.'

'Now everyone will know not to mess around with you.'

'They couldn't before, anyway.'

The lift came to a halt, pulling what felt like several negative Gs.

'One day . . .' Müller said again. 'Sorry I can't drop you off,' he went on as they entered the garage. 'I'm going in the opposite direction.'

'It's alright. My little car's back. They were quicker than I thought. I picked it up this afternoon. Passed every test. It's perfect.'

'Good.' Müller looked at the bag slung from her shoulder. 'You haven't forgotten your gun.'

'I haven't forgotten. Stop worrying.'

'Alright. Drive care—' He stopped, and smiled. 'Alright.'

She nodded, and turned away to go towards her car. As she

walked, she glanced over her shoulder and saw he was standing there. He moved a hand slightly in farewell.

She walked on, a tiny smile on her lips.

A medium-sized mansion, Schlosshotel Derrenberg had seen some rough old times during its DDR days. It had not been a hotel then. Once used by the Party elite, it had been left derelict and overgrown, through years of disuse. Aunt Isolde had been fortunate enough to find and regain appropriated family property that had at least been still standing, just after the fall of the Wall. She had lovingly renovated it to its former glory.

It had been a labour of love that had transformed it into what it now was: part family home, and part luxury hotel. The main structure and the right wing were reincarnated as the hotel. The left wing served as the owner's residence, with its own secure entrance, and a garden and courtyard behind a high wall.

Strategically positioned about the main gardens were ground-level spotlights that floodlit the building, and which illuminated the gardens at night. A stream with raised, prudently constructed banks of earth and concrete to protect against flooding, flowed with a mellow quietude across the garden from the far, wooded part of the vast grounds, and past the rear of the hotel. It emptied itself a kilometre or so later, into the river Saale. A small wooden bridge spanned it.

Berlin to the Schlosshotel Derrenberg was just over 300 kilometres. Müller arrived at 19.45.

At the same moment, Willi Helmer was landing at Dulles International. It was 13.45 Washington time.

Böhmen was waiting, as promised, for Willi. He was dressed as a chauffeur, cap atop shoulder-length grey hair. He wore mirrored sunglasses that effectively hid his eyes.

'Good flight?' Böhmen asked in English as he shook hands with a public show of respect, and took Willi's suiter.

'I slept most of the time.'

'Life is hard,' Böhmen said without the trace of a smile. 'Welcome to Washington, centre of the world.'

Willi sniffed. 'I'm here to do a job, and leave. You sound very American,' he added.

'Could be because I am American.'

'And, despite your hair, you don't look as old as I thought you would, even though the general said—'

'Rule number one, you never say that word in public while you're here. Rule two, you listen to what I tell you without question. Third rule, you never ask me about myself. Fourth rule, if you feel like breaking any of those, remember numbers one, two, and three. I will not be compromised under any circumstances. It that clear?'

'Very.'

'Glad to hear it. The car's over there.' The 'car' was a shiny black limousine. 'You're a high-flying businessman. You get to sit in the back. The separating glass is armoured, and I can lock you in from the front. If you're not who you're supposed to be, I can gas you, and there'll be no trace left when it's all over. I'll talk to you through the intercom.'

Thus put firmly in his place, Willi got into the back while Böhmen put the suiter away.

'Problems with customs and immigration?'

'None.'

'Good. Everything's going smoothly.'

They were on the Beltway, going wherever Böhmen had decided to take him.

'As you can imagine,' Böhmen continued, 'the airport is riddled with security cameras. You will have been seen, a businessman arriving, and will be seen later, the same businessman leaving. In between, you must complete the job. Look in the drinks cabinet.'

The glass-lined cabinet opened as Böhmen spoke, lighting up as it did so.

'Don't bother trying the drinks. You're looking at props. The thing that looks like a bobbin is real. Take it. That's your weapon.'

'*What?*'

'Take it!'

Willi took out the small, plastic cylinder with a hole at each end, and stared at it uncomprehendingly. 'What the hell is it?'

135

The drinks cabinet closed upon itself.

'Hold it between finger and thumb, and squeeze . . . gently.'

Willi did so. The cylinder popped, each half opening wide. The holes at each end now became a channel in each half.

'You simply snap this over a brake, or steering feed. The cylinder will do the rest.'

'How?'

'A small charge will go off, rupturing the cylinder, and releasing a solution that will eat into the pipe in a heartbeat. No brakes, or steering, in the middle of traffic. A tragic accident, and no one the wiser. There will be no traces of the substance used. The bobbin will also be consumed. You'll be back across the Atlantic before anyone even begins to suspect what happened, if at all.'

Willi looked at the tiny cylinder with scepticism, but said nothing.

Böhmen looked at him through the rearview mirror and noted the expression, but did not comment.

'As you've slept on the plane,' he went on a short while later, 'no time like the present. You'll have at least four hours to relax before we're ready to go. We get to the place she usually goes to during this part of the week, just before she does.'

'Where is that?'

'She likes seafood.' Böhmen did not elaborate. 'I'll take you to your hotel. Drop you at the entrance. You're all booked in. It's of a grade suitable for the kind of person you're meant to be. At sixteen thirty, you leave the hotel for a walk. Take the first corner to the right. A cab will be waiting. Get in, I'll drive you to a place where you will change into workman's clothes; then we'll take a van to the place she will park when she stops for her seafood.

'While she's inside, you quickly snap the cylinder on a brake or steering feed. You come back to the van. We leave. Because you're flying business class, you're flexible. You can alter your flight to suit, or, if you feel secure enough, take your original return flight. Either way, you're clean. The cylinder you'll be using is not the one you've got. That's a dummy. Practise opening and closing it so that the whole routine is as familiar as zipping your fly. You'll get the real

136

one just before you do it. The micro charge is set to go off when she's on the turnpike, or the Beltway, tomorrow, on her way to work. She uses either one when it suits her, depending on the traffic. Got it all?'

Willi nodded. 'Yes. I'm looking forward to doing it.'

'They told me you were keen. That's a plus.'

'Why don't I just shoot her? No timing, no guesswork, and it's done . . .'

'*That* is a big minus. What planet have you been on? Snipers are not popular around here. You'd have a hornets' nest up your ass in no time.'

'I was not talking about sniping. I'm talking about getting in her car and—'

'Wait wait wait. *Hold* it right there! This is not up for discussion. Rule number two. You got that?'

Willi was silent.

'*Have you got that?*' Böhmen repeated. His eyes glared from the mirror. '*Listen, you!* You will do *nothing* without my permission. You will do *nothing* that compromises my position, and you will *not* countermand me, *at any time. Now. Have you got that?*'

Willi took his time, but he answered, 'I've got it.'

There was a hostile silence all the way to the hotel.

Müller drove the Porsche slowly on the long, curving driveway that led to the mansion, and pulled up before the colonnaded entrance of the hotel. There were many parked cars.

Christian, familiar in his hussar's uniform, and one of Aunt Isolde's favourite employees, almost bounded out when he spotted the Porsche.

'*Herr Graf!*' he greeted enthusiastically, bending slightly to peer into the car. 'So nice to see you! Can I be of service?'

'Hello, Christian. No need. I'm going through to the residence. Are you well?'

'Very well, thank you, Herr Graf. Yourself?'

'Doing fine. Is Aunt Isolde in?'

'Yes, Herr Graf. Also the major.'

'Good.' Müller glanced at the many cars. 'Full house?'

'Absolutely. The hotel is doing fine business.'

'Always good to hear. Well, thank you, Christian. I'll let myself in.'

'Of course, *Herr Graf*.' Christian gave a little bow, and went back into the hotel.

Müller shook his head slowly as Christian disappeared inside. 'No matter how often I tell him not to bow to me, he still does it.'

Two gates led into the residential grounds, which were made private by a high wall. One was secured by a keypad for pedestrian entrance; the other, for vehicles, opened by remote control.

Müller pressed a button on the console and the larger gate swung open quietly. He drove through into the wide court-yard that had a line of garages tucked against the far wall. Beyond them was a landscaped garden that almost rivalled the main gardens in size. By the time he had parked in one of the five bays next to the garages, the gate had swung shut behind him.

He cut the engine and climbed out. There was a side door next to the kitchen, and a large window looked out upon the courtyard. It had its own keypad, but there would be no need for him to use it. The door was already opening; and Aunt Isolde, followed by Greville, came out, both smiling wide in greeting.

The tall and elegant Aunt Isolde gave him a tight embrace. 'Hello, Jens.'

'Aunt Isolde.'

'Dear boy,' Greville said, holding out a hand, which Müller shook while still being embraced by Aunt Isolde. 'Heard that beautiful monster machine and said to Isolde, that's the beautiful monster machine. Always glad to see you, dear boy. Always.'

'Glad to see you too, Greville.'

'If you two will excuse me,' Aunt Isolde said, releasing Müller. 'I was about to go to the hotel. We're quite busy.'

She spoke English, not so much because of Greville, but because she enjoyed doing so. Now that he was back, it gave her the excuse. Her accents were classic Sandhurst, which she had picked up from Greville all those years ago.

'I know,' Müller said. 'Saw all the cars, and Christian told me.'

'We're booked for months ahead. We're doing far better than I'd dared hope when this mad idea of making the old place earn its living first took hold.'

'All well deserved,' Müller said.

She looked at each of them. 'I'll leave you two to chat. We'll have a fine dinner together, the three of us. Pity Carey isn't with you, Jens. She's a lovely girl.'

'Are you playing cupid, Aunt Isolde?'

'Not at all, my dear. You two need no help from me.' She gave his check a gentle pat, and went back inside.

Both men were silent until she had gone.

Greville, looking exactly as he had on that day when Müller had first seen him sitting in Aunt Isolde's kitchen, was in his customary white suit. Burnished by thirty or so years of sun, he looked Arabic in complexion; but his very pale blue eyes were the giveaway. Bareheaded, he normally wore a wide-brimmed white hat. An otherwise full head of cropped white hair was marred only by the merest hint of a receding hairline.

'She has blossomed, Greville,' Müller said, 'since you came back.'

'And she has regenerated me,' Greville said softly. 'Didn't trust me at first, did you, old boy,' he went on, 'when you first saw me that day? Don't blame you at all. Wouldn't have trusted meself, under similar circumstances.'

'Knowing what I know,' Müller began, and paused, 'I was wrong.'

'Nonsense! You were protecting your aunt. You're a son to her . . . and quite, quite proud of you, she is.'

'Well, she did bring me up after my parents were killed. She's very precious to me.'

'And to me. Always has been. Thinking of her sustained me in many a hell hole. Pure gold.'

'Tell me,' Müller began, looking at Greville, 'how's the . . .'

'DNA time bomb? Ticking away. Care for a walk outside? Rather a lot of guests, but I like it by the stream. Soothing. Many of the guests are out and about somewhere, so, if we're lucky, we might have the stream to ourselves.'

'I saw all the cars, as I said . . . but no one seemed to be in the garden.'

'Then we are lucky. Earlier in the day,' Greville continued as they went through the pedestrian gate, 'lunchtime . . . got a slight twinge. Told Isolde it was probably trapped wind; but, to be quite frank, old son, I'm not sure what it was. Could have indeed been wind . . . or it could have been my nemesis sending out an early warning.'

They walked past the hotel entrance, and into the garden.

Müller gave him an anxious look. 'How do you feel?'

'Absolutely right as rain. Apart from the twinge, nothing. Not a single sign that anything untoward is happening. Amazing horror. Death by stealth. One could almost admire the psychopathic bastards who created it. Even though it's a rough prototype, it is still a clever little piece of evil work. Had I known what I know now, I'd have shot them all myself in that lab. As it was, the team destroyed it anyway.

'But something has been nagging at me for years. You may remember that I mentioned the lab was in the Middle East. Given what you now know about the Semper, and the rather odd people whose paths crossed mine out there, it occurs to me that perhaps, just perhaps, the real owners were not the host country.'

They had arrived at the stream, and Greville looked down at the lazily flowing water.

'Aah,' he said. 'Will you just look at that calmness. He just keeps rolling . . .' Greville's words faded into his reverie.

'You mean the lab was outsourced.'

Greville brought himself back from wherever he had travelled. 'Either that, or a sort of quid pro quo was established to get the lab set up.'

'You give us space to build the lab, no questions asked, and . . .'

'We'll see you're alright,' Greville finished. 'Precisely. Money, weaponry, judicious lobbying, preferential trade facilities. How long is a piece of string? Just give a wish list. Not the first time such deals have been done and, by far, not the last.'

'The Semper?'

'It may not be the Semper. But they certainly would like to get their sweaties on my DNA cocktail. I am, after all, the only laboratory going.'

'They don't know that.'

'They came close to finding out last May, old boy.'

'Close is a million miles away.'

Greville stared at him. 'Where did you hear that?'

Puzzled, Müller answered, 'My father. He was talking about school results. I had just missed getting a pass mark in general knowledge. I knew the answer but, in a hurry to finish, I gave one I did not intend. I told him I'd got close. That was when he said it. Take your time, and get it right, he said. I never forgot.'

'Neither have I. I heard that very phrase out in desert land. But it was not your father who said it. I am quite certain. Strange that. Hearing the same phrase, all those years apart.'

'Which reminds me . . . Greville, have you ever heard of a Jack and Maggie Hargreaves?'

Greville answered without hesitation. 'Never, old boy.' He peered at Müller. 'I can see that disappoints you. Important, is it?'

'Someone sent me information suggesting that they may hold a key answer – perhaps even *the* key answer – to the killing of my parents, and to the Semper.'

'If really so, I would say the Hargreaves are probably living on borrowed time, and under assumed names.'

'That would explain something, at least.'

'How so?'

'The Hargreaves are in Australia.'

'Ah.'

'According to my informant, they have a station of sorts out in Western Australia. Out in the bush, in the general area of Broome.'

'The *outback*? Dear boy, you do realize this could be a trap? Dangle your parents' crash as bait, get you rushing out there in the middle of nowhere and, *bang*. It would take years to find your body, if at all. Another outback mystery goes into legend.'

'I would tend to agree, but this is from a source that has

never given me false information. I have been steered into many a right direction by him.'

'I see. Then perhaps the Hargreaves are themselves exercising some prudence, and hiding themselves out there. Or perhaps your informant wants you to find them for him. Bang, bang, bang. The Hargreaves, *and* the questing policeman. The three were never seen again.'

Müller looked at him with mild scepticism. 'This from you, Greville? The man who went to destroy a laboratory in the middle of hostile territory?'

'In your place, I'd go, of course. But be aware . . .'

'I am, Greville. Believe you me . . . I am. If I do go, just don't die before I get back. We have a rendezvous.'

'Which I shall hold you to. My remains are to be cremated as agreed, and so disposed of that no one will ever be able to desecrate them.'

'You have my word, Greville.'

Greville nodded, staring at the water. 'There is something else, isn't there?' He did not look up.

'I will ask Pappenheim to send two of the Ready Group down here, sufficiently well armed . . .'

'Bodyguards?'

'Of a kind. They'll pose as guests. Nothing might happen to cause alarm. It's just a precaution.' A smile flitted across Müller's face. 'I know you can handle yourself, Greville. You could almost certainly teach the Ready Group boys a thing or two; but we both worry about Aunt Isolde. They'll be under your command. Pappi will ensure they are aware of this.'

'I don't know about being under my command. If they give me good advice, I shall take it.'

'A good commander knows when to listen to his sergeant?'

'That sort of thing.'

'Now to sell the idea to Aunt Isolde.'

Washington.

At the prescribed time, Willi left his hotel and took the first turning on the right as Böhmen had instructed. He walked for about five minutes until he came to a parked taxi, with Böhmen at the wheel.

It was a very different Böhmen to the one who had picked him up at the airport. Gone was the chauffeur's uniform. In its place were the ordinary working clothes of a cab driver. The hatless head was no longer covered by long, grey hair. It was now a shortish blond.

Willi said nothing about the change in appearance, and got into the back. Neither man spoke during the fifteen-minute drive.

Böhmen finally stopped at what looked like a small deserted warehouse. He got out to unlock a set of double doors. He pulled them open, got back into the taxi, and drove in. He got out again, to shut the doors and lock them from the inside.

Willi climbed out and looked about him. In what used to be a large storage area, there was now just the taxi, and a white delivery van with a refrigeration unit. A logo of seafood on a large platter was on the sides, bearing the legend MAX'S SEAFOODS encircling it.

Böhmen next went to the van, and opened the passenger door. He took out some clothes and handed them to Willi. They were a set of blue overalls, a white shirt, blue baseball cap, a soiled pair of gloves, and workman's shoes.

'Change into this stuff. Wear the cap back to front. There's a second set of thin gloves inside of these, remove an outer glove when you put the cylinder in place.'

They both changed quickly. Both wore the caps back to front. They got into the van, which Böhmen drove to the entrance. He got out, and went through the routine with the doors to the building. When they were again outside and the warehouse locked, he set off for Little River Turnpike.

'We'll park, and wait for her to arrive,' Böhmen said.

'What if she doesn't come?'

'We try tomorrow.'

'And if not even then?'

'We abort, and you go back. Going there twice with a seafood-delivery van that does not deliver is risky enough. I will not do so a third time. Better if today's the day she comes for her seafood.'

They did not speak again until they were approaching Annandale from the Beltway junction.

'Nearly there,' Böhmen said as they left the turnpike to head for their destination. A little later, he pulled into the parking area and reversed into a slot that would allow a fast exit. 'We're in time. She's not here yet. Now we wait.'

Böhmen took out a clipboard and pretended he was writing down delivery details.

Their wait was just five minutes. The red BMW M3 pulled into a space just seven slots away. They saw Carey Bloomfield get out, and lock her car. She was not in uniform.

Willi sucked in his breath as he watched her walk off.

'Wait till she's inside,' Böhmen cautioned. 'Here.' He handed over the new cylinder.

'It's heavier,' Willi said.

'Of course it's heavier. This one's loaded. When I say go, you go, do it, then get back here in a heartbeat. I'll have the engine running.

Willi, primed like a hound about to be unleashed, nodded. 'OK.'

'That's it. She's in. Go!'

Willi climbed out of the van.

Eight

Carey Bloomfield had taken Müller's warning to heart. Whenever she left her car unattended in public areas, she made certain she could keep an eye on it from wherever she happened to be.

Which was why she frowned when she saw the workman approaching the BMW.

'Excuse me,' she said to the woman who was attending to her, and who knew her as a regular customer. 'I think I forgot something in my car. I'll be right back.'

'No problem, Miss Bloomfield.'

She went out, surreptitiously taking her gun out of the shoulder bag she carried, slung across her body. She reached the car just as Willi, lying sideways, was about to reach under it.

'Found anything, Willi?'

He was so startled to hear his name called, he jerked upwards, lacerating his arm on the car bumper.

He could not stifle the cry of pain. *'Aargh, Scheisse!'*

'Shit is right, Willi boy. And you're deep in it. *On your fucking feet!'*

Willi's grey eyes looked into the menacing and unwavering snout of the big automatic, pointing down two-handedly at him. He froze in shock as he looked up at the face of his intended target.

Carey Bloomfield glanced at the cylinder in his hand.

'Going to put that under my car, were you?' she snapped. 'What does it do? Blow it up? Wreck my fucking brakes, or my steering? *On your feet I said, you piece of dogshit!'*

'I think not, Miss Bloomfield,' a soft voice said behind her.

'Shit!' she said, annoyed with herself.

'Oh indeedy, Miss Bloomfield. Now let's do this nice and

145

easy, before we attract undue attention. You will put your gun back into your bag. You will do nothing stupid, like shouting to attract attention. When you have put your gun away, you will remain where you are. I do not want to shoot you, because of all the trouble it will cause me; but if you do not do exactly as I have said, I *will* shoot. If you do not die from a bullet in the spine, you will certainly not walk again. Your career will effectively be over. Your life will effectively be over, except that you will be around to see it crumbling. Now, do we have an agreement?'

Willi was looking angry. '*Erschieß sie!*' he snarled. '*Erschieß sie!*'

'Do you understand what he is saying?' the soft voice asked.

'Yes.'

'Of course you do, talented lady like you. But this is not your day to be shot, unless you force me to do so. My . . . colleague is a little primitive. He does not appreciate the bigger picture. He has not thought through the ramifications of shooting an air-force lieutenant-colonel out in the open like this . . .'

'You've done your homework.' She put the gun back into her bag.

'Good,' said the voice in approval. 'Common sense reigns. Homework? Yes, we did. I must leave you now, Colonel. You have been very lucky. Please do not look back. The bullet that will hit your spine can do so from a greater distance than this. You may move after five minutes. Come on, Willi. And bring the cylinder.'

Reluctantly, a glaring Willi did as he was told. He kept his enraged eyes upon Carey Bloomfield until he could no longer do so.

She heard the sound of the van leaving, but did not turn when her five minutes were up, deciding to give it a little longer, just to be sure. When she did move, nothing further happened. She let out a sigh of relief.

'Jesus!' she uttered softly.

In the van, Willi was furious.

'Why didn't you just shoot her?'

146

'You're not thinking very straight, are you, Willi?' Böhmen said calmly as they headed back to the warehouse. 'The whole idea was to do this without complications. A subtle, mysterious hit. An accident on the freeway. Simple. Now compare that with the shooting of an air-force offcer in a public place. If you can think that far, imagine the reaction.'

'She knew my name!' Willi was not listening. 'Someone talked. Someone betrayed me!'

'Did you tell anyone you were coming to Washington, Willi?'

'Of course not! What do you think I . . . am?'

The hesitation at the end was not lost on Böhmen.

'A fool.' he suggested. 'Who did you tell, Willi?'

'I just said to my girlfriend . . . But who could she tell? She's too stupid to know anyone who could have warned that woman.'

'You should know. So, you have a girlfriend. I thought you liked Mary-Anne.'

'I did. But she was not my girlfriend.'

'But you wished she'd been.'

'Yes. And that *bitch* killed her!'

'Shit happens.'

When they got back to the warehouse, Böhmen got out, and opened the rear doors to the refrigerated compartment of the van.

'Willi!' he called.

Willi got out, and came round to the back. 'What?'

'Get in.'

'*What?* I'll freeze!' Then he stared at the silenced gun in Böhmen's hand. 'What's this?'

'*In!*'

'You can't . . .'

'You can get in, or I can shoot you in the kneecap and you can drag yourself in. Your choice.'

Willi climbed into the back of the van.

Then Böhmen shot him. Twice.

Willi gasped in pain and astonishment as he stumbled deeper into the van, before falling untidily. When he died, an expression of betrayal slowly spread across his face.

Böhmen shut and secured the doors. He took a mobile phone out of his overalls, and called a number that was answered immediately.

'Someone to be checked out of the hotel, then the van to be disposed of. You know where both are.'

He ended the call, changed his clothes then threw the ones he'd been wearing into the cab of the van.

An hour later, dressed completely differently, he went into a building with a large sign above the entrance.

DENNISON BIOMETRICS, it said.

The security man at the desk jumped to his feet.

'Dr Dennison, sir!'

'Hi, George.'

'Good trip, sir?'

'So, so. I'll be working late tonight.'

'Of course, sir.'

Berlin, after midnight, local time.
Pappenheim picked up the phone at the third ring. 'Pappenheim.'

'Don't you sleep, Pappi?'

'Miss Bloomfield! A pleasure to hear! As for sleeping, it was suggested to me only recently that I should get some.'

'And you answered . . . ?'

'Plenty of time when I'm dead.'

'Ghoulish, Pappi. Very ghoulish. I haven't tried him as yet,' she went on. 'I'm assuming he's not with you.'

'He isn't. But I can—'

'No need. Just tell him that his warning was just in time. I got a visit from Willi.'

Pappenheim sat up straight. 'As you're talking to me, he obviously failed. What happened?'

'I spotted him, had him cold. Then I'm afraid I behaved like a rookie. I forgot to watch for the partner.'

'It happens. Are you OK?'

'Nothing but a bruised ego. The partner was a thinker. Sounded very educated. American. I never saw him. He could have shot me, but didn't. He was actually against it.'

'A thinker indeed. Not like our Willi.'

'Not like him at all. Willi wanted me shot there and then, and hang the consequences. The other one would have none of it. He warned me not to move or he would give me a spine shot . . .'

'Educated, and cold.'

'And how. I did not doubt him for a second. Then they left. I don't think Willi will be much longer for this world. The other guy did not sound like someone who tolerates loose cannons.'

'From what you've said, it seems a certainty that Willi won't make it back. I'll call Jens,' Pappenheim went on. 'But I'd suggest you call his mobile. I'm certain you can do so securely.'

'Is that a smile I smell, Pappi?'

'Now, would I be smiling?' Pappenheim said, smiling.

'Yes, you would be.'

'Hmm,' he said.

'I might call him,' she said.

'I think you will.' Pappenheim was still smiling when they hung up. 'Hmm,' he said again, lighting up.

A big, round man, Pappenheim's cuddly exterior was an effective cloak that hid an almost sage-like wisdom, backed by a sharp cunning. The baby-blue of his eyes, exuding innocence, effectively aided and abetted a persona that had been carefully constructed over the years. His rumpled and ash-speckled attire helped underscore that impression. Yet his choice of ties, an apparent anomaly that had so impressd the general, was impeccable. His fingers, quite unexpectedly for a compulsive smoker, were scrupulously clean.

In describing Pappenheim as a Sancho Panza, the general, however, had erred. He had missed something beneath the cloak: another predator; another pike to accompany Müller's; a pike which Reindorf's instincts were warning him about, but that was a thought which Reindorf allowed to remain unvoiced.

It was a mistake that many had made – to their cost – about Pappenheim.

*　　*　　*

149

Müller was in his bedroom at the Derrenberg, when Pappenheim called.

'Don't tell me you're still in your office,' Müller said.

'I'm still in my office, and you'll be getting another call soon. I'll even bet on it.'

'I'm not betting against you. I'd lose. So who will it be?'

'Miss Bloomfield.'

'Is she alright?'

'Don't sound so anxious. She is in fine health, despite a visit from Willi.' Pappenheim relayed what Carey Bloomfield had said.

'She was lucky,' Müller said.

'She certainly was. But we all need a bit of luck now and then. Willi's has certainly run out, I think.'

'That I would certainly bet on. Interesting to know where the "educated" one she mentioned fits into all this.'

'She did say he was American. I'm certain she can spot a fake American accent a light year away, if you get my meaning. So he must be the genuine article.'

'Well, we do know the Semper is international to a certain extent.'

'Like a national firm with an extensive foreign network.'

'Exactly. And all ready and waiting for the big day.'

'Which we're not going to let them get to.'

'We're certainly not,' Müller said.

Pappenheim could almost hear Müller thinking about his parents.

'I've got the two Ready Group colleagues,' Pappenheim said. 'They volunteered.'

'Volunteered?'

'They all wanted to do it.'

'Then thank them all for me.'

'Already did. What it is to be popular, eh? So, the two are going to be the same ones who helped out last night. Hartwig Olinsky, and Daniel Stau. They'll be sufficiently armed. They have been told that the major calls the shots, and that they are to properly identify themselves when they get there. They'll be down tomorrow morning. Personally, I think they're looking forward to living in luxury for a few days.'

'Perhaps that's why they all wanted to come.'

'Oh ye of little faith,' Pappenheim finished with a laugh.

Carey Bloomfield's call came within ten minutes of Pappenheim's. 'Hi, you,' she greeted.

'Hi, you,' he responded.

'That's a change. No "Miss Bloomfield".'

'It is still there, Miss Bloomfield.'

'I should have guessed.'

'Pappi told me what happened. Are you quite certain you're alright?'

'As I said to Pappi, damaged ego only.'

'You did leave yourself open . . .'

'Thanks. Make me feel better about it.'

'I won't rub it in.'

'You just did.'

Müller paused. 'Can we start again?'

'Start.'

'The one you call educated . . . was there anything about his voice that rang any bells? Phrasing, inflection, anything like that.'

'Nothing whatsoever. A total stranger. Zilch.'

'It was a long shot. Given what we're dealing with, I thought there might have been a possibility of his being someone who crossed your path in the past.'

'If he had, I think I would have remembered him . . . and, of course, he me. In that case, he might not have been so generous with his gun.'

'There is that,' Müller agreed. 'I'm glad . . . nothing went wrong.'

'The warning came in time.'

'Don't assume it's over.'

'I won't. Count on it. So, Müller, doing any travelling?'

'Might be going south.'

'How far?'

'To the coast, but stopping along the way . . . where we went to last month.'

'If you do go as far as the coast, say hi to Miss Dubois.'

'There was a needle in there.'

'Of course.'

151

'Not fair.'

'Of course it wasn't. I'm a woman.'

'Why don't you try to find a few days off?'

'Is that an invitation?'

'I may also be going much further afield,' he said by way of an answer.

'What are you up to, Müller?'

'You won't find out if you stay over there.'

'That's blackmail.'

'Yes.'

'I'll see if I can find reasons.'

'Knew you would.'

'Don't be so damned sure of yourself, Müller.'

'I never am.'

'Oh sure. And my name's Boudicca.'

'I never knew that.'

There was a moment's silence, then, 'Müller?'

'Yes . . . ?'

'Just . . . oh hell.' And she ended the call.

'See you in Australia, then,' he said, as he put the mobile down.

The general was in a deep leather armchair in his study, reading Juvenal's *Saturae*, in Latin, when the phone on the small table next to the chair warbled at him. He put the book down before answering.

His face hardened as he listened. 'Thank you,' he said neutrally, when the caller had finished, and hung up.

He picked up the phone again, and pressed a button.

In another part of the mansion, Reindorf was preparing to leave for his own home. He maintained a semblance of autonomy, by never sleeping at the general's house like the hired help.

He picked up the phone. 'Yes, General?'

'Did you know Willi had a girlfriend?'

'I did not. I thought Mary-Anne . . .'

'He *lusted* after Mary-Anne,' the general snarled. 'She was never his girlfriend!'

Reindorf read the signals. 'What has happened, General?'

'I have just received a secure call from America. Willi failed. The target *knew*, and caught *him*!'

'But that's not possible!'

'Well it *is*, Reindorf!' the general barked angrily. 'Colonel Bloomfield found Willi by her car. Caught him red-handed at the point of a gun. She would have had him arrested, or most certainly shot him, had Willi done anything stupid, if our man had not intervened. That man is one of our most important people. He risked exposure by going to Willi's aid. Luckily, he was able to keep the colonel covered in a way that prevented her from seeing him. He could not have shot her, for all the obvious reasons. Now tell me, Reindorf . . . how do you think Colonel Bloomfield knew what to expect? How was she fore-warned?'

Reindorf was genuinely baffled. 'I have no idea, General . . .'

'*No idea? Willi*, man! Willi broke the rules. He told his girl-friend he was going to Washington.'

'Doing such a thing is forbidden.'

'I know that! But Willi had other ideas. He disappointed me.'

Reindorf knew what that meant, and noted the use of the past tense.

'I don't expect you to know everything that goes on in the head of every man under your command,' the general was saying, 'but we cannot afford breaches in security. However they did it, it is obvious Müller came by that information. So first, go and find this . . . this girlfriend. We must have a talk with her. I don't care how you do it – subtly, unsubtly – just get her here! And start *now*! Tonight!'

'Yes, General,' Reindorf said with sinking heart.

He put the phone down. Willi had made no mention of a girlfriend, as far as Reindorf knew. Where to start? Was she even in Berlin?

'So much for the pincer, General,' Reindorf said to himself. '*Our* flanks are becoming exposed. And as for the smaller pike, Müller has more than one to call on. A small guerrilla force can defeat a large army. You may yet lose the koi.'

Pappenheim received a call from Australia.

'You awake yet?' the cheerful voice enquired.

153

'I haven't been to sleep.'

Laughter sounded in Pappenheim's ear. 'You haven't changed.'

'Oh I have. You should see the gut.'

'And still smoking?'

'Listen,' Pappenheim said. He drew loudly on his Gauloise.

'Oh, I know that sound! I seem to remember a different kind of cigarette . . .'

'I'm a policeman, you can't say such things to me.'

A chuckle followed this. 'Yep. Same old Pappi. How are you, Pappi?'

'Keeping the wolf from the door. And you, Peter?'

'Same here. Got three extra voracious mouths to feed, but holding steady. How's that beautiful girl of yours? Married her?'

'Married her, and lost her,' Pappenheim replied heavily.

'Jeez, Pappi. I'm sorry, mate. What happened? We never thought you two would break up.'

'We didn't. She . . . er . . . died.'

'Oh jeez, mate. So, so sorry. Put my foot in it . . .'

'You couldn't know, Peter. One of those things. Happened a while ago. Five years.'

Peter Waldron fell silent for long moments. 'Jeez, Pappi. This is terrible. This is what happens when you lose touch.'

'Don't feel guilty about this, Peter. I was not in a fit state to see, or talk to, anyone. You would have hated me. Better this way.'

'Don't know what to say mate.'

'As I said, these things happen . . .'

'Well, we don't let the years pass like this again. None of us is getting any younger. When I'm next in Europe, we get together and crack open a few. Or better yet, you come down under . . .'

'I can't for now, but I'll definitely consider it.'

'Everything for the others arranged to your liking?'

'Perfectly arranged. Thank you, Peter.'

'No worries, mate. Least I could do. When I got the call, couldn't believe it at first. Not mad Pappi, I thought . . .'

'Don't you dare give away that secret . . .'

'A *policeman*? Nah, I said.' Waldron laughed again. 'Who would have thought it?'

'You can talk.'

'Well . . . being a diplo is sort of in the family. Almost no choice in the matter.'

'Enjoying it?'

'I get to meet some strange people.'

'You should see those *I* get to meet.'

'I can imagine. If I can manage it, I'll meet your people personally. Smooth things out more easily.'

'I'd appreciate that, Peter.'

'From what I heard, you've got a hot potato on your hands.'

'And the rest.'

'You must be a special kind of copper, from what I've been told.'

'Not so special.'

'I think I can read something into that, so I won't push. Anything you need, Pappi, consider it done. And no worries.'

'Just make sure things are smooth for them. I'll owe you one.'

'I'm the grateful one, Pappi,' Peter Waldron said, this time very seriously. 'You owe me nothing. I've got me a lovely home, lovely wife, lovely kids, a good career. I've got you to thank for that, mate.'

'Nonsense, Pete,' Pappenheim said, uncharacteristically hiding his light under a bushel. 'Things happen.'

'Not like that one, they don't.'

Pappenheim put down the phone as they ended their conversation. 'Where did the years go?' he asked of himself.

He stared at the ceiling, and blew smoke rings at it.

Müller was standing by his bedroom window, looking down on the stream. The hotel lights played upon it. As he watched, something jumped just beneath the surface. Ever since the reconstruction had been completed, the presence of fish in the stream had been haphazard, to say the least. But of late there seemed to be more, possibly because the rivers in the area were now becoming cleaner, recovering after the damage of previous decades.

As he watched, another fish jumped. He wondered how big it was, and what predators were waiting for it.

He frowned suddenly, went to his phone, and called Pappenheim.

'I thought you'd be asleep by now, in all that luxury,' Pappenheim said.

'And I thought you'd gone home. You haven't been home for at least forty-eight hours, Pappi.'

'Thirty-six,' Pappenheim corrected. 'It will be forty-eight at eight a.m. If I were being paid overtime, I'd be rich. Besides, I've got a change of clothing, a fresh tie, and I can have a shower . . . but I'm rambling. You called me for a reason.'

'Finished?'

'Just about.'

'Then consider this – if you were the general, how would you be feeling right now over Miss Bloomfield's escape, and what would you do about it?'

'Since it is certain that the man who surprised her will have reported Willi's abject failure, I would want to know the why, and the how. I would want to know who spilled the beans. I would . . .' Pappenheim stopped. 'Willi's girlfriend. The transmission Willi made to her . . .'

'Via the mobile-radio hybrid she's not supposed to have . . .'

'And which we piggybacked,' Pappenheim finished. 'I would also immediately change frequency, once I'd found out about Willi's bad behaviour . . .'

'But the goth has assured us our piggyback rider can't be shaken off. So the primary aim is . . .'

'To find the girlfriend before they do.'

'Can we?'

'We need the goth,' they said together.

'She'll probably be asleep,' Müller said.

'She'll do it for you.'

'Glass houses, Pappi.'

'I didn't say a word.'

'I'll call her.'

'Better you than me.' Pappenheim hung up with a distinct snigger.

'Very funny,' Müller said, dialling the goth's number.

156

She answered immediately.

Müller was apologetic. 'Sorry. Didn't mean to wake you.'

'I am awake. I'm watching a movie about Kafka.' Sensing Müller was not totally happy about having to call her out, she added quickly, 'But if you need me . . .'

'We do, I'm afraid. Very important. A car will be sent to get you. No need for you to drive. How soon will you be ready?'

'I'm ready.'

Which was not strictly true. Dressed in a long, flowing nightdress that was as translucent as a Roman blind, she was in fact almost ready for bed.

'Thanks, Hedi.'

'Any time.'

Müller called Pappenheim. 'She's ready.'

'See? Wasn't so hard, was it?'

'I won't even answer that. Send a car, lights flashing. We need her at the gallery as fast as possible.'

'As I was certain she'd do it for you,' Pappenheim said, 'one is already standing by. We can also use it to go get the girlfriend . . . if we're lucky.'

'Then I'll let you get on with it.'

'Keep you updated?'

'Please. And Pappi, heard anything of Kaltendorf since I left?'

'He continues to be conspicuous by his absence.'

'Long may that be so . . . until I'm ready for him.'

'Sounds like a prayer to me.'

Hedi Meyer was virtually running up the corridor. She had rapidly changed back into the clothes she had worn during the day, and had prepared herself so quickly she looked as coolly elegant as always.

Pappenheim was waiting by the door to the gallery. 'Thanks for coming,' he greeted.

'No problem, sir.' Almost casually, she glanced further up the corridor, towards Müller's office.

Pappenheim saw the look but pretended he hadn't, as he tapped in the entry code.

'It will be just the two of us,' he said to her as they went in.

She said nothing, but a covert glance from Pappenheim caught a fleeting look of disappointment.

She went directly to the computer and powered it up. 'What are we looking for?'

'Do you remember that transmission we picked up between Willi and his girlfriend?'

'I do. I can call it up from the audio files.'

'We need a little more than that. Can you not only call it up, but give a location as well?'

'I can do better than that. I can give you a street, if that's what you want, sir. The trace program in here can do that. It's all been saved. Watch.'

She ran the program. First, a map of Germany appeared; then, as the audio transmission started, a pulsing line went from the source to the receiver. Both were located within an area covered by Berlin and its immediate outskirts.

Pappenheim pointed to the first location, which was just outside Berlin itself. 'The general's house. That will have been Willi. The next is the girlfriend. How far can you expand it?'

'I can give you the exact location – street and house number. If it's an apartment, that too.'

'And the person living there?'

'I can hack into the necessary databases, and not leave a trace.'

'I did not hear that.'

'No, sir.'

'And we are trying to prevent a possible murder.'

'Yes, sir.'

The goth was already doing the search, even as they spoke. The street was located in the northernmost district of Pankow, and the house number, which had six apartments, was also in there.

'Right next to Prenzlberg,' the goth said. 'Not really far from me.'

She went online, and hunted out the most likely databases. She found one she thought would yield a fast result, and took all of thirty seconds to break through.

'That quickly?' Pappenheim said, astonished.

'My little program is a fast worker. It needs improvement, though.'

'You could have fooled me.'

'Here we are. Resident . . . Cornelia Mott. We could have done a standard map search once we had the address; just as any kid with a computer could have. But that would only have given us a location on the map, and not who is actually living there at the time. This way, we've got a fully up-to-date result. Even a postal database would not necessarily be accurate. This one is.'

'You're a genius, Miss Meyer.'

'I know.'

Pappenheim picked up the phone, called the Ready Group, and gave them the information. This was relayed to the waiting car, which set off, lights flashing, but no siren.

'Another car will take you home,' he said to the goth, 'unless you want to play your flying game.'

She shook her head. 'Thank you, sir, but I think I'll just shut down and head for bed.'

He nodded. 'Wise choice. The car will be waiting at the front. Thank you again for coming.'

'No problem,' she said as she shut down the machine. 'If they do try to change frequencies, we'll still pick them up. We're stuck to them like glue, and they don't know it.' She stood up. 'Goodnight, sir.'

'Goodnight, Hedi.'

At the general's mansion, Reindorf and three men were taking Willi's living quarters apart. Everything Willi had was searched. He had been one of the privileged of the general's coterie, who lived on the premises, and in a suite big enough to virtually qualify as an apartment. There was a bedroom, living room, and a full bathroom suite.

'*Nothing!*' Reindorf snarled in frustration. He wanted to go home, and every fruitless search delayed that.

The men knew it, kept searching, and wisely remained silent. They treated the place with respect, well aware that what they were searching belonged to the general, and not to Willi.

Then one of them put a probing hand beneath a large sofa. 'I've got something, sir.'

They all stopped to look.

'I wouldn't mind some help.'

The other two men came forward.

The searcher pointed. 'Just lift that end.'

'Be careful not to scrape the floor!' Reindorf cautioned.

'We'll be careful, Colonel,' one of the men said as they lifted the sofa.

'Got it!' the one who had probed beneath the sofa said in triumph. 'OK. Put it back down.'

He had found a letter.

He handed it to Reindorf. 'Must have fallen out of a pocket, and just slid under. Willi probably didn't even realize it.'

Reindorf immediately looked at the back for the sender's address, which should normally be there. Sometimes, people tended not to – despite the requirement. But the return address was there, in a careful, large hand.

Someone uncertain, Reindorf thought gratefully, and who needed to assert herself.

'We have it,' he said with relief. 'Cornelia Mott. She lives in Pankow.' He removed the letter from the envelope, and dropped it on a table. He passed the envelope to the man who had made the find. 'Here. Take this with you. Find her, and bring her here. Go!'

The men went out.

Müller had taken his mobile and gone back to the window, looking for fish. He had been rewarded with several jumps.

'You really are jumping tonight,' he said.

The mobile rang.

'Yes, Pappi,' he answered, moving back into the room.

'We've located her, and a car with two Ready Group colleagues is on its way. The goth strikes again.'

'Good news, and a great effort from the goth. Let's hope our colleagues get there ahead of the competition.'

'My hope too. Of course, we don't know whether Willi's friends know of the girlfriend, or whether he kept it a secret. He may well have, considering he gave her one of those fancy phones he shouldn't.'

'If so, it should take them just that bit longer to find out who she is, which might work in our favour.'

'Time will tell.'

'It has a habit of doing that. And the goth?'

'On her way home in another car.'

'Thanks, Pappi. I'll keep waiting.'

'And I'll get back to you when.'

Müller went back to the window as they ended the call. He looked down at the stream. A short while later, he spotted two jumps.

'You're not the only ones jumping tonight,' he said.

Nine

The unmarked Ready Group car, its detachable blue light flashing, came to a sharp halt in front of the building where Cornelia Mott lived.

The two men inside, in civilian clothes topped by black leather jackets, wore pistols in underarm holsters, and each had a Heckler & Koch MP5N sub-machine gun in the car. The sub-machine guns had silencers screwed to their short barrels.

The flashing light was turned off. Both men got out quickly, and glanced up at the six-storey building.

The driver, Werner Ostmann, said, 'You go, Nico. I'll watch things.'

'Right,' Nico Kovacs said. 'Thank God she's on the ground floor.' He hurried up the three steps to the main door, and pressed the button. He kept it pressed.

Ostmann, HK in hand, kept a watchful eye on the sleeping street, scanning each direction non-stop.

At the building, Kovacs was tensely saying in a low voice, 'Come on, come on!'

At last, a cross voice shouted through the intercom, '*Piss off, whoever you are, or I'll call the police!*'

'We are the police, Frau Mott,' Kovacs told her, and, turning to grin at Ostmann, he added, 'I always wanted to say that.'

'Oh,' came the voice from the intercom. 'Just . . . just a minute, I must . . .'

'You must hurry, Frau Mott! This is urgent!'

'Alright, alright . . .'

The intercom fell silent as Kovacs waited impatiently.

By the car, Ostmann kept up his unceasing vigilance.

Minutes passed.

'What the hell is she *doing*?' Kovacs said crossly.

'Probably looking in the mirror and wondering which make-up to use.'

'There's no bloody time for make-up!'

'Then tell her.'

Kovacs pressed the button again, and again kept doing so.

'Can't you wait?' the intercom blared at him.

'No, Frau Mott! Open up!'

There was a loud sigh and, finally, the main door buzzed. Kovacs pushed it open and hurried in. A light led him to Cornelia Mott's door. He stared when he got there. She was still in a short, transparent nightie and knickers. That was it.

'What the . . . ? Get dressed, Frau Mott. *Now!*'

'Alright,' she sulked. 'Don't shout! You'll wake the neighbours.'

'They're already awake. They just don't want to get involved.' Kovacs quickly got out his ID, showed it to her and said, 'Kovacs,' then entered before she could object.

He found himself in an expensive-looking apartment.

At that moment, a man with nothing on came into the room, peering groggily.

Kovacs whipped his pistol out and pointed it at the man. 'Who the hell are you?'

Cornelia Mott, hair a mass of blonde curls that owed much to the hairdresser's skill, froze, gave a little squeal, then put a hand to her mouth as she stared wide-eyed from Kovacs to the man and back again.

The man glared at Kovacs. 'None of your damned business! And who the hell are you?'

'Nikolaus,' Kovacs said with grating sarcasm, playing a game with his own name. 'What do you think? Frau Mott,' he went on, 'please put some clothes on now and come with me! *Do it!*'

'Now look here,' the man began. He took a step forwards, then stopped quickly, eyes on Kovacs' pistol.

'Moving is a bad idea,' Kovacs said. 'I'll ask again . . . who are you? Frau Mott, if you're still standing there like a frozen statue in the next few seconds, I'll shoot him in the balls.'

She fled.

Kovacs stared hard at the man. 'I'm waiting.'

The man's attitude changed suddenly. 'Just a friend. My name is Grösche. Walter. I . . . I was just . . .'

'Screwing Willi's girlfriend.'

The man paled. 'You *know* Willi?'

'We go way back,' Kovacs lied, enjoying himself.

'Shit! I know Willi knows some police, but . . . oh shit. Shit, *shit*!'

Cornelia Mott rushed out, half-dressed, struggling to put things on, now suddenly at speed.

'*Willi?*' she squealed. 'He's back already? Walter! You must go. You must get out of here!'

'Walter's going nowhere at the moment,' Kovacs said. 'But you are, Frau Mott. If you're not ready in two minutes, I'll drag you out. We've wasted enough time already.'

'What are you talking about? Why do you want me? I haven't done anything!'

'The hospital, Frau Mott,' Kovacs said off the top of his head.

Her eyes widened in alarm. 'My father! What happened!'

'How ill was he, Frau Mott?' Kovacs asked, improvising.

'*Was?*' The alarm rose exponentially.

'He's not dead,' Kovacs assured her, which was true enough. 'But we must hurry.'

'Yes, yes.' She was panicking even more. 'He's a heavy smoker, you see. My mother always told him to give up. And he never listened. Now look what has happened . . .' She went on, spinning a scenario that had nothing to do with reality.

'Are you *ready*?' Kovacs said, cutting into her wild meanderings.

'Yes. I think so.'

'Good. Let's go. Oh wait. Willi gave you a phone. Better bring it with you.'

'Yes, yes. I'll get it.'

As she hurried out again, Grösche said, 'Can I put some clothes on now?'

'You don't move until we get out of here.'

'Shit.'

'Happens,' Kovacs said.

'I've got it.' Cornelia Mott came back, curls flying. She whirled to give Grösche a quick kiss. 'Sorry.'

'Frau Mott!'

'Alright. God! You policemen!'

'The time you're taking, your father could be dead by now!'

She shot him an outraged stare. 'Don't talk about my father like that.'

As they went out, she absentmindedly locked the door.

'Hey!' they heard faintly.

'Oh no! I've locked Walter in! He doesn't have a key! If Willi finds him . . .'

'Hard luck, Frau Mott. No time to go back.'

Kovacs put his gun away and bundled her, struggling, out of the main entrance.

Ostmann was staring at them. 'What the hell kept you?'

'What . . . do . . . you think?' Kovacs growled.

Ostmann gave an amused smile as Kovacs shoved her into the back, and snarled, 'Now *stay* there!'

'*Company!*' Ostmann called sharply. 'Here!' He passed the HK to Kovacs and hurried to get behind the wheel.

Kovacs grabbed the gun and turned to look up the street. A car, with lights blazing, was hurtling towards them.

He saw a flash, and something whizzed past him.

Christ, he thought. They're shooting at me! Are they mad?

He fired a short, silenced burst as the car drew nearer. The lights on one side shattered and went out.

He swung round and leapt into the passenger seat. The door was still open as Ostmann sent the car surging away.

'Christ!' Kovacs said as he finally shut the door. 'Whoever they are, they're crazy.'

'What's going on?' Cornelia Mott shouted. 'What's going on? Why are those people shooting? Are you really police? Are—?'

'*Shut up!*' both men said together.

'Better call the chief,' Ostmann said. 'See what he says.'

Kovacs called Pappenheim. 'We've got her, Chief.'

'Excellent!'

'You won't believe what happened.'

'Tell me when you get here.'

'That's just it, Chief. We've got company. They shot first. I shot back. They're driving a black Mercedes, lights on the right side shot out.'

'Leave it to me. Just get here.'

'Right, Chief.'

'Police?' one of the men in the Mercedes said.

Then a blue light began flashing on the roof of the car in front.

'That answer your question?' another asked.

'Well, they've got her.'

'I think we should go back and see what's in her place. There might be something useful to the colonel.' He was the one who had found the letter.

'No,' the driver insisted. 'We try to get her. The colonel ordered it.'

Then, suddenly, the place was full of police cars, blocking them.

'You were saying?' the man who had found the letter said.

'Shut up!'

The Mercedes came to a halt. Police with guns stood behind their cars.

The men got out calmly. The police did not approach, neither did they speak.

'What's happening?' the letter finder asked softly. 'No shouting, no *Get your hands in the air . . .*'

'Shut up,' the driver repeated.

The silent stand-off lasted a full ten minutes. Then the police cars suddenly began to move off.

The driver looked at the last one to start moving. One of the policemen was still out.

'When we take over,' the driver of the Mercedes shouted, 'things will be very different.'

The policeman looked at him coldly. 'In your dreams, *Arschloch*!'

'In your *nightmare*, *Arschloch*!'

The policeman ignored him, got into his patrol car, and it moved off at speed.

'Now what?' the letter finder began.

166

The driver looked at him. 'What do you mean?'

'Are we staying here all night?'

The driver glared at him. 'Let's see if there's anything in that apartment.'

The letter finder smiled to himself, and got back into the car.

When they arrived back at the building, all three got out and went to the entrance.

'Alright, genius,' the driver said to the letter finder. 'How do we get in without waking the whole house?'

'The same way we would have got in, had the cops not got here first.'

The letter finder took something out of his pocket, held it up briefly, then put it against the door. It made no sound. Then the lock on the entrance door buzzed open.

He took his electronic burglar away and they filed in, going to Cornelia Mott's door. He took a set of keys out of his pocket. They were not for the building, but one of them worked. The apartment was open.

'Thank God you're back!' they heard from within.

They glanced at each other, taken aback by this turn of events. Then went in.

The mighty relief on a now half-dressed Walter Grösche's face was transformed into a mixture of uncertainty, and fear.

'Who . . . who are you?' he demanded in a shaking voice. 'How . . . how can you just break into people's homes?'

'"People's homes"?' the driver, already in a foul mood because of their failure, countered. 'This is *your* home, is it? Your name is Willi Helmer, is it? Who are *you*, I should be asking.' He looked Grösche up and down. 'Been playing in the nest while Willi's away, have you? Been *fucking* her? Were *fucking* her when the cops arrived, were you? *Were you?*'

'L–look. I don't know who you are but . . .'

'You're right you don't know who I am, because if you did, you'd be shitting your pants right now.'

The driver looked about him, went into the bedroom, and came back out holding a photograph of Cornelia Mott in a bikini, standing next to Willi. Their arms were about each other's waists.

'I never realized Willi had this little bed warmer stashed away. He kept things from us. The bedroom stinks of fucking,' the driver continued, looking at Grösche. He thrust the photograph towards Grösche. 'You don't look like him.'

Without warning, the driver gave vent to his frustration, and smashed the framed photograph savagely into Grösche's face. Something cracked. Grösche screamed and fell, holding on to his face.

'Hey!' the letter finder snapped. 'What the hell are you doing? Are you crazy? The general—'

The driver, taller, with a sharp face and mean eyes, rounded on him. '*Shut . . . up!*'

'We came here to look for things, not to do this. You're going beyond—'

'I'm getting pissed off with you, smartass. With Willi gone, I'm going to be the one taking charge. The general tells the colonel, the colonel tells *me*, and I tell *you*! Got it?'

Without waiting for an answer, the driver again turned to the hapless Grösche and delivered several vicious kicks to the body of the prone man.

'En–joyed her . . . did . . . you? Eh? *Eh? Was it fun? Was she good?*'

'Stop it!' the one who had found the letter shouted. 'You'll kill him!'

'So fucking what?'

The driver kept kicking.

Then some people in the rest of the house starting banging on the walls and ceilings in annoyance.

Müller got the call from Pappenheim.

'She's safely here. I've put her in a witness-holding room. I'll be interviewing her when we're finished.'

'Well done, Pappi.'

'The bouquet rightfully belongs to Ostmann and Kovacs. They got out of there just as the general's lot arrived. They were shot at, and returned fire.'

'Anyone hurt?'

'Not on our side. Damaged egos on the other. They lost the race, and got the lights on their car shot out for their pains.

Kovacs called for support, I got some patrol colleagues to block the Mercedes, but nothing else. No arrests, no gun battle. Keep it all low key, I thought.'

'As ever, the right decision.'

'We also got the little toy Willi so stupidly – but luckily for us – gave to his girlfriend.'

'That is a huge bonus,' Müller said. 'Give it to the goth to play with. I'm certain she'll find a way to have us listen in even better to what the general says to his minions.'

'You're a mind reader. The beauty is, they don't and won't even know we've got it.'

'The general is after my flanks. Every little helps. This will give us an invaluable advantage.'

'It will. And, talking of minds, I doubt that Miss Cornelia Mott has much of one; again, a blessing for us. Must be the dye she uses on that hairdo.'

'Meaning, had she not pestered Willi, we would never have found out about his trip to Washington.'

'Exactly. But her reasons for pestering Willi,' Pappenheim said with meaning, 'were less than driven by a pining heart. Not bursting with intelligence, but brimming with low cunning. Her real purpose was to find out how long he'd be gone.'

'Let me guess – she likes playing away.'

'You always win these little quizzes. Not only does she like doing it, she was actually in the process when Kovacs made his visit. A naked gentleman, Walter Grösche by name, made a poignant entrance in his birthday suit.'

Müller could not stop the laugh he felt coming. 'You're joking.'

'I joke not.'

'And where's this enterprising cuckoo now?'

'Still in the apartment, accidentally locked in by the airheaded Miss Mott.'

Müller allowed the laugh full rein. Pappenheim's accompanying bellow sounded in his ear.

As their laughter subsided, Pappenheim said, 'At least we got a laugh out of this one. And it's Walter's lucky night. Willi is never coming home again. I've sent Kovacs and Ostmann back with the keys – which Miss Mott kindly handed to us – to get him out of his perfumed jail.'

'Pappi, I can hear you're about to collapse again,' Müller said, grinning. 'I'll leave you to the delightful Miss Mott. I'm off to bed. But call me if anything of interest happens.'

'Well, here's something to make your veins curdle. One of the joy boys in the Mercedes shouted at a colleague that things would be different when they took over. He was just a thug with a loud mouth; but it's interesting that he feels he can say that.'

'I doubt that the general would be pleased. Bravado is not exactly the silent way to power. The Semper way is stealth. Whoever he was, he may have overreached himself.'

'Another Willi in the making, perhaps?'

'Who might well share the same fate.'

'I won't lose any sleep over it.'

'Nor I,' Müller said. 'The more they decimate themselves, the better I like it.'

By the time Ostmann and Kovacs had returned to Cornelia Mott's apartment building in Pankow, the Mercedes and the three men had gone. The street was quiet, the night still. No car went by. Somewhere, a service train clattered, a metallic echo in the night.

Kovacs was shaking his head and laughing softly, as they left the car and made for the building's entrance.

'I just can't stop seeing that little scene. She standing there looking like God knows what in a nightdress that leaves her more undressed than dressed, then in he comes, just as his mother made him.'

'Big baby,' Ostmann said with a chuckle.

'And then, she locks him inside!'

Their shoulders shook with silent mirth as Kovacs opened the main door and they entered. They made for Cornelia Mott's door.

Kovacs began to insert the key. The door moved slightly.

'What the f—' he said. 'It's open! He must have managed to get out.' He pushed the door wider. 'Oh God in Heaven!' he uttered in a shocked whisper.

Ostmann pushed forward slightly to look, and saw Grösche. 'Oh shit!' he said.

The witness-holding room was more than a standard interview room. It was, in fact, more like an ordinary suite with better than average fittings, which included a separate bedroom, and en suite bathroom. Pappenheim was talking to Cornelia Mott in what served as the living room. They were sitting opposite each other at a basic table. A female sergeant in civilian clothes, her escort, was standing by.

'When will I see my father?' Cornelia Mott asked.

'Frau Mott,' Pappenheim said patiently. 'There's nothing wrong with your father.'

'But that policeman told me . . .'

'He never did. He mentioned hospital. *You* mentioned your father. He never said anything was wrong with your father. He knew nothing about your father until you brought up his smoking history.'

'You smoke, don't you? I know the signs. You'll be just like my father.'

Pappenheim stared at her. 'Frau Mott, I haven't slept for . . . too many hours. This can sometimes strain my patience. I hate it when my patience is strained, and I hate it even more when people strain my patience. Let me ask you very nicely . . . are you on the same planet as the rest of us? Why do you think you are here?'

'How should I know? Those men pushed me into a car, and people started shooting . . .'

'*Frau Mott!*' Pappenheim said in exasperation. 'The "people" were shooting because they wanted to kill you! They would have kidnapped you if they had arrived in time. They were coming for you! My men got to you first, and, if you hadn't delayed them, you would have got away without being seen.'

'So now you're saying it's my fault?'

Pappenheim sighed. 'Where is Willi?'

'Washington. He'll be back tomorrow.'

'He may be in Washington, Frau Mott . . . but he is not coming back.'

'Willi would never leave me.'

171

Pappenheim passed a hand across his face. The brazenness of it, he thought. He glanced at the escort sergeant and saw she was trying hard not to laugh.

Pappenheim gave another sigh. 'Frau Mott, perhaps Willi would never leave you, but I think, in this instance, he had no choice.'

'Walter was just a fling. Nothing serious . . .'

'Frau Mott! Willi is probably *dead*, and you would have been as well, by the time those men, or their bosses, had finished with you. You were very lucky that my officers beat them to it. Now, will you please understand how serious—'

There was a knock. A uniformed sergeant opened the door and looked in. 'Call from Kovacs for you, sir. Will you take it in here? Or . . .'

'I'll take it outside.'

The sergeant nodded and left.

Pappenheim got to his feet, and shook his head slowly. Cornelia Mott stared blankly back at him.

Pappenheim went out. When he returned, his expression was a grim one.

He did not mince words. 'Frau Mott, Walter Grösche has been badly beaten up. The officers went back to let him out of your apartment, and found him bleeding on your living-room floor. Those were Willi's colleagues . . .'

'He came back early! It was a trap . . .'

'No, no, *no*! This has nothing to do with your sexual activities!'

The sergeant looked at him sternly.

'Then you tell her,' Pappenheim said to the sergeant, allowing his exasperation to flow unchecked. 'Frau Mott,' he went on, trying again, 'those men did not go to your place to avenge Willi, they went there to ransack your place; to see if there was anything they could find that would tell them how much you knew about Willi. They had planned to take you to their bosses. They failed. That is why they went back to your apartment. Unfortunately for Walter, they found him instead. They beat him up so badly, he might not live. He's on his way to hospital right now . . .'

She stood up suddenly. 'I must go to him . . .'

'You are not going anywhere!' Pappenheim roared, so suddenly, both women jumped. 'Get it into your head, Frau Mott. Your life is at stake! You mean nothing to these people. You're just like a . . . un . . . an insect they would like to squash.'

He stared at her, the full force of his eyes impaling her as if she were herself a butterfly specimen in a display cabinet.

For the first time, the seriousness of her predicament at last seemed to dawn upon her.

The general was not looking pleased.

The three men who had been sent to get Cornelia Mott were standing before him in a room of baronial proportions that sometimes doubled as a conference room. Along its walls, like mute sentries, stood suits of armour from various periods of history. All gleamed in the lights from the walls and ceiling, evidence of meticulous attention. There were no carpets on the equally gleaming floor, which was surfaced with interlocking Spanish red and white tiles, fitted in an alternating diamond pattern.

The men stood before the general, looking very much like soldiers on parade. Behind them, a quiet presence, was Reindorf.

'Hart, Schonert, Auerberg,' the general began. 'You three, like Willi and others here, are privileged to live in this house. You are here because each of you is seen as having special qualities which our Order of the Bretheren values. In previous centuries, orders like our own sustained themselves through *discipline*. When that was allowed to become corrupted, the seeds of their eventual destruction were planted.

'Like the Romans before them, they were the instruments of their own demise. They fragmented into warring factions. They became corrupt, mendacious, greedy, lustful for individual power. What they received in return smears the pages of history. Our order has meticulously, over *decades*, prepared itself, and is *still* preparing itself for the goal it intends to achieve. It has done so by acting *invisibly*; by drawing as little attention to itself as possible, by remaining in the background while it goes about its business.

173

'Like any such power – and we *are* a power – it has international capabilities and representatives. Borders mean little to us. We retain our close, tight-knit strength through our very invisibility, and our presence throughout many strands of society.' The general paused, and looked directly at Hart, the driver with the mean eyes. 'Some of you came to us from the military services. Some from the streets. We have moulded you. Given you purpose.

'In the days when our predecessors wore armour, it was not only the knights of whom the highest standards were expected, but their squires, and their men-at-arms. Those of you who live here are the modern versions of the squires and men-at-arms. Hart, you were expected to replace Willi. I want a factual report of what happened in the woman's apartment.'

The general stopped, and did not take his eyes off Hart.

'We went in, General, and found a man—'

'You found a man. And what did you do to him?'

'We . . .'

'"We"?'

Hart glanced at Auerberg, the one with the electronic burglar.

'*I* am talking to you, Hart! *Not* Auerberg!'

'I . . . talked to the man . . .'

'"Talked"?'

Hart became uncomfortable.

'If you do not tell me exactly what happened, I shall ask Auerberg, or Schonert. I will expect the same exactitude from them. The choice is yours.'

'I . . . roughed him up a bit . . .'

'"Roughed him up a bit."' The general paused again. 'It may interest you to know, Hart, that we intercepted an ambulance report. A man was found in the woman's apartment so badly beaten, he is not expected to live. We also have information that your car was blocked by police, but you were not arrested, and not spoken to. And you were heard to shout that, when we took power, things would be different. Your car has some of its lights shot out. Your weapon has been fired. The thing about discipline, Hart, is that you *never* exceed the limits of your power; that you understand how far you can go, or, if you do decide to push your boundaries, that you are aware

174

of the risks of doing so. If you do not, you become a liability. We do *not* appreciate unwanted attention being brought upon ourselves, Hart. I think the colonel has something to say.'

'Hart,' Reindorf said.

Hart turned, and stared, wide-eyed. The other two men remained as they were, facing the general.

The silenced gun in Reindorf's gloved hand coughed three times. Hart was propelled backwards with each shot, going past the general as he staggered. He gave a wheezing gasp as he went.

The general, standing, legs slightly apart, hands behind his back, twisted his upper body briefly to follow Hart's stagger.

He turned back to Schonert and Auerberg. 'I despise indiscipline. Get rid of that. Have it buried in the forest. Auerberg, you now have charge.'

'Yes, General.'

'Wait, Auerberg,' Reindorf said.

He went to the body, and placed the weapon into the shoulder holster where it belonged. Hart had been shot with his own gun.

Reindorf then stood up, and began removing the gloves. He went to the door, opened it, and spoke to someone outside.

'Alright.'

Two men entered with a body bag and, with Auerberg and Schonert, began to place Hart's body into it.

'And don't let it bleed all over the floor!' Reindorf told them sharply.

Reindorf and the general watched dispassionately as the laden bag was carried out of the room. A few spots of blood had nevertheless dropped on to the pristine floor.

The general looked at them, but said nothing.

'I'll see to it,' Reindorf said.

'I know you will. One of the things I have liked and admired about you, Reindorf,' the general went on, 'even when we served together, is your clinical efficiency.'

'Thank you, General.'

'No need to thank me for the truth, my dear Reindorf.' The general paused. 'How the devil did he manage to get ahead of us?'

'Müller? Somehow, he continues to get hold of sensitive information. Willi is intercepted by the target, in Washington. They beat us to the Mott woman and, despite being shot at, made no move to arrest Hart, Schonert, and Auerberg. They unearthed Mainauer, luckily too late. He walked boldly in here. He has the rings. He has found the real recorders . . . He got General von Mappus last winter. The list continues. General . . . he, is attacking *our* flanks.'

The general remained silent for several moments.

'Müller would have remained in blissful ignorance, had it not been for that distaff cousin of his, Dahlberg. Dahlberg pushed the limit, and alerted Müller to something we had spent decades keeping in the shadows. Dahlberg was always a loose cannon, even during the days of the DDR. Must be a genetic fault with that family, even the distaff members. Discipline is clearly not their strongest suit. See how he behaves towards Kaltendorf.'

If Reindorf believed the general to be wrong about Müller, he said nothing. He also thought that Mainauer was himself as loose a cannon as Dahlberg had been.

He had not told the general about Mainauer's personal threat to him; but, like many an advisor throughout history whose instincts were at times more accurate than those of the boss, self-preservation made Reindorf keep his counsel. Mainauer was the general's own protégé. Messengers, after all, tended to be shot for their pains in situations like these. History was replete with such examples.

'Still nothing from our people at the airports?' the general now asked.

'Nothing. It is clear that, for their own reasons, Müller's people are not interested in the airports . . . just as they had reasons for not apprehending Hart and the others.'

'At least we got Mainauer safely on his way.'

'He'll have arrived by now.'

'Yes. He will.' The general glanced at his watch. 'The darkest hour. It will soon be dawn, Reindorf. You should go home for some sleep.'

'I will, General, as soon as I've had these blood spots attended to.'

176

'Very well. Goodnight, Reindorf.'
'Goodnight, General.'

'Jens.'

Müller came awake with a start. The soft voice had been close to his ear. He put on the bedside light. There was no one in the room. He would have been very surprised if there had been; which was putting it mildly.

The voice he'd heard had been his mother's.

He turned off the light and lay in the gloom, listening to the race of his own heartbeat. As he calmed himself, he realized he could see remarkably well, by the diffused glow of the lights from the garden.

'A dream,' he muttered. 'Just a dream.'

But it had been a strange one. He was not aware of having actually been *in* a dream. It had just been the voice, waking him. But why?

The last time he'd dreamt of her had been in May. On that occasion, he had been in the cockpit of his parents' aircraft, and he and his mother had been hauling on the yokes, desperately trying to gain altitude, and failing.

Just before the aircraft hit, he'd heard himself say, 'Oh God!'

And his mother, in those final moments, had uttered just the one word: 'Jens!'

That dream had been instrumental in driving him to hunt for the real flight recorders, which he had found.

He paused, a thought coming with sudden clarity.

'She wants me to go to Australia,' he remarked softly into the gloom.

Sunrise was still ninety minutes away.

Reindorf drove at an easy pace to his substantial home near a small lake, about twenty kilometres away.

For a man who had just coldly executed one of his own lower-ranking comrades, he was surprisingly thoughtful; but it was not because he felt any regrets about Hart. Hart had not been his first.

Unlike the general, Reindorf had a family: a wife, and an eleven-year-old daughter. Unlike the general, he did not have a large staff, nor members of the order living in his house. His sole help was a gardener who came to keep the grounds from becoming overgrown. In a strangely unexpected way, given the general's comments about his being clinically efficient, Reindorf was a man who liked a wild garden.

Unlike the general, he was not sanguine about Müller's ability to seriously damage the order.

When he got home, Reindorf entered quietly and went upstairs. He turned on a single light on the soaring ceiling above the landing, to avoid disturbing either his wife or his daughter.

Cautiously, he opened the door to his daughter's room. He stood there for long moments, just looking at her. She tended to sleep half in, half out of the bedclothes, one of her pillows clutched tightly like a teddy bear. Her long hair was spread like a dark sunburst about her head. She had always slept like that, ever since she had moved out of her cradle.

He smiled fondly, and softly closed the door.

He went to the master bedroom, and did the same. He looked at his wife, who slept exactly like her daughter.

Again, he smiled, shut the door, and went into his study. He went up to a safe that was hidden behind a false panel, which was itself hidden behind the sliding section of a bookcase. The safe was protected by a keypad with both numbers and letters upon it. He tapped in a ten-unit code, opened the safe and pulled out a thick, leatherbound journal. He took the journal to an antique rolltop desk. At the desk was a matching chair with green leather panels on the seat and the high back. He opened the rolltop, sat down, and carefully opened the journal at a marked page. He opened a drawer, and took out a fountain pen of ribbed gold. Then he began to write.

Daylight was beginning to filter through the drawn curtains when he at last finished. He put the journal back into its hiding place, and closed the rolltop.

The journal was a mixture of a report, and a diary, which he regularly compiled. Its eventual destination would be the higher echelons of the Semper.

Reindorf left his study, satisfied with his work.

*   *   *

Annandale, 00.10.

Carey Bloomfield woke suddenly and, for brief seconds, was unsure of where she actually was.

'Shit!' she said. 'I fell asleep in front of the damned television. The shock of seeing that asshole under my car is turning me into a couch potato.'

In T-shirt, a loose pair of shorts and barefoot, she had been half-reclining on her sofa, watching a science channel about freshwater bull sharks. The programme had long since changed to another, which was now coming to an end.

She stood up, stretched luxuriously, bending her body in a way that would have seriously disturbed Müller; and yawned with all the delicacy of someone in a beer hall, at the end of a heavy night of drinking.

'Mmmm,' she said. 'That felt good. Now for bed.'

'And we thank Drs Annette Morris of Graham Electronics,' the presenter was saying, 'Harry Holt of Michaels and Sloane, Rachel Tanleyn of Evergreen Earth, and James Dennison of Dennison Biometrics. Thank you for being with us, Doctors. Very intriguing subject.'

'Thank you,' three of them said, almost in concert.

'Thank you,' Dennison said. 'It is intriguing, and fascinating. The strides in DNA research are quite spectacular.'

Carey Bloomfield, who had previously not been paying attention, had been in the act of switching off. Her hand froze inches from the button.

'What the . . . ?' she began. 'That's his voice! That's the bastard who sneaked up behind me! But it can't be . . .'

The credits were running.

'*No, no!*' she cried. 'What was his name? What company? Oh shit, shit, *shit*! Run it in the credits,' she pleaded to the television. 'Run it . . .'

She waited, hoping.

Then the name, and the company, appeared, moving quickly upscreen.

'Dennison,' she said, memorizing. 'James Dennison, Dennison Biometrics.'

She hunted for a pen, found one, and quickly began to write it all down on a pad near the living-room phone.

'Spectacular research, is it?' she muttered, suddenly thinking of Greville. 'Like DNA poisons?'

She paused. She could be wrong, and the man totally innocent. The date at the end of the credits increased her uncertainty. The programme was over two years old. Graveyard-hour programming.

'The way companies fold these days,' she said, 'or get bought out, Dennison Biometrics might not even exist any more.'

But she went to her laptop, turned it on, and went online. She searched for Dennison Biometrics, and soon found a home page. She opened it, and found nothing out of the ordinary, just the usual, bland company publicity, saying how wonderful the company was. She went off, and shut down. She tore the note she had written into tiny pieces, and put it into a waste bin.

'Well, anything really interesting would not be on a home page, anyway. I need someone who can get into the places angels would fear to tread. And I know just who.'

Her first thought was to call a fellow officer – an expert hacker – who worked in her department, who liked her, and who would certainly do the probe if she asked. Then she had another thought.

'I know someone else, with no connection to me over here.'

She picked up her secure mobile, and called Müller. 'It should be after six in Germany,' she said to herself as she waited for the connection. 'He should be awake.'

Müller, still asleep, came groggily awake and picked up his own mobile.

'Müller?' he heard. 'Why are you still asleep? I thought you were the crack-of-dawn guy.'

'I had a long night. And why are you still awake?'

'I had a slow evening. That invitation still stand?'

Müller came fully awake. 'Why the abrupt switch from "I'll see" to this blinding flash of certainty?'

'Hey, this is good. We're speaking in questions. I've got some time off.'

'I thought you had none.'

'Have you any idea how many vacation entitlements I haven't

used? If I took them all at once, I'd be off for a year. I can arrange for a few days.'

'Alright. When are you coming over?'

'I can fly in the morning.'

'Something must have excited you.'

'Could be I just miss you guys.'

'Could be. On the other hand . . .'

'Lighten up, Müller, for Pete's sake.'

'Blame the time of day. I've got a suggestion.'

'Suggest away.'

'Don't come to Berlin. Meet me in Perth.'

'Perth, Australia? Or Perth, Scotland?'

'You'd be enjoying the land of the thistle alone.'

'Very cryptic, Müller. Don't you want to fly with me?'

'Precaution. Discretion. Forewarned.'

She thought about that. 'There's something that needs to be done in Berlin. It will interest you. We need your favourite lady, the goth.'

'*My* favourite lady?'

'Well, you're certainly *her* favourite man,' Carey Bloomfield retorted, barb just touching acid.

'I felt that one,' Müller said. He paused, interested in knowing what she wanted the goth to find. 'Can you tell me over this? I can ask her to do it, then let you know the results when we meet.'

'We're still secure, but we should not stay on much longer.'

'Alright. Go ahead.'

'Dennison Biometrics. I'm certain she'll know what to do.'

'Dennison Biometrics,' Müller repeated. 'She certainly will. I won't ask you why. I'll wait to hear.'

'I'm doing this on a hunch that's probably way off base,' Carey Bloomfield said. 'But you never know. So when do you expect to be there?'

'Within forty-eight hours. Can you do it?'

'I can.'

'Alright. Everything's arranged. I'll meet you. Send Pappi your flight number. He'll get it to me.'

'*Arranged?*' she said, ignoring the rest of the sentence. 'You *expected* me to say yes?'

'Pappi thought you might. Don't forget the flight number.'
'Müller . . . !'
'See you there, Miss Bloomfield.'
In Annandale, Carey Bloomfield glared at her phone. *'Urrrgh!'* she said in frustration. 'Sometimes, that man . . .'

Ten

Autobahn A9, 07.30.

Müller was driving at speed, heading back to Berlin. He'd had one of Aunt Isolde's great breakfasts, and had set off as soon as was decently possible. He had said nothing to her about his experience with the voice, nor had he mentioned he had decided to go to Australia as soon as he could.

But Greville had been watching him surreptitiously, and had come out to the car with him.

Their conversation replayed itself in Müller's mind.

'Been watching you, old son,' Greville had begun. 'Know the signs. Twitchy, what? Something happened?'

Müller had nodded. 'Something has. I'll be going to Australia sooner, rather than later.'

'The Hargreaves.'

'Yes.'

But Greville had still been looking curiously at him. 'What . . . ?' And Greville had paused. 'What's really up, old boy?'

'You'll think me mad.'

'Why? Why on earth would I?'

'I heard my mother call my name. I . . . think she wants me to go to Australia. As soon as possible. There. Now you'll think I *am* mad.'

Greville had repeated his question. 'Why? Dear boy, when you have lived as long as I have, and been to the most outlandish places on this earth, you will come to realize there are many things which, if you saw, or heard, would lead you to consider yourself harbouring a few bats in the belfry. Your bond with your mother was very close. Isolde has told me. Hearing her voice now and then . . . par for the course. As you're going to Oz, the odd passing Aborigine

183

might well tell you things that would surprise you . . . to say the least.'

Müller smiled as he remembered that remark.

'Have you ever heard of something called Dennison Biometrics?' he had then asked Greville.

'That's an easy one. No. Any particular reason?'

'Not that I know of . . . yet.'

'Biometrics. DNA stuff.'

'Fingerprints, eyescans . . .'

'But you think there could be more.'

'There is always that possibility.'

'Who gave this to you?'

'Miss Bloomfield. She called me at six.'

'Midnight in White House country. Then, my boy, she must have considered it sufficiently important. If I were to follow the train of thought I'm having right now, I'd reach a point where I'd be asking myself whether someone is trying to recreate my nemesis. Not a recommendation for peace of mind.'

'We don't know that, Greville. But I am going to look into it, as soon as I'm back in Berlin.'

'If these biometrics people are indeed trying to reincarnate the monster, that would be very bad news indeed. I want this infernal thing to die with me, not have its more advanced cousin loose in the world . . .'

'If Dennison Biometrics are reaching anywhere into that territory, we'll find a way to stop them. That's a promise.'

'Then do not forget the other promise, Jens. See that you are back here before the monster gets me.'

'I'll do that.'

'Then I'll be waiting. Do hope you find what you're looking for down there.'

'So do I.'

They had shaken hands.

'Just continue to keep your monster chained, Greville,' Müller now said quietly.

He had also called Pappenheim to warn him to alert the goth; but had as yet said nothing to him about Dennison Biometrics, nor of the decision about Australia.

By 10.30, Müller was parking the Porsche in the underground

184

garage. A few minutes later, he was tapping at the keypad of the rogues' gallery. He entered, and called Pappenheim from there. Moments later, Pappenheim joined him,

'You've been burning the wind,' Pappenheim said, giving him a searching look. 'You look like a man who's discovered the meaning of life and found that it's worse than you thought.'

Pappenheim did not look as if he had not gone home. His clothes still looked as if he had slept in them, as they always did, even when new; but he had on a fresh tie, impeccably chosen as ever . . .

'That bad?' Müller asked.

'Well . . . like a man on a leash.'

'Interesting concept, Pappi. I'd better let you have both barrels, then. I'm not going to Grenoble for now . . .'

'As you're back here, that did cross my mind.'

'The flight recorders are safe where they are, for the time being,' Müller said, 'under the flagstones in the kitchen of the Lavaliere house. The Lavalieres are themselves safe, up in the mountains, and will not return until they have heard from me. The retired gendarme contact you gave me in July, Alphonse La Croix, whom they know, will keep an eye on the house in Grenoble, in case the Semper go sneaking.

'I'd also like you to warn your Cap Ferrat contact about Solange Dubois. Her maternal grandfather, as we know, was once a colonial policeman. Your contact should let him know they should keep an eye on her, just in case the general thinks it a good idea to have her kidnapped, to keep Kaltendorf in line.'

'Consider that done.'

'Talking of which, has he put in an appearance today?'

Pappenheim shook his head. 'Not so far.'

'Getting to be a habit, but a pleasant one as far as I am concerned. With luck, I'll be out of here before he decides to show his face, if at all.'

'You're going down under.'

'The first flight I can get.'

'I'll warn Pete Waldron while you're in the air. And Miss Bloomfield?'

'The second barrel. She'll join me down there.'

Pappenheim raised an eyebrow. 'Things have been moving fast.'

'A few things did come up on the radar . . . which is where the goth comes in.'

'She's on her way,' Pappenheim said.

'Miss Bloomfield called me at six this morning,' Müller said, 'wanting a check done on something called Dennison Biometrics. She gave no other information. But the fact that she wants it done here, and not in Washington, says enough.'

'She does not want even her own people to know.'

'That must be her reason. I am certain of it. Now here's something a little mad for you, Pappi,' Müller added.

'I'm a policeman. I am mad.'

'I heard my mother call my name, in the early hours of this morning. As clearly as I hear you.'

'Why is that mad?' Pappenheim asked seriously. 'There are times when I have heard Sylvia call my name.'

Müller looked at him in surprise. 'I never imagined . . .'

'The mind sometimes does strange things,' Pappenheim explained with a sheepish smile. 'I wouldn't worry about it; and I'll tell no one, if you don't.'

'I mentioned it to Greville.'

'And?'

'His reaction was generally similar to yours.'

'By a consensus of two, you are not losing your marbles.'

'I think she wants me to go to Australia, Pappi. I feel it.'

'Then there's only one thing to do. You go. Afraid I've got some bad news,' Pappenheim went on. 'Grösche didn't make it.'

Müller said nothing for a few moments, then he hit one of the cabinets with the palm of his hand. Hard. It boomed through the room.

'I know you'd like that to be the general's face . . .' Pappenheim said, glancing at the cabinet.

'But we can't move against him. Not just yet.'

Pappenheim nodded. 'I know. Kovacs is kicking himself,' he added.

'Why?'

'He seems to believe that if he had allowed Cornelia Mott to go back, Grösche would still be alive.'

'That is nonsense, and he knows it. Going back could have left all four of them dead. He knows that. His job was to get her out alive. He did. Cornelia Mott was cheating on Willi. *She* is responsible for Grösche being in the wrong place at the wrong time. Where is Kovacs now?'

'On the way to your aunt's with Ostmann. I thought it best to send them down there. They should be arriving any moment now. They've got direct and secure communication with us.'

'Good,' Müller said in approval. 'Going down there should help keep his mind off his imagined miseries. And where is *she*?'

'Still sleeping.' Pappenheim replied. A long-suffering sigh escaped him. 'Before she went down, she demanded that we get her fresh make-up, plus a few other . . . er . . . womanly things. I talked to the financial department. Seems they can cover it with contingency funds. I have the terrible feeling that, before we're finished, we're going to wish we had left her in that apartment. Would you like to interview her?'

'No thanks. I've got a plane to catch. She's all yours.'

'Thanks for nothing.'

A single knock sounded. The armoured door was so thick, the knock itself was barely perceptible.

'The goth, I believe,' Müller said.

'The Great White would have been trying to break it down,' Pappenheim commented drily as he went to open up.

It was indeed Hedi Meyer. She was dressed all in black: black clinging jeans, black shirt, sleek black trainers with black side stripes. Black-shaded eyelids; but green fingernails.

'Morning, sir,' she greeted Müller warmly.

'Good morning, Miss Meyer.'

Pappenheim looked at her closely. 'Miss Meyer, is one of your eyes green?'

'It shows?' This seemed to please her. 'I thought so this morning before I left home, but wasn't sure.' She looked at Müller. 'You may remember I mentioned a while ago that one sometimes turns a little green.'

'Yes,' he said. 'I remember.'

'So, I'm calm and fertile today. Blue for calm, green for

187

fertility. What are we hunting?' she went on before a bemused Müller could say anything.

'Er . . . Dennison Biometrics.'

'Just standard information? Or something deeper?'

'As deep as you can get without sounding any alarms.'

'I love challenges. Let's see how interesting this one will be.' She took her seat at the computer, and switched it on. 'Alright, lets see what you've got, Dennison Biometrics.' She came to the homepage that Carey Bloomfield had found. 'Tourist stuff,' she said dismissively, and began to seriously probe. 'I want something you haven't got on the page.'

A minute later, she had found a laboratory database.

'Shall I go in?'

'Until you're stopped,' Müller told her.

She made a scoffing sound, as her fingers flew across the keyboard. She seemed to be hitting pages that threw up password requirements which she broke easily, only to be presented with another.

'Oh, they are hiding something,' she said with glee. 'Their firewalls are not coping and, so far, I've got five password entries, but no meat. You don't have so many guards for empty space. Now hitting the sixth.'

'How can you get through those firewalls, and break those passwords so easily?' Müller asked.

'Sir, you shouldn't ask questions whose answers you don't really want to hear.'

Müller glanced at Pappenheim, who raised an amused eyebrow at him.

The goth made it through the sixth . . . only to be met by a seventh.

'What *are* they hiding in there?' she asked herself.

'Couldn't that be a time waster? Giving you all these to play with while they track you?'

'It *is* a time waster, just for that purpose. Thing is, they don't even know I'm there. Number eight coming up.' Her fingers seemed to blur, then their flurry was suddenly halted. 'We're in! No such thing as total security . . . that's why I keep tinkering with our systems to continuously upgrade and update them.' She paused. 'And *what* the hell is *that*?'

188

Müller and Pappenheim went closer, to stare at the screen. A familiar pattern was going through a series of mutations.

PRIMARY SPECIMEN ZERO, a caption informed them.

'My God,' Müller uttered softly. 'I hope it's not what I think it is.'

'I think it is what you hope it isn't,' Pappenheim said. 'Question is, are they succeeding? Or are we looking at a failure?'

'You don't have to be a scientist to recognize a strand of DNA,' the goth said. 'What does "Primary Specimen Zero" really mean? You sound a little . . . anxious, sir.'

'I would put it at stronger than "anxious", Miss Meyer,' Müller said. 'Could you delete all the data in there?'

'I have control of the database. I can do anything to it.'

'Kill it.'

She hit a key. DO YOU REALLY WANT TO DELETE? a small window asked.

She confirmed. It responded with a password request.

'We've really hit the meat,' she said. 'Perhaps it's the only one they've got. That's why delete is protected by a password. I do that myself. Sometimes, being asked is not a sufficient guard against accidental deletion.'

'Can you find that password?'

'Already working on it.'

'Let us hope no one there's yet at work.'

'Or working through all hours,' Pappenheim suggested.

'That too.'

'There is no indication of location,' the goth said, 'but, wherever it is, if someone's working on this at the moment, they will have seen the delete question, but won't be able to do anything about it.'

'And they still won't be tracking you?'

'They'll be too worried about trying to save it first; but they may also have independent trackers trying to find out what the hell's going on. So I'd still like to be out of there soon. This . . . one . . . is a little trickier, but I'll get it.'

A minute went by as the codebreaking program she was using raced on.

'Clever,' she said.

'What do you mean?'

189

'This is a very long code. Digits and letters. The program is working very fast, so as not to hit the time limit. I think I may have another forty seconds, then it will shut down. Security mode. But . . . *Hah!* Got you!'

DELETED, the window announced.

The goth quit the database she had invaded, then swung round to look at Müller and Pappenheim. 'Someone's in for a nasty surprise when he or she comes in to work. Or, if they're there, I just ruined the rest of their day.'

'And there is no trace of your having been in?' Müller asked.

'I don't think I'll answer that,' she said.

Müller gave a slight, jokey bow. 'My apologies, Miss Meyer.'

'I should think so too. You're not going to tell me what that was about, are you?'

Müller shook his head. 'For your own protection.'

The blue eyes looked at him for long moments. Müller actually noticed one turning slightly greener.

'I believe you,' she said. She turned back to the computer. 'Anything else? Or shall I shut down?'

'That's it for now. You can shut down.'

She did so, and stood up. 'Keep finding me these challenges, and I'm all yours. Sir. Now I think I should go back to *Kommissar* Spyros.'

They watched her leave.

'Was she talking to me?' Müller began. 'Or to you?'

'I'm too big,' Pappenheim said, 'crumpled, don't have a ponytail, don't drive a Porsche . . .'

Müller stared at him.

'You did ask,' Pappenheim said, grinning.

Müller got out his mobile. 'What numbers did you give Ostmann and Kovacs? I need to ask Greville something, if they're already there.'

'Ostmann is twenty-one, Kovacs twenty-two.'

Müller called Kovacs.

Almost immediately, Kovacs came on. 'Two-two.'

'Nico, Müller.'

'Hello, sir. Sorry about—'

'Nothing to apologize for. Do you hear? You did your job, and did it well.'

'Thank you, sir. But I still feel—'

'It is quite understandable to feel the way you do, but it was *not* your fault. Alright?'

'Yes, sir.'

'Where are you now?'

'We've arrived, sir. Fantastic place you've got, sir.'

Müller gave a brief smile. 'It isn't mine, Nico. It belongs to my aunt.'

'Wish I had an aunt like that.'

'That's better,' Müller said. 'Your humour's coming back. Is Mr Greville with you? Or anywhere close?'

'He's right here, sir. We're discussing the arrangements.'

'Oh good. Would you put him on, please?'

'Yes, sir.'

There was a slight pause, then Greville was saying, 'Dear boy . . .'

'Can you put some distance between you?'

'Doing it.' There was another pause, then, 'Should be far enough.'

'Greville, think back. Have you ever heard of Primary Specimen Zero?'

There was a long pause.

'Greville?'

When Greville finally responded, his voice was full of shock. 'My God. They're trying again, after all these years.'

Müller felt cold. 'Trying?'

'PS0,' Greville said. 'That's for Primary Specimen Zero. It's the culprit which alerted our lot in the first place. It was the template for the monster I'm wearing . . . or which is wearing me. But PS0 by itself was not working. Something was missing. It took them a long time to identify the missing ingredient, so to speak. That little gem was christened PS-01. Primary Specimen Zero One. Call it the genesis of the nightmare. From that source, all manner of variations could be produced, to target specific DNA. You could decide to eliminate only redheads, or blondes, or men, or women, or people of a specific age group, ethnic group, the entire range of skin

191

colour, so forth. To cut a long nightmare tale short, dear boy, the variations were potentially endless.'

'Jesus . . . !'

'Well you might. When I nabbed the original PS-01, I shut Pandora's box but, as you know, ended up carrying it meself. I am, if you like, the source code. The destruction of the lab meant they needed to start, literally, from zero. It's taken them years, but they're trying to open the damned box again. A plague on their houses!'

'But can they make progress?'

'Progress is always possible. But the original maker of the nightmare has long shuffled off the mortal coil. His work was destroyed with the lab. That was our intention.'

'Are you saying that, without what you're carrying, they are stuck where they are?'

'Let's put it like this, old man. Progress is always possible, as I've just said; but . . . given how long it took the man who managed to make the original PS-01 to do so . . . PS0, by itself, is a dead end. Should they, however, discover for certain that I am the bearer and do manage to get their hands on me . . . or my body . . . then, dear boy, they've got the gold mine. That thing must have refined itself in me by now, and is quite possibly ready and willing to share its dark secrets, and proliferate. It has lived within a human body, almost symbiotically, but it is also killing its host . . . stealthily. Rather like our pals with a penchant for medieval symbolism. In fact, I would say PS-01 is their viral equivalent.

'Strange thing is,' Greville went on, 'although it is killing me, I have the bizarre feeling that it is also prolonging my life. Making me healthier, while carrying on its deadly work. Can't explain it. Must be something to do with my own DNA. Perhaps there's a bit of tiffin in there it likes. Makes the entire damned nightmare even more horrible. Like executing a man only just so, prolonging the time it takes.' There was a pause as Greville considered this possibility, then he asked, 'Did the name you mentioned earlier lead you to this?'

'Yes.'

'I won't ask how. What did you do?'

'Killed what we found.'

192

'You were able to do *that*?' Greville sounded most impressed.

'Mightily chuffed, old boy.'

'Of course, they could have made copies . . .'

'If you reached the PS0, you will have found the current source. They may well have outsourced bits of it, but without PS0 itself, the outsourcees might as well be playing with putty. In the days when I went to that other place, things had to be written down, or printed. These days, it all goes into the computer; easier when you can watch your nightmare take root, and the risk of papers falling into the wrong hands is lessened. Of course, disks can be made, but that too is fraught with potential for security breaches. Safest to keep no copies, and hide behind a rigorously secure electronic barrier. But this is also a two-edged sword. Once your data is gone, it's gone. I do hope, for all our sakes, Jens, you really did kill it.'

'So do I,' Müller said fervently.

'Stroke of luck, that. On such small things, as they say.'

'Yes.'

'Well, I'll let you get on with it, dear boy. Give you back to your man, shall I?'

'Yes, please.'

'And Jens . . . don't worry about us down here. We'll manage.'

'Thank you, Greville.'

'I raise a phantom glass, old son. Real one when you get back.'

'Count on it.'

When Kovacs was back, Müller said, 'Nico, if anything goes hot and Mr Greville needs a gun, give it to him.'

'Can he shoot?'

'Can you walk?'

'Er . . . I get the message, sir. He wants a gun, he gets one.'

'Thank you, Nico.'

'Well, Pappi,' Müller said as he ended the conversation with Kovacs, 'how much did you get?'

'I filled in some spaces.'

'Then here's some more space filling,' Müller said, and went on to give Pappenheim a short version of his chat with Greville.

'Such nice people,' Pappenheim commented grimly when Müller had finished. 'Playing with a fire they cannot put out. If they were the only ones who would be burnt . . .'

'Unfortunately, they never are. We've got to hope we did kill that PS0. I would not like to risk another probe, no matter how good the goth's programs are. I'm hoping Greville is right.'

'At least we did kill the one we found,' Pappenheim said.

'I wish that made me feel totally secure.'

'No such thing,' Pappenheim said. 'You heard the goth.'

'I heard the goth.'

Somewhere on the edges of the Arizona desert, 04.28 local. The laboratory was behind a high, electrified security fence, and patrolled by armed security guards. If Müller and Pappenheim could have seen them, the demeanour of those guards would have reminded them of Willi, Hart and the others.

Inside the lab itself, a man sat down at a computer, and called up a page with a fast sequence of keys. He did not even look at the keyboard, so familiar was he with the routine.

He got a response he would never have expected on his worst of days.

ERROR. NO DATA. PATH UNKNOWN.

He paled. '*What?*' he whispered.

He tried again, several times, becoming more frantic with each try. The response was maddeningly, and frighteningly, the same.

ERROR. NO DATA. PATH UNKNOWN.

'Oh God!' he said. 'I'm a dead man.'

With a shaking hand, he picked up a phone that was next to his monitor, and made a call he was almost certain would seal his death warrant.

He paled even more as he listened to the person at the other end. He put the phone down, then left his desk. He went out of the room.

A minute or so later, a shot rang out in one of the toilets.

People ran to check, and found him sprawled off the toilet seat, the gun that had taken his life lying in the partially open palm of his right hand.

*   *   *

194

Washington, 06.35 local.
The shockwaves were spreading fast. Dennison sat at his large desk, staring at one of his office walls. Heads, he knew, would roll; but none would be his. He was too valuable.

He picked up a phone.

The general got the call in his study at 12.40, Berlin time. 'PS0 is gone,' Dennison, who masqueraded under the name of Böhmen, said without preamble.

'*What?* How can this be possible? Are you sure?'

'Do you think I would risk this call on a whim?'

'No, no . . .'

'It is gone, and we are back to square one. Someone, somewhere, attacked the system and killed it. People are trying to find out how, but I can tell you that it does not look good. Whoever did this knew what they were doing. No trail has been left to follow. Somebody, somewhere, talked.'

'What if nobody did talk?' the general asked.

'Don't be ridiculous. Whoever did this was good; but not that good. Some specific information was needed. They did not get into our database by accident. I suggest we make it our primary goal to find that leak. And if we find the intruders . . .' Dennison left the obvious unsaid. 'We must also now step up the hunt for the carrier, if he is still alive, or find his body, wherever it may be.'

'That is an impossible task. If he is already dead – which he should be – his body could be anywhere on the planet.'

'We can start with what we do know. He was in the Middle East. We work from that point, and widen the net . . .'

'We did that, and thought we had probable candidates. All were living. None were positive. We thought we had another, but that seems highly unlikely, especially after our failures with the others. I believe he must have died at least ten years ago. It was an expected side effect.'

'We have no choice but to keep trying.'

Early evening, same day.
While Müller watched from his window seat as his plane lifted into the air, heading for Frankfurt, where he would join the

195

747-400, 23.25 flight to Perth, the general received another call. It came from the airport.

'Müller's taken off,' the caller said.

'Taken off? Where is he bound?'

'Perth, Western Australia. He's joining the flight at Frankfurt.'

The general was stunned. 'Are you certain?'

'Unless the passenger manifest is lying.'

'Thank you,' the general said, and hung up.

He remained thoughtful for long moments; then, rising from his favourite armchair, he went over to a gleaming suit of armour, said to have been worn by one of the Knights of Rhodes. It was a magnificent example with intricate golden patterns. The plumed helm was topped by a bird of prey in attack mode.

'From the moment Müller gatecrashed this house,' the general said to the knight, 'it has been consistently bad news, each report worse than the last. Perhaps Reindorf is correct. Müller is already attacking our flanks, and is able to neutralize our own attacks on his. We have lost the initiative of July. It is time we regained it.'

The general paused, then asked the knight a strange question.

'But how did Müller know about Australia?'

He went back to his desk, picked up the phone, and made a very long-distance call. It was to someone who was halfway around the world.

He made several other phone calls.

At about the same time, Pappenheim received a call from Carey Bloomfield, with her flight number and her expected time of arrival in Perth.

Pappenheim called Müller when he had landed at Frankfurt, and passed it on.

'She'll be arriving,' Pappenheim said, 'about eleven hours after you have; at eleven fifty. Assuming she makes all her connections. Gives you time for some sleep . . .'

'Most of which I'll do on the plane . . .'

'And Peter will meet you . . .'

'No need for him to do that.'

'He wants to.'

'A kind thing to do. I shall look forward to meeting him.'

'He also likes saying "no worries" . . . a lot. You'll get used to it.'

'I'm sure I will. Stay tight on everything, Pappi,' Müller added after a pause.

'No worries, mate. And don't let the crocs get you.'

They ended the conversation with soft laughter.

At that moment, at the general's home, Reindorf entered to find Sternbach standing before the knight's armour.

The general turned his head briefly. 'Ah. Reindorf. Look at this admirable suit of armour. He was a big man, solidly built. Strong enough to wield that great sword; but even his power waned . . . as will Müller's. Müller sees himself as a knight of some kind, slaying all manner of evils . . . he believes. A lone knight, championing what he perceives to be right. Delusion.'

The general turned to face Reindorf. 'He has struck some blows, Reindorf, but whatever he believes he is slaying will continue to come at him until he is overwhelmed. Do you know where he is now headed? I have just received the report.'

'No, General.'

'Australia.'

Reindorf said nothing, but his expression was eloquent.

'Exactly,' the general said.

'But how could he—?'

'Have known? My own question, Reindorf. Whoever is giving him information *must* be found.'

'And you believe this person, or persons, to be among us?'

'Not here . . . but possibly within the order.'

'General,' Reindorf began, 'if I may suggest caution. We cannot make accusations which may subsequently prove to be unfounded. They could rebound . . . with fatal consequences.'

The general remained silent for very long moments. He had once more turned to look at the armour, as if seeking inspiration from it.

'Think of it, Reindorf,' he began at last. 'Someone got into the database, and killed the PSO . . .'

'Not Müller, surely. He would not have known of it, even if he had the capability to do anything.'

'Possibly. Possibly not. But you may be correct. This requires knowledge of a particular kind, and we do know there are others who rival us in this specific area, and who would like to either plunder us, or destroy the PS0 development. They certainly do have the means. Yet . . .'

The general allowed his words to hang.

'I have attended to matters in Australia,' he went on, seeming to change tack. He looked at Reindorf once more. 'And I'm remembering a very high-ranking member of the order whose actions did untold damage, and continue to do so. I am remembering . . . Müller's father.'

'He's dead, General.'

'Yes. But his son isn't.'

Reindorf knew what the general meant.

Müller's plane landed on time at 00.50 local.

'Welcome to Australia,' he murmured as the aircraft taxied in the Western Australian night to its allotted parking ramp. 'I'm down under.'

As he had said to Pappenheim, he had slept for most of the long flight, preferring to relax in the comfortable sleeper seat. Now he felt quite refreshed, and not sleepy at all. He had travelled light, bringing just cabin luggage, deciding anything he might need for the stay and journey to the outback could be purchased on arrival.

He was off the plane and approaching passport/immigration control when a young woman came up to him.

'Mr Müller?'

'Yes.'

'Could you come with me, please?'

Surreptitious glances came his way from some of the other waiting passengers in the longish queue. A few looked grumpy because of the wait after the long flight.

They probably think I'm some drug smuggler, or terror suspect, he thought drily. Must be my ponytail.

The young woman led him down a corridor and towards a small room that had a curious familiarity about it. A tall slim man, slightly older, tieless in a lightweight suit, was waiting. He had a small canvas bag with him.

'Interview rooms look the same everywhere,' Müller said to her as they entered.

She smiled at him, showing twin dimples, but said nothing.

'Thanks, Jan,' the man said, studying Müller.

Jan smiled again and went out, closing the door softly.

The man came towards him, hand outstretched. 'They do, don't they? Welcome to Oz. I'm Peter Waldron. A pleasure to meet you. Please call me Peter, or Pete, if you like. Some people even call me Petey.' Waldron had a strong, pleasant voice.

Müller shook the hand. 'Pappi's Peter,' Müller said with a smile. 'The pleasure's mine. Thank you for meeting me.'

'No worries. Nothing is too much to do for Pappi.' Waldron handed Müller the bag. 'This is yours, I believe.'

'Ah,' Müller said, taking it. 'My Beretta . . .'

'With holster and ammo. I would advise not putting it on,' Waldron added with a grin. 'Some people might not understand, especially the local constabulary.'

'I don't doubt it. What exactly can I do, or not do?'

'You will be given co-operation up to a certain point. You may defend yourself. You cannot arrest anyone without a member of the local force present, wherever that may be. If, of course, you're out in the bush and someone is taking pot shots at you, and there is no constable within shouting distance, you may take such action as is appropriate to save your life, and anyone else with you. Don't frighten the citizenry, and they won't frighten you.' Waldron grinned. 'Don't go near the crocs in the bush, and they won't come near you . . . unless it's a saltie. Watch where you walk. It is true that we have the top deadliest snakes in the world. Just let them get on with it, and they'll let you get on with it. When on the roads, look out for three main denizens: roos, cattle and road trains. The first two are self-explanatory; the third one you've got to see to believe.'

Waldron looked amused as he said that. Then he pointed to the bag. 'In there, all the outback advice you should need. There's a four-wheel-drive waiting for you at Broome. It's a

199

dark-green Oz Explorer, and it has everything you can wish for; from air-conditioning to detailed maps to satellite phone. Bags of space. For two people, more than enough. I would suggest visiting the nearest police station or post, before you go off into the bush. This is not only for your own safety in case something goes wrong, but also to let them know you're an international police colleague on a job. There's an instruction for you to show, with the stuff in the bag. It's on headed paper they will recognize. You'll get co-operation if and when you need it. You won't have jurisdiction over them, irrespective of rank.'

'I would not expect it.'

'Good-oh. Then that's it. When's the lady arriving?'

'Eleven-fifty,' Müller said.

'Perfect. Time to get some sleep, buy any extra clothes . . . and a hat, and some good outback shoes, and probably a Longhorn, if you want that kind of thing. Or would you prefer to wait till she gets here and do the shopping together?'

'That might be best.'

'No worries. Then let's get you out of here. We live on the outskirts, but we've also got a place by the river. Jenny and the kiddies are at the house, so we've got the place to ourselves.'

'Pete, you don't have to. A hotel—'

'Nobody who comes from Pappi turns old Pete down.'

'An offer I can't refuse?'

'Too right,' Waldron said with another grin. 'Now let's get out of this interview room. We'll come and fetch the lady when she lands.'

Müller could not have known that someone on the observation deck had taken particular interest in the arrival of his plane.

The apartment was spacious, with high ceilings, and did not just 'overlook' the river. Müller went on to the huge balcony. The river seemed almost directly below.

'So this is Swan River,' he said, looking from the water to the constellation of lights on the tall, modern skyscrapers. To Müller, looking upon the lights reflected upon the dark surface of the water, great smears of colour that flamed towards him,

200

it felt like being in an alien galaxy. He assumed it was a kind of dislocation.

He looked further out. Marked by borders of lights, the river widened in the direction of Fremantle, then seemed to close upon itself in the distance.

Waldron joined him on the balcony with a bottle in each hand. 'Fancy a drop of the nectar? Or . . .'

Müller reached for one of the bottles. 'I'll have a few drops.'

Waldron handed one over. 'Take the load off your feet.'

They lowered themselves on to comfortable recliners.

'Ahh,' Waldron sighed with pleasure. 'That's the stuff. I love this view. Never tire of it.' He leaned across to clink the bottles. 'Welcome to the land of Oz, the lucky country.'

'Glad to be here.'

They took generous mouthfuls. Waldron sighed again, then said, 'I know it's burning in your mind. How did I get to meet Pappi?' he went on. 'How do you meet anyone? By accident. Twenty years ago, I was doing the usual Aussie thing before settling down to make something useful of my life – the great Aussie trek to Europe, VW combi included, bought in Germany. I headed for Belgium with some mates, to cross the channel for the mother country. The mates and I eventually went our separate ways, because by then I'd met the woman I would one day marry. Jenny's a Pom.

'To cut a very long story short, I was parked where a lot of combis parked in those days, on the South Bank in London, near the Festival Hall. I had a problem with the van. If I couldn't fix it, I was stuck. I was living in it. Then this German-registered Beetle pulls up, and this guy says in German-accented English, "Can I help you?" He had this darling beauty with him. I later got to know she was Sylvia, and he planned to marry her.

'I thought, great, he sees a VW, and thinks he can fix it. I let him have a go. He fixed the bloody thing! I was so happy I took them out on a tour of London. Even introduced them to the pleasures of Earl's Court, home from home for wandering Aussies. We got pissed and hit the joyous weed. Sylvia had to drive us back to the combi. We walked along the Thames, and I had the crazy idea to go down to the water. Now, the

Thames can be bloody dangerous when it wants to be. It's got a high body count.

'I fell in. Of course I fell in. I remember thinking . . . shit, you're pissed and stoned out of your brain, Petey. You're never going to see Oz again. Then there's this splash as I start going downriver, even though I'm swimming as hard as my foggy brain would let me. Sylvia is screaming. Pappi has jumped in to save me. Now, that guy is tough. He is pissed, he is stoned, but he hangs on to me, I'm feeling weak, and I can't help him. I tell him to let me go. We can't both drown, and there's Sylvia to think about. Does he let go? It's as if I'd told him not to. He hangs on like a damned St Bernard. He hauls, drags, God knows what, using the flow to bring us back to the bank. We pass Hungerford Bridge. Still Pappi would not let go. Of course, we made it, or I wouldn't be here, nor perhaps Pappi, up there in Berlin.

'That's the short version. At the time it happened, it was the hairiest thing I had ever experienced. Pappi married his Sylvia and became a policeman. I persuaded Jenny to marry a crazy Aussie, and dragged her out here with me. That's how I met Pappi.'

Müller had listened to this in wonder. 'I never knew. He's never mentioned a word about this.'

'That's Pappi. He never again talked about it to me, either. We lost touch. These things happen. But he never let me feel I owed him anything.'

'That's definitely Pappi. He took a bullet for me once.'

'Jeez!' Waldron raised the bottle. 'To Pappi. A warrior and a scholar.'

'I'll drink to that.'

'And to Sylvia. Beautiful, beautiful woman. Never knew she had died.'

They toasted Pappi's wife.

'He never talks about that, either,' Müller said. 'But he grieves still.'

'No wonder, mate. She was an angel.'

Waldron peered at his bottle. 'Mine's had it. Yours?'

'Close.'

'More needed.'

'Definitely.'

'And besides, it's a long way to eleven fifty.'

'It is indeed.'

'Don't fall into the river,' Waldron joked. 'It's a long way down.'

'Any crocs?'

'Who knows?' Waldron said with a cackle.

He returned with a fresh supply.

'Reinforcements!' Müller exclaimed gratefully.

'D'you . . . d'you know what, Jens?' Waldron said as he clinked a bottle against Müller's. 'Your English is excellent. If you don't mind my saying so . . . you talk like a Pom . . . a certain kind of Pom.'

'Blame Oxford,' Müller said cheerfully. 'Blame my aunt who married a Brit. She speaks English like her husband used to. She brought me up.'

'*She* brought you up?'

'That—' Müller burped. 'Sorry.'

'I can do better than that.' Waldron burped loudly.

They laughed.

'That's right,' Müller continued. 'After my parents died. Plane crash.'

'Shit, mate. You poor bugger. Sorry.'

'Not your fault. Happens.'

'You said "used to" about her husband. Where is he?'

Müller's mind was suddenly very clear. Waldron might be exactly what Pappenheim had said he was: an honourable man in the diplomatic service. But diplomacy had many coats, and it had been years; and people changed.

'He's dead too,' Müller heard himself say.

Waldron paused in the act of putting the bottle to his lips. 'Jeez!' he said. It could have meant anything. 'Still,' he went on, brightening. 'No worries, eh?'

'No worries,' Müller said.

Waldron grinned. 'We'll make an Aussie out of you yet.' Then he paused again. 'What the hell's that?'

They listened.

'My phone,' Müller said, after the sound had come a fourth time. 'Where . . . where the . . . where is it?'

'Your jacket?' Waldron suggested.

'My jacket. My jacket. Where's my jacket?'

'That thing on the chair next to your right shoulder?'

'Ah! Yes.'

Müller gingerly put his bottle on the small table to his left, then reached for his jacket. He finally got the phone out after the sixth ring.

'Yes, Pappi!' he greeted brightly.

'Are you alright?' Pappenheim enquired.

'I can almost see your frown, Pappi. I am absolutely fine, and Petey is fine too.'

'*Petey?*'

'He says people call him that.'

'Are you drunk?'

''Course not! Am I drunk, Pete?'

'No, he's not!' Waldron yelled.

'Do you have neighbours, Pete?' Müller asked. 'They just heard that.'

'Nooo worries.'

'As you can hear, Pappi, Pete is giving me a royal welcome to the lucky country. Talk to him.'

Müller handed the mobile to Waldron, who stared at it in wonder.

'Never seen anything like this,' Waldron said. 'Does it fly a plane too?'

'Talk to the man, Pete.'

'Hi, Pappi,' Waldron said.

'Pete. Is he OK?'

'Wow!' Waldron exclaimed. 'You are so clear. This is fantastic. Yes. He is fine. Turning into an Aussie.'

Pappenheim laughed. 'Well, just make sure he doesn't go native. We need him back here.'

'I'll make sure he . . . does . . . not forget.'

'Thanks for helping out, Pete.'

'No . . . no worries, mate. For you, Pappi, anything.'

'Thanks, Pete,' Pappenheim said again. 'Can I have him back?'

'Sure. Mind how you go, Pappi.'

'You too, Pete.'

Waldron passed the phone back to Müller.

'I'm back.'

'Not much happening,' Pappenheim said. 'Seems very quiet. Almost too quiet.'

Müller said nothing.

Pappenheim got the message. 'Knew you weren't *that* drunk. Being cautious?'

'Something like that.'

'Alright. Call me when you feel less inhibited. And have fun.'

'If Pete has his way, I shall have fun.'

Waldron grinned, then took a long swig.

'Then we'll talk tomorrow?'

'At some stage. Yes.'

'Watch your back.'

'Definitely.'

'Enjoy Oz.'

'I am enjoying it. We'll talk again.'

As Müller switched off, Waldron said, 'He worries about you.'

'You know Pappi.'

'I know Pappi.' Waldron raised the bottle. 'To Pappi.'

'To Pappi.'

In Berlin, Pappenheim put the phone down and wondered about Müller's caution.

'I hope Pete does not turn out to be dirty,' he said, lighting up and blowing three rings at the ceiling. 'That really would shatter some more of my beliefs in people.'

The time was 20.30 local.

By 03.30, Perth time, there were a lot of empty bottles on Pete Waldron's balcony.

Müller looked out at the city, air so clear, everything seemed to sparkle. A city at the other end of the world, with its own mysteries; alien, yet familiar. For the briefest of moments, he imagined himself still in Berlin; the river, light as well as dark, a liquid Friedrichstrasse.

'Feeling homesick?' Waldron asked.

'No. Just thinking how very different this city is . . . and how familiar. Does that make sense?'

Waldron looked out on the view. 'In a way, yes,' he said.

From his hotel bedroom on the other side of the river, a man made a call to Berlin.

'He's here.'

'You know what to do,' the voice at the other end said.

'I do know what to do. However, right now I've lost him.'

'*What?*'

The man was not perturbed. 'I'll find him again. I'm very good at tracking people, as you know. I saw him come off the plane,' the man continued, 'but he did not come through to the arrivals lounge. He was obviously met inside.'

'Obviously.'

'He's not at the usual hotels you'd expect someone like him to use. I've checked. This could mean he knows people down here. Probably staying with one of them.'

'Then you'd better find him, before he finds you.'

'Up yours,' the man said, when the called had ended.

Eleven

Perth, 09.30 local.

Müller, looking remarkably refreshed, came out of the bedroom and smelled the freshly made coffee as he went out on to the balcony. Waldron was already there, fully dressed, a pot of coffee and two cups waiting on the table. The empty bottles were all gone.

Waldron turned as Müller approached. 'You look indecently healthy,' he said, looking at Müller with respect. 'After our post-midnight binge, I expected to see you come out here holding on to your head like a sick wallaby.' A quick grin appeared. 'Coffee?'

'Please.'

Waldron filled the cups and handed one to Müller, before turning again to look out over the river, and the city. The day was bright, clear, and mildly warm.

'Now isn't this beautiful?' Waldron said.

'I can see why you never tire of looking at it. I would not.'

'August is our February, but, as you can see, it's milder, as they would say in the UK. We are sometimes called the most isolated city in the world. And we are. Darwin to the north, and Adelaide to the east, are the nearest. Between them and us is the outback.' Waldron spoke as if he considered this an asset. 'Gives us individuality. Edward John Eyre and his Aborigine guide Wylie walked it; from Adelaide to Albany, in the early 19th century. No roads . . . just beautiful, hellish country. It was raining when he arrived. Wylie was not with him right at the very beginning; but for nearly all of that crazy nightmare trek.

'Without Wylie, he would not have made it. He lost most of his party, his horses – some of which they ate. He lost his best friend, Baxter. Twelve hundred miles of near-starvation and death. It took him from November to July. I'd say Wylie was his best mate. Reliable as hell. Kind of bloke you want with you. Bit like Pappi.

'A wartime supply road made the first connection,' Waldron continued. 'It used to take a month to drive it. They sealed it thirty years after the war. Today, you can drive it in, oh . . . two days, depending on what you're driving, and how fast you dare go. Imagine that.

'So, yes, we are isolated. Kind of. It's like Berlin being Adelaide, and we're Nice in France, with nothing much in between. I know you can drive from Berlin to Nice in under twelve hours non-stop; but you've got all those nice fast Autobahns and autoroutes. The Eyre Highway is no Autobahn.'

When Waldron had finished speaking they stood there on the balcony, admiring the view in silence as they drank their coffee.

'You've still got over two hours before we meet your lady from the States,' Waldron at last said, finishing his coffee. 'How about some breakfast near the river?'

'Sounds good to me.'

'How's the head?'

'Clear.'

'No worries?'

Müller smiled. 'No worries.'

'Then let's go.'

'I'll get my jacket.'

'But no gun.'

'No gun.'

It was during the breakfast that Müller felt he was under surveillance. He spotted no one, and said nothing about it to Waldron as they set off for the airport.

They arrived just as Carey Bloomfield's plane taxied to its parking slot. Waldron took him to the same room where they had met for the first time, to wait. Ten minutes later, a bemused Carey Bloomfield, in jeans, white shirt worn over them, and a denim jacket, carrying a suiter and a shoulder bag, was led in by another young customs staffer. When she saw Müller, her expression brightened instantly, her eyes lighting up with both pleasure and relief.

Waldron nodded his thanks to the customs official, who went out again.

'Müller!' Carey Bloomfield exclaimed. 'Thank God! I wondered what the hell was going on.' She came up to him, beaming. She took him by the hand and gave it a little tug. 'Hey, you.'

'Hey, yourself. Good flight?'

'Some stops and changes, but OK. I slept most of the way.'

'So did I. Er –' he turned to Waldron, who was looking at them with a speculative smile – 'this is the man to thank for the fast-track clearance. Pete Waldron, Carey Bloomfield.'

They shook hands. 'Pete.'

'Carey. Welcome to God's own.'

'I know some Americans who would dispute that.'

'I'm sure you do,' he said, with a quick grin. He looked at the suiter. 'That all the luggage?'

She nodded. 'I travel light.'

'Like Jens here. If you'll wait a mo, there's something else.'

A couple of minutes later, the same customs woman returned with a small bag like the one Waldron had given to Müller, when he too had been in the room on arrival.

Waldron passed it to Carey Bloomfield. 'I think you'll be wanting this.'

'Ah,' she said. 'Yes. Thank you. I wondered if I'd see it again before it was time to leave.'

'As I said to Jens, you're getting this back with a caution. He'll explain the rules.'

'OK,' she said, putting the bag into the side pocket of the suiter.

Müller took the suiter from her. 'I'll carry that.'

She gave him an enigmatic smile. 'Thank you.'

Waldron cleared his throat. 'We drop everything at my place, then you can take your time shopping for the things you'll need. We respect the outback out here. It can kill, and has killed, often because people – Aussies included – forget. Your flight to Broome is at five past ten tomorrow. Broome's two thousand two hundred kilometres north of here – like going from Berlin to Nice twice in one go. You'll be in the Kimberley, and it'll be a lot warmer, even at this time of the year. You're talking in the low thirties in temperature. In the outback itself, it can be even hotter. Driving it would cost you at least twenty-four hours. Non-stop. Tiredness is also a killer. First principle, *never* take chances with anything. That's the lesson for the day.' He grinned at them.

'He sounds like you, Müller,' Carey Bloomfield said.

'*He* sounds like a Pom,' Waldron protested, looking shocked. 'What are you trying to do to me?'

'I was talking about his lectures,' she said, smiling too sweetly at Müller.

They were heading for Waldron's car. Waldron touched Müller's arm slightly, to slow him down.

'Something going on with you two?' he whispered.

'Of course not,' Müller whispered back.

Waldron smirked in disbelief.

When they got back to the apartment, Carey Bloomfield put her luggage into the bedroom she had been given, and went out on to the balcony. Waldron went into another room to call his wife.

'Oooh yes!' she said to Müller. 'This is some view, and this is some apartment. Relax, Müller. Yours is still king.'

'I made no comment.'

'You didn't have to,' she countered, deliberately needling.

'You've been here for three seconds and you're already picking fights?'

'Lighten up, Müller. Just joking. Alright,' she continued before he could respond, 'decision made. I'll just lie on one of these recliners, and soak up the view. You two can go shopping.' She backed her words with action. 'What do I need, anyway?' she finished, looking up at him.

'You heard Pete. This is winter, but it's still in the thirties up there in Broome. In the outback itself, bound to be higher. I had a look at the advice booklet in the bag he gave me. There should be one in yours as well. Three things stand out: light shirts or tops, solid walking boots or shoes, especially for protection against things you might step on . . .'

'Step on? What are we talking about here?'

'Mainly snakes . . .'

210

She sat bolt upright. '*Snakes?* You're taking me where there are *snakes*? You know me and snakes. Müller, are you *crazy*?'

'You know Australia has snakes.'

'Some of the meanest,' she said. 'Most of the world knows that. I was just hoping we would not be going anywhere near their territory.'

'Everywhere's their territory. Even houses, in some instances.'

'Oh great.'

'That's yes to the solid boots. Next, shorts.'

'Brought some.'

I could . . . just grab her, Müller thought.

'Alright,' he said aloud. 'Bush hat. It is wise to have one, even though you don't wear it all the time.'

'A hat's a hat. OK.'

'Next, a Longhorn . . .'

'That's a breed of cattle.'

'That's a breed of weather coat out here. Perfect for the wet. Although it's not really the season. That's the stockman's long coat that makes you look like the heroes and baddies in stylish westerns.'

'You're rich. Why not?' She smiled at him. 'So, I really have to leave this nice view, stop enjoying just lounging here, and go do all that walking about to shop?'

'It won't take long, and I can't buy shoes for you. My feet are too big.'

'Hah!'

'Alright, campers!' Waldron called from inside. 'Dinner tonight! Called Jenny to see if she could join us, but one of the kiddies is a bit under the weather, and she doesn't want to leave him with anyone; so it looks like the three of us. I'm gooseberry, but I promise you'll love the place. Anyone hate seafood?'

'You're looking at the wrong people,' Carey Bloomfield said.

'Fantastic. Imagine hating seafood out here.'

'Where are we going?' Müller asked.

'Freo . . . ah . . . that's Fremantle, our river-mouth port. The restaurant's right on the water. It's less than half an hour

211

from here. It's casual, easy, but great, great food; and great, great location. Right among the yachts. Are we on?'

'We are indeed,' Müller said. He glanced at Carey Bloomfield.

'I'm not looking at the night view from up here alone, while you two kill some lobster, or whatever.'

Waldron looked at each in turn, smiled to himself, and said, 'Definitely.'

'Definitely, what?' she asked.

'Going shopping,' Waldron replied.

He went out, still smiling.

'You two are up to something,' she accused Müller.

'Innocent,' Müller said.

'You were never born innocent, Müller.'

'Remind me to tell you something quite amazing about Pappi.'

'Changing the subject?'

'No. It is something incredible, and very brave. Something he never told me about himself.'

She saw that he was serious. 'OK. We haven't talked about Dennison. Did you . . . ?'

'We will. In Broome. Prepare to be . . .' He paused. 'Wait till Broome.'

'OK,' she repeated.

Shopping was painless. They had completed their purchases when Müller again felt under scrutiny.

He deliberately chose not to turn round, so as not to alert whoever the watcher happened to be. When he did eventually turn to look, it was part of a movement naturally begun. Even so, he still spotted no one.

As with the morning incident, he again chose to say nothing.

That evening in the white-topped marina restaurant, the feeling again came to him. This time it was so strong, he felt as if the person were standing right next to him. Once more, he did not turn round to look.

He did not allow this to spoil the evening and, as before, chose not to mention it, giving every impression of someone obliviously enjoying himself; which he was.

Some two hours later, when they were walking back to Waldron's car, he did not feel the unease.

I'm twitchy, he thought. Why?

Waldron had walked on to the car, deliberately, it seemed.

'This is a great place,' Carey Bloomfield said. 'Pete was right. Great food. I just found another favourite restaurant. When we're done with whatever we're doing up there in the Kimberley, let's come back. That's for the snakes. Deal?'

'Deal,' he said.

She glanced towards Waldron. 'I think he's giving us some room.'

'You're imagining it.'

'Oh sure. Like I'm imagining you're on edge about something?'

'It's that obvious?'

'No. But I know you by now, Müller. Perhaps still only a little; but enough to tell me something's bugging you.'

'Someone's been watching us, or me . . . because it's the third time today.'

'You're kidding.'

He shook his head. 'The first time was at breakfast. Pete and I were at a riverside café in town, just before we came to get you. Next time was during our little shopping spree . . .'

'And the third?'

'Just now. When we were in the restaurant. The feeling's gone now. So whoever it is has decided that's it for the night.'

'We're being *tracked*? All the way down here on the tip of Australia?'

'Looks like it.'

'But who?'

'That is a good question.'

'So what do we do?'

'We wait.'

'To get shot first?'

'They might try to do that, if that's what they're planning. But I think not yet. At least, not here. The real question is why we are being tracked.'

213

'Great,' she said. 'Well, I had a hearty dinner.'

They reached the car, and Waldron was holding a rear door open for her, a knowing smile upon his face.

She paused before him. 'Pete, that was a great dinner. Thank you for bringing us here.'

'A pleasure, Carey.'

'And I just made Müller promise to bring me back when we're done up there.'

'Knew you'd like it.'

'You've got that smile on your face again.'

'And what smile is that?' His smile widened.

'Pete, Pete,' she said, and entered the car.

As they drove back, Müller took surreptitious glances at the wing mirror. Again, he said nothing.

The man was back at his hotel, and was on the phone.

'She's here as well.' He was not speaking English.

'You are quite certain?'

'Definitely. I saw her earlier today. They went to the airport to pick her up, just before noon. She did not come through arrivals, just as it was with him last night.'

'Two birds with one stone.'

'They also went shopping . . . in an outback supply shop.'

There was a long pause. 'Perhaps four birds with one stone, if you're lucky.'

'I never rely on luck, although it can be useful.'

'Have you seen them again?'

'Recently. They went to dinner in Fremantle.'

'See what they do in the morning. Check if they're going to where we believe they are. If they are, it is certain they will intervene. It also means our information was correct. All you need to do is follow, to find the exact location. Charter a plane to their destination. Go to the address you have. You will find a vehicle. Everything is there. When you have finished, use the ticket you will find with the vehicle. Leave the vehicle and all you found with it – except the ticket – where you picked it up. Let us hope they had a hearty dinner.'

*   *   *

214

Next morning, Waldron took them to the domestic terminal. The white building with its blue sign was totally separate, and a few kilometres from the international terminal.

He again took the bags with the guns from them.

'One of the flight crew will hand them back to you,' he said. 'Sorry. Has to be done. But no worries. No one will disturb them. They'll be returned to you when you're off the plane.'

He escorted them to the boarding gate, when he had arranged for the bags to be taken aboard.

Müller held out his hand. 'For everything, Pete, thank you.'

'A real pleasure to meet you, Jens,' Waldron said, shaking hands, 'and just great to be able to do something for Pappi at last. Any problems, you've got my numbers. Don't hesitate.'

'I won't.'

Waldron turned to Carey Bloomfield. 'Carey . . . great, great to meet you. Don't let that fella push you around.'

'I won't.'

He grinned, and gave her a quick hug. 'And watch for the snakes.'

'Don't ruin my day, Pete.' But she smiled at him.

Waldron stood back, looking like a parent sending his kids to school. 'You've got everything. The Oz Explorer will be waiting for you at the airport. Just go to the desk and pick up the docs and keys. You've got your hotel particulars. Don't forget to leave them a general itinerary of your movements. The hire people will also expect it. Keep an eye on the UV index. You'd be surprised how high it can be. Now, you two watch yourselves. I don't want to give Pappi any bad news.'

'We'll make certain you won't have to,' Müller said. 'No worries.'

Waldron grinned at them. He was still standing there when they boarded the aircraft.

'I like him,' Carey Bloomfield said as they took their seats for the two-and-a-half-hour flight.

'Yes. He does seem a very pleasant person.'

'Does seem? Come on, Müller. You don't think . . . No. *No.* I don't buy it.'

215

'I am being cautious. He's done everything to make things work smoothly for us while we're here . . .'

'But?'

'He asked a seemingly innocuous question about Greville . . .' Müller paused as someone went past, heading for a seat. 'I'd better wait till we're on our own.'

She nodded. 'OK.' She had a window seat, and peered out. 'Have you had that feeling of being watched?'

'Yes. When we were in the terminal.'

The man waited until the aircraft had taken off; then, taking his single piece of luggage with him, went to a charter company and booked a small aircraft to Broome.

Carey Bloomfield was still looking out of the window.

'Red earth,' she said. 'It's frightening, and beautiful at the same time.' She looked across at Müller. 'Can you tell me about Pappi? How come he knows Pete?'

Müller told her the story about Waldron and Pappenheim, as Waldron had related it.

'Wow!' she said, when Müller had finished. 'And he never told you about this?'

'Never.' Müller slowly shook his head in wonder. 'Just when you think you know all about him, you hear something like this.'

She gave a sudden giggle.

'What?'

'Pappi smoking the weed way back when. Who'd have believed it?'

'Perhaps he didn't inhale.'

She gave him a critically amused look. 'That's an old one, Müller.'

'It's not that bad.'

The plane landed at Broome five minutes late. The canvas bags were returned to them, and they went to the car-hire counter to pick up the documents and keys of their 4WD vehicle.

'Wow!' Carey Bloomfield said again, as they walked to the Explorer. 'Big hike in temperature.'

216

'We'll change at the hotel,' Müller said. 'Have something to eat, then set off. How does that sound to you?'

'Sounds fine.' They had reached the vehicle. 'Hey,' she continued, 'this looks brand new. Thanks again, Pete.'

Müller unlocked it, and inspected it. The Explorer had been comprehensively equipped for outback travel.

'Everything we need,' he said as they put their luggage aboard, 'is here. Air-conditoned. There's even sleeping stuff. Recline the seats and you've got a bed. He certainly did do a good job. Let's see what the hotel's like. In you get.'

The hotel turned out to be an unexpected gem. A series of suites with balconies, or verandahs, had been created out of what had once been a magnificent home, situated within a lush garden.

Carey Bloomfield's had a four-poster bed. 'Hmm,' she said to herself, looking at it.

She had changed into a loose olive-green shirt, and a pale pair of shorts. She put on the sturdy ankle boots over sweat socks, got out her sunglasses, picked up the bush hat and the canvas bag with her gun, holster, and ammunition in it, and went over to Müller's neighbouring suite.

Müller had also changed. He wore desert-coloured linen trousers, boots similar to hers, a khaki shirt with the sleeves partially rolled up. He had the weapon bag ready and, like her, had his sunglasses and the bush hat. He had also got out the detailed map that the goth had printed. He took his travel documents, police ID, and the letter of authority Waldron had given him.

'It's open!' he called to Carey Bloomfield's knock.

She pushed the door wide and stood at the entrance. 'Well? Do I look OK?'

He looked at her slightly toed-in stance, thinking that the genes of Mr and Mrs Bloomfield had wrought something magical.

'My legs are too big, right?' she said, misinterpreting his silence.

Her legs, he thought, were glorious: sensuous, with every sweepingly gentle curve as precisely sculpted as it should be. Fashionable matchsticks they were not. Thank you, Mr and Mrs Bloomfield, for creating this woman.

Fearing he might say this aloud, he said, 'You look great.'

This pleased her. 'You really think so?'

'I really think so.'

'Don't make it sound so hard, Müller. Let's go eat.'

After lunch, they got into the Explorer.

'Got all your IDs and travel documents with you?' he asked.

'Got them all.'

They set off for Woonnalla Station, and the Hargreaves. Müller hoped Grogan had given him the right co-ordinates.

Either that, he thought, or we've come all the way to this side of the world for nothing.

He drove out of town along Broome Road to join the Great Northern Highway, in the direction of Derby; but they would not be going that far.

'Time to tell me,' Carey Bloomfield said.

'I'll start with Dennison Biometrics.'

He told her about the goth hacking into the database, and what they had discovered. He told her about Willi's girlfriend, and how Grösche had died. He told her about Grogan's co-ordinates, and the Hargreaves. He told her about the killing of Johann Hoventhaler by one of his own colleagues. He told her about hearing his mother call his name.

She listened in complete silence. When he had at last finished, they were approaching the junction with the Great Northern.

'Jesus!' she uttered softly. 'They were trying to recreate that thing in Greville? So, if I hadn't seen that broadcast and had my hunch, you would never have found out.'

'That is certainly true. We were lucky; and you were lucky to have caught Willi in time.'

'It all links,' she said. 'These bastards have their dirty hands in everything. They're spreading.'

'They've been at it for decades.'

'Müller, they won't give up.'

'If we hurt them badly enough . . .'

'I hate to spoil your fun, Müller, but knights in shining armour don't exist.'

'Even if I were one, which I am certainly not, my armour would be tarnished. The general even called me quixotic. That's my level in his eyes. I tilt at windmills.'

218

For a moment, she let her guard down, and glanced at him.
A look came into her eyes that his attention on the road caused
him to miss.

'What does *he* know?' she said.

The small aircraft landed at Broome. The man got out, cleared
through customs, and took a taxi to a beach-front café. He
waited until the taxi had gone, then started walking.

Ten minutes later, he came to a locked garage belonging to
a house that seemed unoccupied. He got out a key, and opened
the garage. The 4WD vehicle was there. He entered the garage,
and began checking the off-roader. To anyone looking, he was
simply someone checking out his vehicle.

He looked beneath, and saw the attached box he was looking
for. Satisfied, he climbed in, and reversed out. He stopped,
locked the garage again, and drove off.

His first stop was a hotel. He went to the reception desk
and asked if his friend were staying there. He gave the names
of Müller and Carey Bloomfield. He repeated this routine until
he found the one they had booked into.

He was supposed to join them, he said, but his plane had
been late. Had they left an itinerary?

The Explorer was nearing a left turn that led off the sealed
road and on to an unsealed road of red earth, when flashing
lights appeared in the rearview mirror.

'I wasn't speeding, officer,' Müller mimicked, and slowed
down.

'Now where the hell did *he* come from?' Carey Bloomfield
asked. 'There isn't a town, village, or house in sight for miles.'

He came to a halt. The police car pulled up behind.

'Police have a way of doing that,' Müller said, straight-
faced. 'Especially in empty landscapes.'

They remained in the Explorer, as the policeman got out,
and walked towards them. In shorts, shirt, solid walking boots,
badged bush hat, and sunglasses, he did not come too close.
He indicated that Müller should lower the window. A blast of
heat swept in.

'G'day. Where to?'

Burnt by years of outback sun, he was a wiry man of about forty.

'Good afternoon, officer. We're looking for Woonnalla Station. Some friends—'

'Woonnalla, did you say?' The policeman was suddenly interested.

'Yes. Do you know it?'

'Can I see your documents, sir?' the policeman countered. 'Please get out of the car. You too, madam.'

'Certainly.'

Müller opened the door carefully, and got out. Carey Bloomfield did the same. Müller handed over his ID, and the instruction note.

The policeman removed his sunglasses. His dark eyes widened slightly. 'So you're *Haup . . . Hauptkommissar* Müller.'

'Yes.'

'Got the news about you on the radio.' He handed the documents back, eyes squinting, keenly studying Müller. 'It says I should give you all co-operation.'

'I'm the guest here. It's entirely in your hands.'

The policeman gave a tight smile. 'Very diplomatic.' He held out a hand. 'Jamie Mackay. Senior constable.' He also shook hands with Carey Bloomfield. 'Ma'am. You're a copper too? The note says you're his colleague.'

'Yes,' she said. 'I am.'

The slight widening of the eyes came again. 'American.'

'Yes.'

He put his sunglasses back on, and looked at each in turn. 'Well, you're on the right track.' He pointed to the road Müller had been about to turn on to. 'That leads to Jack and Maggie's place. Beautiful, it is, in the middle of all this. It's a sort of eco-place. Been here for years and years. They make produce which they deliver themselves. Must make them good money, though. You'll see why. Nice people. They like being on their own. Are they in trouble with the law?'

'No,' Müller replied. 'Absolutely not. It's just an enquiry.'

'You mean they know something you need to find out.'

'I could not have put it better.'

220

'Well, they're twenty kilometres along. You can't miss it. The road stops there.'

'I see. Thank you again.'

The policeman seemed to be peering closely at him.

'Is something the matter, officer?'

'No. It's just that it's . . . amazing.'

'What is, Constable?'

'Have a nice day,' Jamie Mackay said.

They got back into the Explorer, and turned on to the red road. Dust billowing behind them began to obscure the policeman, who gave them a parting wave. Then a left-hand bend took him out of sight.

Jamie Mackay hurried to his radio, as soon as the Explorer had disappeared.

He selected a frequency and began to call, 'Woonnalla. Woonnalla. This is Jamie. Woonnalla. Woonnalla. This is Jamie. Over.'

'Jamie,' came the response. 'Jack here. What's up? Over.'

'This could be the day you told me about all those years ago. A young fella and a young woman on their way to you. He's a policeman. At least, he's got the documents to prove it, and a note from some high-powered people who say he is to be given police co-operation. Could be anyone, of course. But he looks a nice enough fella, and the woman with him's a looker. Could be nothing . . . but thought you'd like to know. Over.'

'Thanks, Jamie. I appreciate it. Did he give a name? Over.'

'Müller. German. He's a *Haup* . . . *Hauptkommissar*, whatever that is. Over.'

There was a long pause. 'Thanks for the warning, Jamie. Over.'

'You and Maggie going to be OK? Over.'

'We'll be fine, Jamie. No worries. Over.'

'Strange thing about him . . .' Mackay paused, sounding puzzled.

'Jamie? Over.'

'Ah. It's nothing. Couldn't be. 'Kay, mate. Over and out.'

*　　*　　*

221

The red road, bordered by stunted clumps of bush, stretched before them in a straight that was at least three kilometres long. Red dust whirled from the wheels, boiling upwards before floating down in spreading, opaque clouds.

'Strange, the way he seemed to be staring at you, just before we left.'

'Yes. It was. Wonder what that was all about.'

'Perhaps you reminded him of some fugitive.'

'Hah.'

Jamie Mackay was still standing by his patrol vehicle wondering whether he should contact Hargreaves again, when another 4WD pulled up behind his car.

Frowning, he began to approach it. 'Getting crowded.'

Thundering towards him, from the direction of Broome, was a vast road train: a triple-carriaged behemoth that was well over fifty metres long.

The person in the off-roader did not get out of his vehicle.

The road train thundered past, the driver greeting Mackay with a roaring toot.

Mackay waved in return, then ducked behind his car to avoid the blast of the slipstream from the huge truck.

As the road train went on its way, Mackay moved out from behind his car to go up to the off-roader. As he got closer, the driver got out. It was the man who had been following Müller and Carey Bloomfield. He wore very dark sunglasses.

He smiled at Mackay, who did not smile back.

'Can I help you?' Mackay began.

'Hope so. I'm looking for some friends. I was supposed to meet them in Broome, but my plane got in late. I'm trying to find them.'

'Didn't they leave you an itinerary back in Broome?'

'That's just it. We arranged a rendezvous, and talked about the route. Because I was late, I hurried on. I know they would be using this road . . .' The man gave a shrug, looking helpless.

'This is the outback,' Mackay said. 'There's no guesswork when dealing with it. Guesswork can kill you. What are their names?'

'Müller, and Bloomfield. Bloomfield is a woman.'

'I see. Can you show me some identification?'

'Of course. The man opened the door of his vehicle, as if to comply. What he took out was not a document.

Mackay looked at the gun that was now pointing at him. 'That would be a very foolish thing to do,' he said with commendable calm. He did not raise his hands.

'Where did they go?' the man asked harshly. 'Don't try to play smart games with me, or be a hero. You answer, or you die.'

'You've pulled a gun on me. I'll die anyway.'

'Turn round!'

Mackay did so.

'Now move!'

Mackay started walking.

'Stop!'

They stopped just where Müller and Carey Bloomfield had turned off. The tyre tracks in the red earth were plain to see.

'No thanks for your help,' the man said, and shot Mackay once.

The policeman staggered, and collapsed against his patrol vehicle. He tried to reach for his radio.

The man watched dispassionately as Mackay fought against encroaching death, to make it to the radio.

He never had a chance. The man shot him a second time.

He bundled Mackay's body into the policeman's own vehicle, then drove it a little way, up to the bend in the road. He got out, and ran back to his 4WD. He drove it close to the patrol car, then stopped. He got a long bag out of the off-roader, and put that into the police car. He then took out what looked like loose-fitting camouflaged combat fatigues with a hood, and put that into the car.

He got in, and drove on.

'We've covered nearly fifteen kilometres,' Müller said. 'We'll soon be there.'

'What's that?' Carey Bloomfield asked, lowering her head to peer up through the windscreen.

A small speck was rising in the distance.

'A plane,' Müller said. 'Flying is sometimes the only way to get to some places out here, in reasonable time. Or it could be the flying doctor.'

'Or it's a search plane looking for someone who's lost.'

'Or sightseers.'

'Are we playing I spy?'

Müller smiled tolerantly.

The aircraft grew bigger as they drove on. In a few minutes, it was passing right over them.

'Probably going to Broome,' he suggested.

They thought no more about it, and continued on their way.

About two kilometres later, Carey Bloomfield said, 'Oh wow!'

The vegetation on either side of the road had begun to change. It had now entered a wide, shallow, cultivated valley in which neat segments formed a patchwork of riotous colour. Small trees were dotted like punctuation marks within it. In the middle of all that was a low, white house.

As they drew closer, they saw that the road ended in a sealed section that went right up to the house, which now looked much bigger than at first thought, surrounded by its big, flourishing garden.

'It's an oasis!' she said. 'Can't see water, but there must be some around.'

'A well, perhaps. There, that tower with the wheel at the top. That's where the water comes from.'

'That house is beautiful. Uh-oh.'

'What?'

'To the right,' Carey Bloomfield said. 'What do you see?'

Müller saw the tell-tale strip that looked like a road in the wrong place.

'That plane,' he said with sinking heart. 'That nice Constable Mackay must have warned them. The Hargreaves decided they really wanted to be alone today. They'll not come back as long as Mackay tells them we're here. All this way, and for nothing.'

They drew up to the house, and stopped. A big outhouse, previously out of view, could now be seen, a short distance behind the house, and bordered by low trees. There was some

224

machinery in front of it. An open garage was attached to it, and two trucks were parked there.

They got out of the Explorer. It was very warm out of the air-conditioned atmosphere of the vehicle. They put on their hats.

'Now what?' Carey Bloomfield asked, looking about her. This close, it was now possible to see what that patchwork really was. 'They grow vegetables, fruit, and flowers. All ecologically. They really made their part of the desert bloom.'

'Well, as Mackay said, they made good money. It bought them a plane.'

'The way you feel is all in that remark, Müller. I sympathize.'

She went up to the house, and peered in. 'Oh wow, wow!' she cried. 'Müller . . . you've got to see this. It's . . . well . . . just beautiful. Whatever the Hargreaves are, they are not your average, stereotyped eco-people. These are stylish ecos. Come look at *this*. You won't believe it. There's furniture in here that comes from some real fancy stores. Come on. Take a look, as we're here. This is what I call open-plan living.'

Müller looked. What he saw was a cool, white, and spacious interior. Terracotta floor. Areas segregated by low walls with columns reaching to the high ceiling, marking the entry space. Huge windows with white Roman blinds let in a flood of natural light. The dining area was carpeted in a neutral colour, and the table and chairs were classic antiques.

Müller stood back, frowning.

She looked at him. 'What?'

'I don't know. I just had the strangest feeling. A very faint memory. Whatever it is, it isn't strong.'

'I'd like to look around some more. I'll bet it's beautiful here at night; with the kind of darkness that really lets you see the sky. They must love this place. It was definitely built with love.'

Müller gave her one of his tolerant smiles. 'You can see all that through a single window?'

'Hey. I know what I'm talking about. Come on, Müller. Let's look some more. Not much we can do around here now, anyway. I'm going to check the back.'

225

Müller remained where he was, a puzzled expression clouding his face. He could not understand why the house seemed to be jogging at his memories.

Then an unease made him turn to look back at the road. In the distance, he could see the police off-roader approaching. If the Hargreaves had literally flown the coop, why was Mackay now coming? To check if they were breaking into the house?

Then the patrol vehicle stopped.

Müller felt his unease grow. He hurried to the Explorer, and got out the gun bags. He then went to find Carey Bloomfield.

She was at the back of the house standing on a huge covered terrace, bordered by a well-tended mixed bed of shrubs and flowers, peering in, through a wide french window, at the kitchen.

'Müller, you've got to see this kitchen. Still not as amazing as yours, but this runs it a close second. Take a look.' When he did not respond, she turned and stared at the gun bags. 'Oh hell. Trouble?'

'Perhaps.' He passed hers over, then began to open his. 'Better to be prepared. Something's not right. The Hargreaves are gone. Why would Mackay still come all the way here? He takes a detour of twenty kilometres – forty, counting the return journey – just to see if we're breaking in? It smells.'

He got out his Beretta, still in its holster, and put it on. He checked his spare magazines. All were there, and full.

Carey Bloomfield followed suit, her holster being the original waxed, lightweight canvas rig she had used the first time they'd met.

She looked at him closely. 'Do you have that feeling you had in Perth?'

He nodded.

'Jesus. You think he's *here*?'

'I can't explain it. But why would Mackay come all the way here, then stop some distance from the house?'

'He was forced?'

'Or he's dead. This is a trap; for me, for both of us, or even for the Hargreaves.'

'The *Hargreaves*?'

'Grogan must know that they have very crucial information

226

that I need to help me sink the Semper. Perhaps the Semper knew of that too, but not where they were . . .'

'Shit. You're telling me we *led* them here?'

'It's beginning to feel like it,' he replied grimly.

'Oh Jesus!'

'We were the foxes sent after the chickens, and the hunter is out there to take all four.'

'See the outback and die. That doesn't sit well with me.'

'Nor with me.'

'So what's the next move?'

'You stay here.'

Müller began to move round to the front of the house.

'Müller! Hey, Müller, damn it!'

He disappeared.

'Damn that man!'

Müller crept towards the Explorer, and pretended he wanted to get in. Something hummed viciously and smacked into a small, ornamentally positioned boulder close by. The boulder split in two. There was no report.

'Now I know,' he muttered, ducking back into cover. 'Silencer, so shortened range. He's close in.'

The firing position could be a clump of bushes on rising ground not far from the police car, but not necessarily.

He went back to the terrace.

Carey Bloomfield stared at him. 'What was that noise?'

'A cracking boulder, courtesy of a sniper.'

'*What?* Are you kidding me?'

'I wish I were. I also have a feeling I may know who the sniper might be. If it is who I think . . .'

'Bad news?'

'Very.'

'Oh great. Do we have a plan B?'

'We have a plan. It's dangerous.'

'I can feel my confidence vanishing already.'

'We'll split his attention,' Müller said.

'Doesn't that usually take two sitting ducks?'

'Only one gets hit, if we do it well. Perhaps no one gets hit.'

'Müller, remind me to hit you . . . hard, one day.'

'I'll be the target duck. You move to get around him.'

'Müller . . .'

'What?'

'It's snake country out there! You promised . . .'

'If that person out there is the one I think he is, your worries are not snakes.'

She had her automatic out, pointing down at the floor. She looked at the gun for long moments, then drew a deep breath and let it out slowly.

'I'm ready.'

'Alright. Mark his position near the police car. He is within that area; the only question being precisely where. He is a master of camouflage. Don't even waste time trying to spot him before he fires. When he does, try to spot anomalies. Usually, a sniper's probable position is not known in advance. He does not rate us highly, so feels he has no need to apply all his capabilities. We are merely flies he's going to swat.'

'Well, I agree with him there.'

'You are Lieutenant-Colonel Bloomfield. You're not a fly to swat.'

'Damned right.'

'Come. I'll show you where he may be positioned.'

They worked their way back until they could see the police car while still in cover.

'You will go left, work your way round, going wide as you dare, to force him to make large corrections when he tries to get one of us. Remember, he probably does not know that the Hargreaves are gone. So he will need to concentrate on the house as well. This will split his attention, more than he would like. This could be the window we need.'

'Müller . . .'

'Yes?'

'It sucks.'

'I know. But let's not forget pressure of time for the sniper. He has to do this reasonably quickly. If Mackay really is dead, his colleagues will soon start looking for him. That's an important pressure on the sniper. He has to get away before this happens. It's the best we have. We'll each count out erratic periods before we move; but never more than ten seconds, and never in concert. This would give him a fixed pattern and he would adjust to it. The next time one of us moved, he'd be waiting.'

She looked at him for long moments. 'You get yourself killed, Mister, and I'll come back and shoot you again.'

He smiled. 'I'll do the same for you. We leave the hats,' he finished.

She kept looking at him. 'You going to kiss me, or what?'

'Or what,' he said, and kissed her quickly on the lips.

'It will have to do, I suppose,' she grumbled to herself as he moved swiftly away.

Müller started off at a run, and dropped almost immediately.

Nothing happened. He waited. Then he tried again, heading for one of the small but thick-stemmed trees. He made it at the same time that a high-powered round slammed into its base. The tree shook with the force of the blow.

Müller did not move. The tree was broad enough to give him all the cover he needed. He hoped Carey Bloomfield had moved.

She had. Working her way round the back of the house towards the outbuildings, she was grateful to discover that there was far more cover available to her than the open killing ground that Müller had chosen. At the same time, she worried that his deliberate choice was going to get him killed very quickly.

She decided to bring some attention to herself. There was plenty of material about, to allow her to extend her reach. She found what looked like a fence upright. It was partway into some bushes, and seemed light enough to wield easily. She put the gun back into its holster.

Lying flat on her stomach, she pulled the piece of fencing towards her, trying hard not to think about disturbing a snake. There was no snake. The bit of fence was at least three metres long. She used the length of rounded wood to poke at a shrub. Instantly, something smashed into the shrub.

'OK,' she said. 'I know you're out there. Better move, Müller. I'm about to, and I'm not ready to become the duck.'

She moved, taking the piece of fencing with her. Nothing came near her.

They worked their way like this, each decoying, Carey Bloomfield using her length of wood to draw fire away from her.

She orientated herself on the police car, moving in a wide arc. Then she stopped. She had to cross open ground, and there was still no way to see where the sniper was positioned. She had no idea where Müller was, and without communication, no idea whether he was still alive.

She remained where she was.

Müller was behind another tree, now far enough around the sniper's position to force a wide swing each time the unseen shooter wanted to take an alternate shot.

Like Carey Bloomfield, he waited.

The sniper was not too bothered. He felt the advantage was still his. Their ploy was only delaying the inevitable. But he knew he had to finish this soon, and leave, before the police started looking for their dead colleague.

And there were still the people in the house.

A soft slithering made him remain completely still. He was so well hidden, the big, speckled mulga snake had no idea he was there. Highly venomous, it would leave well alone; but if touched or threatened, it would strike; repeatedly.

The sniper watched the snake pass almost directly across his vision, well within reach. He hated snakes with a passion. Infinitely slowly, he reached for a big, sheathed knife that was strapped to his right leg.

The snake paused.

The sniper stopped. He now wanted to test himself against the snake, certain he would win.

The snake began to move again. He smiled.

He continued to ease the knife out of its sheath. The snake was still moving lethargically. With a single sweeping motion, he brought the knife savagely down on the snake, pinning it to the ground just behind the head. The knife went in to the hilt. There was no way the snake, coiling and uncoiling

230

frantically, could free itself. Its jaws kept opening and closing, its fangs spewing venom uselessly each time.

The sniper watched, smiling as the animal took a long time dying.

Carey Bloomfield had spotted the sweeping movement. She had not realized he was so close!

As she focused on the position, she slowly began to see the outlines of his body. He seemed to be facing away from her, and was looking at something on the ground. It was her chance. She would never get another.

Leaving the piece of wood and drawing her Beretta, she rose from cover and ran across the open ground. She had reached a position about a metre from the soles of his feet before he realized something new had happened.

The gun was pointed two-handedly at him.

'Enjoy torturing snakes, do you?'

He calmly looked at her over his shoulder, his face totally hidden by his camouflage. Only the dead eyes could be seen.

'Do you *really* think you can take me?'

She got the impression he was smiling.

Legs spread, gun unerringly pointing, she said, 'I have taken you. Try to use any weapon, and you're dead.' She was amazed how calm she was. 'You don't sound Australian; but then, all things considered, you wouldn't be, would you?'

He ignored the question. 'Ah . . . but can you just *shoot* me? Because, if you don't, you're not going to take me anywhere. Are you going to stand here for the rest of the day and into the night? If you try to warn Müller by pointing away from me to fire, that will give me all the time I need.'

'OK.'

She fired. The shot smashed into his right thigh.

'*Jeeezuss!*' he hissed, astonished that she had done it. '*You bitch!*'

'Right first time. Better stay as you are. I might get bitchy again.'

Müller heard the shot, and feared the worst. Then he calmed down and realized he had *heard* a shot. That meant Carey

231

Bloomfield, not the sniper. He risked being punctured by the Dragunov and ran in a direct line towards where the police car was parked. Nothing came his way.

Emboldened, he ran on.

Carey Bloomfield did not relax her stance.

'He'll have heard that,' she said. 'He's on his way.'

The sniper risked a move. Suddenly twisting his body and swinging the Dragunov in a sweeping motion, he tried to bring it to bear on her. The wound in his thigh made him give a half-grunt, half-scream with the pain of it.

She was waiting for the move. Her second shot tore into an upper arm. He dropped the rifle.

'*Aaarghh shit! Shit! You fucking whore!*'

'That, I'm not.'

Müller heard the second bark of the Beretta, and actually smiled.

'That's my girl!' he said, racing to get there.

The sniper was making low noises. Carey Bloomfield had quickly reached down to pull the rifle away, but she did not stay close, knowing that, even wounded, he was still dangerous. She was certain he had another weapon, and was only waiting for an opportunity to get at it. She was not about to try and search him, and so risk being grabbed herself.

Then movement at the corner of her eye made her glance swiftly. The biggest sparkling snake she ever saw was crawling towards the sniper. Its eventual path would be directly across his midriff. She stifled her fear.

'I wouldn't move, if I were you,' she said to the sniper. 'I think either daddy, mummy, or the boyfriend/girlfriend of that dying snake, is coming your way.'

'Fuck off, bitch! Think I'll fall for that?'

'Suit yourself.'

She saw him trying to go for his hidden gun. The snake, clearly having thought it was approaching just another piece of vegetation, paused, tongue flicking.

'I really . . . would not move,' she said quietly, emphasizing each word.

'Piss off!'

And he moved, grabbing for the pistol he had inside his suit.

The big mulga struck, and kept striking.

The sniper thrashed about, the snake wrapped about him now, and still striking. With a potential of up to 600mg of venom, it had plenty to go around.

It was clear that the first strikes had not penetrated the suit, or had at least been deflected. But one strike went in through the opening made by the bullet that had gone into his thigh.

He screamed hoarsely within the muffling of his hood. His eyes seemed to be trying to leave their sockets.

'Get it off me! Get it off me!'

Carey Bloomfield stood back, and let the snake do its work.

She was still standing there, when Müller arrived. The sniper was no longer moving. At last, she lowered her weapon.

He put an arm about her shoulders. 'Are you alright?'

She nodded, but said nothing.

'That's a big snake,' he said, looking on as it uncoiled itself and moved off the sniper's body.

It slithered away, totally ignoring the pinioned, dying mulga.

'I guess they weren't related, after all,' she said.

'Am I missing something?'

'I never thought I'd feel solidarity with a snake.'

'I am definitely missing something,' he said.

He took his arm from her shoulders to go over to the sniper. He removed the hood. The contorted face and staring eyes were still recognizable.

'Mainauer,' he said quietly. 'You've come a long way to die.'

'You *know* him?'

'That's the ex-police officer who killed his colleague.'

'*He* was a contract sniper for the Semper?'

'Among many other things. Mackay is dead. I paused to have a look at his car. He's in there.'

'Oh God.' She looked at Mainauer. 'Bastard.'

'Let's get back,' Müller said. 'We'll leave things for the local police. It's their territory, and their colleague who was murdered.'

'What about the rifle? Don't you need it for evidence against the Semper?'

'It's coming with us. We'll need Pete's diplomatic skills. You did well, Carey. I'm proud of you.'

'Hold me. I'm going to faint.'

Back down by the house, Müller was still looking bemused as they got ready to leave.

Carey Bloomfield stared at him. 'What is it, Müller?'

'I really don't know. It's as if something is pulling at me, but I really don't know what it could possibly be.'

'It's this house. It's so beautiful, you don't want to leave it.'

'It has to do with the house,' he agreed. 'But what it is, I just can't tell. Let's go. Do you mind driving?'

'Of course not.'

'I'll be right back.'

Puzzled, she watched as he disappeared round the back of the house.

Müller had taken one of his business-type cards from his wallet. He placed it beneath a small flowerpot on the terrace in an unmissable position, leaving it peeping out. Then he hurried round to climb into the Explorer.

He did not look back as Carey Bloomfield drove off.

Jack and Maggie Hargreaves had landed at Cape Leveque on the Dampier Peninsula, overlooking the Indian Ocean. They were now walking along their favourite beach, which was virtually deserted. The whiteness of the beach, the bright red of the rising pindan cliffs, the blue of the ocean, was a postcard from another world.

'We knew this would happen one day,' he said to her.

'I know. It was still . . .' She paused. 'This is so hard.'

'I know,' he said softly. 'I know.'

'He got very close.'

'Close,' he said, looking out across the water, 'is a million miles away.'